JIM AN

ҍ ͵

MARY GRANT BRUCE

CHAPTER I
WAR

"For one the laurel, one the rose, and glory for them all,

All the gallant gentlemen who fight and laugh and fall."

Margery Ruth Betts.

THE trench wound a sinuous way through the sodden Flanders mud. Underfoot were boards; and then sandbags; and then more boards, added as the mud rose up and swallowed all that was put down upon it. Some of the last-added boards had almost disappeared, ground out of sight by the trampling feet of hundreds of men: a new battalion had relieved, three nights before, the men who had held that part of the line for a week, and when a relief arrives, a trench becomes uncomfortably filled, and the ground underfoot is churned into deep glue. It was more than time to put down another floor; to which the only objection was that no more flooring material was available, and had there been, no one had time to fetch it.

It was the second trench. Beyond it was another, occupied by British soldiers: beyond that again, a mass of tangled barbed-wire, and then the strip of No-Man's Land dividing the two armies—a strip ploughed up by shells and scarred with craters formed by the bursting of high explosives. Here and there lay rifles, and spiked German helmets, and khaki caps; but no living thing was visible save the cheeky Flemish sparrows that hopped about the quiet space, chirping and twittering as if trying to convince themselves and everybody else that War was hundreds of miles away. The sparrows carried out this pleasant deception every morning, abandoning the attempt as soon as the first German gun began what the British soldiers, disagreeably interrupted in frying bacon, termed "the breakfast hate." Then they retreated precipitately to the sparrow equivalent to a dug-out, to meditate in justifiable annoyance on the curious ways of men.

In the second trench the men were weary and heavy-eyed, and even bacon had scant attractions for them. It was their first experience of trench-life complicated by shell-fire, and since their arrival the enemy had been "hating" with a vigour that seemed to argue on his part a peculiar sourness of temper. Now, after two days of incessant artillery din and three nights of the strenuous toil that falls upon the trenches with darkness, the new men bore evidence of exhaustion. Casualties had been few, considering the violent nature of the bombardment; but to those who had never before seen Death come suddenly, an even slighter loss would have been horrifying. The ceaseless nerve-shattering roar of the big guns pounded in their brains long after darkness had put an end to the bombardment; their brief snatches of sleep were haunted by the white faces of the comrades with whom they would laugh and fight and work no more. They were stiff and sore with crouching under the parapets and in the narrow dug-outs; dazed with noise, sullen with the anger of men who have been forced to endure without making any effort to hit back. But their faces had hardened under the test. A few were shrinking, "jumpy," useless: but the majority had stiffened into men. When the time for hitting back came, they would be ready.

Dawn on the fourth morning found them weary enough, but, on the whole, in better condition than they had been two days earlier. They were getting used to it; and even to artillery bombardment "custom hath made a property of easiness." The first sense of imminent personal danger had faded with each hour that found most of them still alive. Discipline and routine, making each officer and man merely part of one great machine, steadied them into familiar ways, even in that unfamiliar setting. And above all was satisfaction that after months of slow training on barrack-square and peaceful English fields they were at last in the middle of the real thing—doing their bit. It had been conveyed to them that they were considered to be shaping none too badly: a curt testimonial, which, passing down the line, had lent energy to a hard night of rebuilding parapets, mending barbed-wire, and cleaning up battered sections of trench. They were almost too tired to eat. But the morning—so far—was peaceful; the sunlight was cheery, the clean breeze refreshing. Possibly to-day might find the Hun grown weary of hating so noisily. There were worse things than even a trench in Flanders on a bright April morning.

Jim Linton sat on a small box outside his dug-out, drinking enormous quantities of tea, and making a less enthusiastic attempt to demolish the contents of an imperfectly heated tin of bully beef. He was bare-headed, owing to the fact that a portion of shrapnel had removed his cap the day before, luckily without damaging the head inside it. Mud plastered him from neck to heels. He was a huge boy, well over six feet, broad-shouldered and powerful; and the bronze which the sun of his native Australia had put into his face had been proof against the trench experiences that had whitened English cheeks, less deeply tanned.

Another second lieutenant came hastily round a traverse and tripped over his feet.

"There's an awful lot of you in a trench!" said the new-comer, recovering himself.

"Sorry," said Jim. "I can't find any other place to put them; they will stick out. Never mind, the mud will bury them soon; it swallows them if I forget to move them every two minutes. Come and have breakfast."

"I want oceans of tea," said Wally Meadows, dragging a biscuit-tin from the dug-out, perching it precariously on a small board island in the mud, and seating himself with caution. He glanced with disfavour at the beef-tin. "Is that good?"

"Beastly," Jim answered laconically. "Smith's strong point is not cookery. It's faintly warm and exceedingly tough; and something with moisture in it seems to have happened to the biscuits. But the tea is topping. I told Smith to bring another supply presently. Bacon's a bit short, so I said we preferred bully."

Wally accepted a tin mug of milkless tea with gratitude.

"That's great," he said, after a beatific pause, putting down the empty mug. He pushed his cap back from his tired young face, and heaved a great sigh of relief. "Blessings on whoever discovered tea! I don't think I'll have any beef, thanks."

"Yes, you will," Jim said, firmly. "I know it's beastly, and one isn't hungry, but it's a fool game not to eat. If we have any luck there may be some work to-day; and you can't fight if you don't eat something. The first mouthful is the worst."

His chum took the beef-tin meekly.

"I suppose you're right," he said. "If we only do get a chance of fighting, I should think we'd have enormous appetites afterwards; but one can't get hungry hiding in this beastly hole and letting Brother Boche sling his tin cans at us. Wouldn't you give something for a bath and twelve hours' sleep?"

"By Jove, yes!" Jim agreed. "But I don't mind postponing them if only we get a smack at those gentry across the way first. Did you see Anstruther?"

"Yes—he's better. He dodged the R.A.M.C. men—said he wasn't going to be carted back because of a knock on the head. He's tied up freshly and looks awfully interesting, but he declares he's quite fit."

Captain Anstruther was the company commander, a veteran of one-and-twenty, with eight months' service. The two Australian boys, nineteen and eighteen respectively, and fully conscious of their own limitations, regarded him with great respect in his official capacity, and, off duty, had clearly demonstrated their ability to dispose of him, with the gloves on, within three rounds. They were exceedingly good friends. Anstruther could tell stories of the Marne, of the retreat from Mons, of the amazing tangle of the first weeks of war, which had left him, then a second lieutenant, in sole command of the remnant of his battalion. To the two Australians he was a mine of splendid information. They were mildly puzzled at what he demanded in return—bush "yarns" of their own country, stories of cattle musterings, of aboriginals, of sheep-shearing by machinery, of bush-fire fighting; even of football as played at their school in Melbourne. To them these things, interesting enough in peacetime and in their own setting, were commonplace and stale in the trenches, with Europe ablaze with battle all round them. Anstruther, however, looked on war with an eye that saw little of romance: willing to see it through, but with no illusions as to its attractions. He greatly preferred to talk of bush-fires, which he had not seen.

Yesterday a shell which had wrecked far too much of a section of trench to be at all comfortable had provided this disillusioned warrior with a means of escape, had he so wished, by knocking him senseless, with a severe scalp-wound. Counselled to seek the dressing-station at the rear, when he had recovered his senses, however, he had flatly declined; all his boredom lost in annoyance at his aching head, and a wild desire to obtain enemy scalps in vengeance. Jim and Wally had administered first-aid with field dressings, and the wounded one, declaring himself immediately cured, had hidden himself and his bandages from any intrusive senior who might be hard-hearted enough to insist on his retirement.

"It was a near thing," Jim said reflectively.

"So was yours," stated his chum.

"Oh—my old cap?—a miss is as good as a mile," said Jim. "I'm glad it wasn't a bit nearer, though; it would be a bore to be put out of business without ever having seen a German, let alone finding out which of us could 'get his fist in fust.'" He rose, feeling for his pipe. "Have you eaten your whack of that stuff?"

"I've done my best," said Wally, displaying the tin, nearly empty. "Can't manage any more. Let's have a walk along the trench and see what's happening."

"Well, keep your silly head down," Jim said. "The parapet is getting more and more uneven, and you never remember you're six feet."

Wally grinned. Each of the friends suffered under the belief that he was extremely careful and the other destined to sudden death from unwittingly exposing himself to a German sniper.

"If you followed your own advice, grandmother," he said; "you being three inches taller, and six times more careless! I always told your father and Norah that you'd be an awful responsibility."

"I'll put you under arrest if you're not civil," Jim threatened. "Small boys aren't allowed to be impertinent on active service!"

They floundered along in the mud, ducking whenever the parapet was low: sandbags had run short, and trench-repairing on the previous night had been like making bricks without straw. The men were finishing breakfast, keeping close to the dug-outs, since at any moment the first German shell might scream overhead. The line was very thin; reinforcements, badly enough wanted, were reported to be coming up. Meanwhile the battalion could only hope that the shells would continue to spare them, and that when the enemy came the numbers would be sufficiently even to enable them to put up a good fight.

Captain Anstruther, white-faced under a bandage that showed red stains, nodded to them cheerily.

"Ripping morning, isn't it?" he said. "Hope you've had a pleasant night, Linton!"

Jim grinned, glancing at his hands, which displayed numerous long red scars.

"One's nights here are first-class training for the career of a burglar later on," he said. "Mending barbed-wire in the dark is full of unexpected happenings, chiefly unpleasant. I don't mind the actual mending so much as having to lie flat on one's face in the mud when a star-shell comes along."

"Very disorganizing to work," said another subaltern, Blake, whose mud-plastered uniform showed that he had had his share of lying flat. In private life Blake had belonged to the species "nut," and had been wont to parade in Bond Street in beautiful raiment. Here, dirty, unshaven and scarcely distinguishable from the muddiest of his platoon, he permitted himself a cheerfulness that Bond Street had never seen.

"Sit down," Anstruther said. "There are more or less dry sandbags, and business is slack. Why didn't you fellows come down to mess? Have you had any breakfast?"

"Yes, thanks," Jim answered. "We fed up there—our men were inclined to give breakfast a miss, so we encouraged them to eat by feeding largely, among them. Nothing like exciting a feeling of competition."

"Trenches under fire don't breed good healthy appetites—at any rate until you're used to them," Blake remarked.

"The men are bucking up well, all the same," said Anstruther. "I'm jolly proud of them; it's a tough breaking-in for fellows who aren't much more than recruits. They're steadying down better than I could have hoped they would."

"Doesn't the weary old barrack-square grind stand to them now!" said Jim. "They see it, too, themselves; only they're very keen to put all the bayonet-exercise into practice. Smith, my servant, was the mildest little man you ever saw, at home; now he spends most of the day putting a bloodthirsty edge on his bayonet, and I catch him in corners prodding the air and looking an awful Berserk. They're all chirping up wonderfully this morning, bless 'em. I shouldn't wonder if by this time to-morrow they were regarding it all as a picnic!"

"So it is, if you look at it the right way," said Blake. "Lots of jokes about, too. Did you hear what one of our airmen gave the enemy on April the First? He flew over a crowd behind their lines, and dropped a football. It fell slowly, and Brother Boche took to cover like a rabbit, from all directions. Then it struck the ground and bounced wildly, finally settling to rest: I suppose they thought it was a delay-action fuse, for they laid low for a long time before they dared believe it was not going to explode. So they came out from their shelters to examine it, and found written on it 'April fool—Gott strafe England!'"

His hearers gave way to mirth.

"Good man!" said Anstruther. "But there are lots of mad wags among the flying people. I should think it must make 'em extraordinarily cheerful always to be cutting about in nice clean air, where there isn't any barbed-wire or mud."

Feeling grunts came from the others.

"Rather!" said Garrett, another veteran of eight months' service. "There was one poor chap who had engine-trouble when he was doing a lone reconnaissance, and had to come down behind the German lines. He worked furiously, and just got his machine in going order, when two enemy officers trotted up, armed with revolvers, and took him prisoner. Then they thought it would be a bright idea to make him take them on a reconnaissance over the Allied lines; which design they explained to him in broken English and with a fine display of their portable artillery, making him understand that if he didn't obey he'd be shot forthwith."

"But he didn't!" Wally burst out.

"Just you wait, young Australia—you're an awful fire-eater!" said the narrator. "The airman thought it over, and came to the conclusion that it would be a pity to waste his valuable life; so he gave in meekly, climbed in, and took his passengers aboard. They went off very gaily, and he gave them a first-rate view of all they wanted to see; and, of course, carrying our colours, he could fly much lower than any German machine could have gone in safety. It was jam for the two Boches; I guess they felt their Iron Crosses sprouting. Their joy only ended—and then it ended suddenly—when he looped the loop!"

The audience jumped.

"What happened?"

"They very naturally fell out."

"And the airman?" Wally asked, ecstatically.

"He had taken the precaution to strap himself in—unobtrusively. Didn't I tell you he appreciated his valuable life?" said Garrett, laughing. "He came down neatly where he wanted to, made his report, and sent out a party to give decent burial to two very dead amateur aviators. The force of gravity is an excellent thing to back you up in a tight place, isn't it?"

"Well, it's something to get one's chance—and it's quite another to know when to take advantage of it," said Anstruther. "I expect an airman has to learn to make up his mind quicker than most of us. But there's no doubt of the chances that come to some people. A Staff officer was here early this morning, and he was telling me of young Goujon."

"Who's he?" queried Blake, lazily.

"He's a French kid—just seventeen. He was one of a small party sent out to locate some enemy machine-guns that were giving a good deal of trouble. They found 'em, all right; but when they were wriggling their way back a shell came along and wiped out the entire crowd—all except this Goujon kid. He was untouched, and he hid for hours in the crater made by the explosion of the shell. When it got dark he crept out: but by that time he was pretty mad, and instead of getting home, he wanted to get a bit of his own back, and what must he do but crawl to those machine-guns and lob bombs on them!"

"That's some kid," said Blake briefly.

"Yes, he was, rather. He destroyed two of the three guns, and then was overpowered—that wouldn't have taken long!—and made prisoner: pretty roughly handled, too. But before he could be sent to the rear, some of our chaps made a little night-attack on that bit of German trench, and in the excitement Goujon got away. So he trotted home—but on the way he stopped, and gathered up the remaining machine-gun. Staggered into his own lines with it. They've given him the Military Medal."

"Deserved it, too," was the comment.

"And he's seventeen!" said some one. "He ought to get pretty high up before the war is over."

"I know a man who's a major at nineteen," Anstruther said, "Went out as a second lieutenant and was promoted for gallantry at Mons; got his captaincy and was wounded at the Aisne; recovered, and at Neuve Chapelle was the sole officer left, except two very junior subalterns, in all his battalion. He handled it in action, brought them out brilliantly—awful corner it was, too,—and was in command for a fortnight after, before they could find a senior man; there weren't any to spare. He was gazetted major last week."

"Lucky dog!" said Blake.

"Well, I suppose he is. They say he's a genius at soldiering, anyhow; and, of course, he got his chance. There must be hundreds of men who would do as well if they ever got it; only opportunity doesn't come their way."

"They say this will be a war for young men," Garrett said. "We're going back to old days; I believe Wellington and Napoleon were colonels at twenty. And that's more than you will be, young Meadows, if you don't mend your ways."

"I never expected to be," said Wally, thus attacked.

"But why won't I, anyhow, apart from obvious reasons?"

"Because you'll be a neat little corpse," said Garrett. "What's this game of yours I hear about?—crawling round on No-Man's Land at night, and collecting little souvenirs? The souvenir you'll certainly collect will come from a machine-gun."

Wally blushed.

"Well, there are such a jolly lot of things there," he defended himself. "Boche helmets—I've got three beauties—and belts, and buckles, and things. People at home like 'em."

"Presumably people at home like you," Anstruther said. "But they certainly won't have you to like if you do it, and it's possible their affection might even wane for a German helmet that had cost you your scalp. Verboten, Meadows; that's good German, at any rate. Understand?"

Wally assented meekly. Jim Linton, apparently sublimely unconscious of the conversation, sighed with relief. His chum's adventurous expeditions had caused him no little anxiety, especially as they were undertaken at a time when his own duties prevented his keeping an eye on the younger boy—which would probably have ended in his accompanying him. From childhood, Jim and Wally had been accustomed to do things in pairs: a habit which had persisted even to sending them together from Australia to join the Army, since Wally was too young for the Australian forces. England was willing to take boys of seventeen; therefore it was manifestly out of the question that Jim should join anywhere but in England, despite his nineteen years. And as Jim's father and sister were also willing to come to England, the matter had arranged itself as a family affair. Wally Meadows was an orphan, and the Linton family had long included him on a permanent, if informal, basis.

"It's jolly to get V.C.'s and medals and other ironmongery," Anstruther was saying; "but I'd like to be the chap who organized the Toy Band on the retreat from

Mons. He was a Staff officer, and he found the remains of a regiment, several hundred strong, straggling through a village, just dead beat. The Germans were close on their heels; the British had no officers left, and had quite given up. The Staff chap called on them to make another effort to save themselves, but they wouldn't—they had been on the run for days, were half-starved, worn out: they didn't care what happened to them. The officer was at his wits' end what to do, when his eye fell on a little bit of a shop—you know the usual French village store, with all sorts of stuff in the window: and there he saw some toy drums and penny whistles. He darted in and bought some: came out and induced two or three of the less exhausted men to play them—it's said he piped on one penny whistle himself, only he won't admit it now. But you know what the tap of a drum will do on a route-march when the men are getting tired. He roused the whole regiment with his fourpence-worth of band and brought them back to their brigade next day—never lost a man!"

"Jolly good work," said Blake.

"He won't get anything for it, of course," said Anstruther. "You don't get medals for playing tin whistles; and anyhow, there was no one to report it. But—yes, I'd like to have been that chap." He rose and stretched himself, taking advantage of a section of undamaged parapet. "Brother Boche is rather late in beginning his hate this morning, don't you think?"

"Perhaps he's given up hating as a bad job," Wally suggested.

"We'll miss the dear old thing if he really means to leave us alone," said Anstruther. "Just as well if he does, though: our line is painfully thin, and it's evident to anyone that our guns are short of ammunition: we're giving them about one shell to twenty of theirs. And don't they know it! They send us enormous doses of high-explosive shells, and in return we tickle them feebly with a little shrapnel. They must chuckle!"

"I suppose England will wake up and make munitions for us when we're all wiped out," said Garrett, scornfully. "They're awfully cheery over there: theatres and restaurants packed, business as usual, bull-dog grit, and all the rest of it: Parliament yapping happily, and strikes twice a week. And our chaps trying to fight for 'em, and dying for want of ammunition to do it with. I suppose they think we're rather lazy not to make it in our spare time!"

"I'm afraid they won't appoint me dictator just yet," Blake remarked. "If they would, I'd have every striker and slacker out here: not to fight, but to mend barbed-wire, clean up trenches, and do the general dirty work. First-rate tonic for a disgruntled mind. And I'd send what was left of them to the end of the world afterwards. Will you have them in Australia, Linton?"

"Thanks; we've plenty of troubles of our own," Jim returned hastily. "Don't you think we were dumping-ground for your rubbish for long enough?"

"You were a large, empty place, and you had to be peopled," said Blake, grinning. "And a good many of them were very decent people, I believe."

"Well, they might well be," Jim responded—"you sent them out for stealing a sheep or a shirt or a medicine-bottle: one poor kid of six was sent out for life for stealing jam-tarts. Many excellent men must have begun life by stealing jam-tarts: I did, myself!"

"If you're a sample of the after-effects, I don't wonder we exported the other criminals early," laughed Blake.

"Well, if any of their descendants grew into the chaps that landed at Gallipoli the other day, they were no bad asset," said Anstruther. "By Jove, those fellows must be fighters, Linton! I wouldn't care to have the job of holding them back."

"I knew they'd fight," said Jim briefly. Down in his quiet soul he was torn between utter pride in his countrymen, and woe that he had not been with them in that stern Gallipoli landing: the latter emotion firmly repressed. It had been the fight of his boyish dreams—wild charging, hand to hand work, a fleeing enemy: not like this hole-and-corner trench existence unseen by the unseen foe, with Death that could not be combated dropping from the sky. His old school-fellows had been at Gallipoli, and had "made good." He ached to have been with them.

An orderly came up hurriedly. Anstruther tore open the note he carried.

"There's word of an enemy attack," he said crisply. "Get to your places—quick!"

The subalterns scattered along the trench, each to his platoon. They had already inspected the men, making sure that no detail of armament had been forgotten, and that rifles were all in order. Garrett, who commanded the machine-gun section, fled joyfully to the emplacement, his face like a happy child's. The alarm ran swiftly up and down the trench: low, sharp words of command brought every man to his place, while the sentries, like statues, were glued to their peep-holes. Jim and Wally fingered their revolvers, scarcely able to realize that the time for using them had come at last. Field officers appeared, hurriedly scanning every detail of preparation, and giving a word of advice here and there.

"Thank 'eving, we're going to have a look-in!" muttered a man in front of Jim: a grizzled sergeant with the two South African ribbons on his breast. "Steady there, young 'Awkins; don't go meddlin' with that trigger of yours. You'll get a chanst of loosin' off pretty soon."

"Cawn't come too soon for me!" said Hawkins, in a throaty whisper, fondling his rifle lovingly. "They got me best pal yesterday."

"Then keep your 'ead cool till the time comes to mention wot you think of 'em," returned the sergeant.

Jim and Wally found a chink in the sandbag parapet, and looked out eagerly ahead. All was quiet. The sparrows, made bold by the extraordinary peace of the morning, still chirped and twittered on No-Man's Land. No sound came from the German trenches beyond. Here and there a faint smoke-wreath curled lazily into the air, telling of cooking-fires and breakfast.

"How do they know they're coming?" Wally whispered.

"Aeroplane reconnaissance, I suppose," Jim answered, pointing to two or three specks floating in the blue overhead, far out of reach of the anti-aircraft guns. "They've been hovering up there all the morning. Feeling all right, Wal?"

"Fit as a fiddle. I suppose I'll be in a blue funk presently, but just now I feel as if I were going to a picnic."

"So do I—and the men are keen as mustard. I thought little Wilson would be useless; you know how jumpy he's been since we came here. But look at him, there; he's as steady and cool as any sergeant. They're good boys," said the subaltern, who was not yet twenty.

"Mind your 'ead, sir!" came in an agonized whisper from a corporal below; and Jim ducked obediently under the lee of the parapet.

"It's quite hot," he said, peering again through his peep-hole. "There's a jolly breeze springing up, though."

The breeze came softly over No-Man's Land, fluttering the wings of the cheerful sparrows. Across the scarred strip of grass a low, green cloud wavered upwards. It grew more solid, spreading in a dense wall over the parapet of the German trench.

"What on earth——?" Jim began.

The green cloud seemed to hesitate. Then the wind freshened a little, and it suddenly blew forward across No-Man's Land, growing denser as it came. Before it, the sparrows fled suddenly, darting to the upper air with shrill chirpings of alarm. But one bird, taken unawares, beat his wings wildly for a moment, flying forward. Then he pitched downwards and the cloud rolled over him.

"What is it?" uttered Wally.

Before the parapet of the British trench ahead of them the cloud stood for a moment, and then toppled bodily into the trench. It fell as water falls like a heavy thing. From its green depths came hoarse shouts, and rifles suddenly went off in an irregular fusillade. Then the cloud rolled over, leaving the trench full of vapour, and stole towards the second British line.

A great cry came ringing down the trench.

"Gas! It's their filthy gas!"

It was a new thing, and no one was prepared for it. Across the Channel, England was shuddering over the first reports of the asphyxiating gas attacks, and the women of England were working night and day at the first half-million respirators to be sent out to the troops. But to the men in the trenches there had come only vague rumours of what the French and Canadians had suffered: and they had been slow to believe. It was not easy to realize, unseeing, the full horror of that most malignant device with which Science had blackened War. A few of the officers had respirators—dry, and comparatively useless. The men were utterly unprotected. Like sheep waiting for the slaughter they stood rigidly at attention, waiting for the evil green cloud that blew towards them, already poisoning the clean air with its noxious fumes.

"Tie your handkerchiefs round your mouths and nostrils!" Jim Linton shouted. "Quick, Wally!"

He caught at the younger boy's handkerchief and knotted it swiftly. The corporal shook his head.

"Most of 'em ain't got no 'ankerchers, sir," he said grimly. "They will clean their rifles with 'em."

Then came another cry.

"Look out—they're coming!"

Dimly, behind the cloud of gas, they could see shadowy forms clambering over the parapet of the enemy trench; German soldiers, unreal and horrible in their hideous respirators, with great goggle eyes of talc. Ahead, the quick spit of machine-guns broke out spitefully; and, as if in answer, Garrett's Maxims opened fire. Then the gas was upon them: falling from above over the parapet, stealing like a live thing down the communication trench that led from the first line, where already the Germans were swarming. Men were choking, gasping, fighting for air; dropping their rifles as they tore at their collars, losing their heads altogether in the horror of the silent attack. A little way down the trench Anstruther was trying to rally them, his voice only audible for a few yards. Jim echoed him.

"Come on, boys! it's better in the open. Let's get at them!"

He sprang up over the parapet, Wally at his side. There were bullets whistling all round them, but the air was more free—it was Paradise compared to the agony of suffocation in the trench. Some of the men followed. Jim leaped back again, dragging at others; pushing, striking, threatening; anything to get them up above, where at least they might die fighting, not like rats in a hole. He was voiceless, inarticulate; he could only point upwards, and force them over the parapet and into the bullet-swept space. Wally was there—was Wally killed? Then he saw him beside him in the trench, dragging at little Private Wilson, who had fallen senseless. Together they lifted him and flung him out at the rear, turning to fight with other men who had given up and were leaning against the walls, choking. Above them Anstruther was getting the men into some semblance of formation to meet the oncoming rush of Germans. He called to them sharply, authoritatively.

"Linton!—Meadows! Come out at once!"

Jim tried to obey. Then he saw that Wally was staggering, and flung his arm round him; but the arm was suddenly limp and helpless, and Wally pitched forward on his face and lay still, gasping. Jim tried to drag him up, fighting with the powerlessness that was creeping over him. Behind him the roar of artillery grew faint in his ears and died away, though still he seemed to hear the steady spit of Garrett's machine-guns. He sagged downwards. Then black, choking darkness rushed upon him, and he fell across the body of his friend.

"Jim Linton sat on a small box outside his dug-out . . ."

CHAPTER II
YELLOW ENVELOPES

"London's smoke hides all the stars from me,

Light from mine eyes and Heaven from my heart."

Dora Wilcox.

THE lift came gliding on its upward journey in a big London hotel, far too slowly for the impatience of its only passenger, a tall girl of sixteen, with a mop of brown curls, and grey eyes alight with excitement. Ordinarily, Norah Linton was rather pale, especially in London, where the air is largely composed of smoke, and has been breathed in and out of a great number of people until it is nearly worn out; but just now there was a scarlet spot on each cheek, and her mouth broke into smiles as though it could not help itself. At Floor No. 4, a fat old lady threatened to stop the lift, but decided at the last moment that she preferred to walk upstairs. At No. 5, no one was in sight, and Norah sighed with audible relief, and ejaculated, "Thank goodness!" At No. 6, two men were seen hurrying along the corridor some distance away, and shouting, "Lift!" But at this point the lift-boy, to whom Norah's impatience had communicated itself, behaved like Nelson when he applied his telescope to his blind eye, and shot upwards, disregarding the shouts of his would-be passengers; and, passing by No. 7 as though it were not there, brought the lift to an abrupt halt at No. 8, flinging the door open with a rattle and a triumphant, "There y'are, miss!"

"Thank you!" said Norah, flashing at him a grateful smile that sent the lift-boy earthwards in a state of mind that made him loftily oblivious of the reproaches of neglected passengers. She was out of the lift with a quick movement, and in the empty corridor broke into a run. Her flying feet carried her swiftly to a sitting-room some distance away, and she burst in like a whirlwind. "Dad! Daddy!"

There was no one there, and with an exclamation of impatience she turned and ran once more, far too excited now to care whether any Londoners were there to be shocked at the spectacle of a daughter of Australia racing along an hotel corridor. She had not far to go; a turn brought her face to face with a tall man, lean and grizzled, who cast a glance at her that took in the crumpled yellow envelope in her hand.

No one with a soldier son looked calmly on telegrams in those days, and David Linton's face changed abruptly. "What is it, Norah?"

"They're coming," said Norah, and suddenly found a huge lump in her throat that would not go away. She put out a hand and clung to her father's coat. "They're truly coming, daddy!"

Her father's voice was not as steady as usual.

"They're all right?"

"Oh, yes, they must be. It says 'Better—London to-morrow.'"

"Better?" mused Mr. Linton. "I wonder if that means hospital or us, Norah?"

Norah's face fell.

"I suppose it may be hospital," she said. "It was so lovely to think they were coming that I nearly forgot that part of it. Can we find out, daddy?"

"We'll go and try," Mr. Linton said.

"Now?" said Norah, and jigged on one foot.

"I'll get my hat," said her father, departing with a step not so unlike his daughter's. Norah waited in the corridor for a few minutes, and then, impatient beyond the possibility of further waiting in silence, followed him to his room, there finding him endeavouring to remove London mud-stains from a trouser-leg.

"You might think when you've managed to brush it off that it had gone—but indeed it hasn't," said David Linton, wrathfully regarding gruesome stains and brushing them with a vigour that should have been productive of better results.

"It does cling," remarked Norah, comprehendingly. "I'll sponge it for you, daddy; those stains never yield to mild measures. Daddy, do you think they'll be long getting better?"

Anyone else might have been excused for thinking she meant the mud-stains. But David Linton made no such mistake.

"I don't know," he said slowly. "One hears such different stories about that filthy German gas. It all depends on the size of the dose they got, I fancy. Jim said it was mild; but then Jim would say a good deal to avoid frightening us."

"And he was able to write. But Wally hasn't written."

"No; and that doesn't look well. He's such a good lad—it's quite likely he'd write and let us know all he could about Jim. But I don't fancy the doctors would let them travel unless they were pretty well."

"I suppose not. Oh, doesn't it seem ages until to-morrow, dad!"

"It'll come, if you give it time," said her father. "However—yes, it does seem a pretty long time, Norah." They laughed at each other.

"It doesn't do a bit of good for you to put on that wise air," Norah said, "because I know exactly how you feel, and that's just the same as I do. And anyone would be the same who had two boys at the Front like Jim and Wally."

"I think they would," said her father, abandoning as untenable the position of age and wisdom. "Thank goodness they will be back with us to-morrow, at any rate." He put his clothes-brush on the table and stood up, tall and thin and a little grim. "It seems a long while since they went away."

"Long!" Norah echoed, expressively. It was in reality only a month since her brother Jim and his chum had said good-bye on the platform at Victoria Station; and in some ways it seemed only a few minutes since the train had moved slowly out, with the laughing boyish faces framed in the window. But each slow day, with its dragging weight of anxiety, had been a lifetime. To them had come what the whole world had learned to know; the shiver of fear on opening the green envelopes from the Front; the racking longing for the news; the sick dread at the sight of a telegram—even at the sound of an unusual knock. David Linton had grown silent and grim; Norah felt an old woman, and the care-free Australian life which was all she had known seemed a world away—vanished as completely as the Australian tan had faded from her cheeks.

Now it was all over, and for a while, at any rate, they could forget. Jim had so managed that no shock came to them—the cheery telegram he had contrived to send before being taken to hospital had reached them two days earlier than the curt War Office intimation that both boys were suffering from gas-poisoning. Jim did not mean that they should ever know what it had meant to send it. The cavalry subaltern who had helped him along to the dressing-station had been very kind; he had contrived to hear the address, even in the choked, strangling whisper, which was all the voice the gas had left to Jim; had even suggested a wording that would tell without alarming, and had put aside almost angrily Jim's struggle to find his money. "Don't you worry," he had said, "it'll go. I've seen other chaps gassed, and you'll be all right soon." He was a cheery pink and white youngster: Jim was sorry he had not found out his name. In the hard days and nights that followed, his face hovered round his half-conscious dreams—curiously like a little lad who had fagged for him at school in Melbourne.

That was two weeks ago, and of those two weeks Mr. Linton and Norah fortunately knew little. Wally had been the worst; Jim had been dragged out of the gassed trench a few minutes earlier than his friend, and possibly to the younger boy the shock had been greater. When the first terrible paroxysms passed, he could only lie motionless, endeavouring to conjure up a faint ghost of his old smile when Jim's anxious face peered at him from the next bed. Neither had any idea at all of how they had reached the hospital at Boulogne; all their definite memories ended abruptly when that evil-smelling green cloud had rolled like a wave above them into the trench.

Out of the first dark mist of choking suffering they had passed slowly into comparative peace, broken now and then by recurring attacks, but, by contrast, a very haven of tranquillity. They were very tired and lazy: it was heavenly to lie there, quite still, and watch the blue French sky through the window and the kind-faced nurses flitting about—each doing far too much for her strength, but always cheery. They did not want to talk—their voices had gone somewhere very far off; all they wanted was just to be quiet; not to move, not to talk, not to cough. Then, as the clean vigour of their youth reasserted itself, and strength came back to them, energy woke once more, and with it their old-time lively hatred of bed. They begged to be allowed to get up; and as their places were badly needed for men worse than they, the doctors granted their prayer—after which they would have been extremely glad to get back again, only that pride forbade their admitting it.

Moreover, there was London; and London, with all that it meant to them, was worth a struggle. Two months earlier it had bored them exceedingly, and nothing had seemed worth while, with the call in their blood to be out in the trenches. Now, after actual experience of the trenches, their ideas had undergone a violent change. The romance of war had faded utterly. The Flying Corps might retain it still—those plucky fighting men who soared and circled overhead, bright specks in the clouds and the blue sky; but to the men who grubbed underground amid discomfort, smells, and dirt, to which actual fighting came as a blessed relief, war had lost all its glamour. They wanted to see the job through. But London was coming first, and it had blossomed suddenly into a paradise.

Some of which Jim had tried to put into his shaky pencilled notes; and the certainty of their boys' gladness to get back lay warm at the hearts of Norah and her father as they walked along Piccadilly. Spring was in the air: the Park had been full of people, the Row crowded with happy children, scurrying up and down the tan on their ponies, with decorous grooms endeavouring to keep them in sight. The window-boxes in the clubs were gay with daffodils and hyacinths: the busy, knowing London sparrows twittered noisily in the budding trees, making hurried arrangements for setting up housekeeping in the summer. Even though war raged so close to England, and its shadow lay on every hearth, nothing could quite dim the gladness of London's awakening to the Spring.

"Those fellows all look so happy," said Mr. Linton, indicating a motor-car crammed with wounded men in their blue hospital suits and scarlet ties. "One never sees a discontented face among them. I hope our boys will look as happy, Norah."

"If there is any chance of looking happy, Jim and Wally will take it!" said Norah, firmly.

"I think they will," said her father, laughing. "The difficulty is to imagine them ill."

"Yes, isn't it? Do you remember when those horrid Zulus battered them about so badly in Durban, how extraordinary it was to see them both in bed, looking pale?"

"Well, I think it was the first time it had occurred to either of them," said Mr. Linton.

"I suppose one could never realize the awful effects of the gas unless one actually saw it," Norah said. "But I can't help feeling glad, if they had to be hurt, that it was that: not wounds or—crippling." Her voice fell on the last word. "I just couldn't bear the thought of Jim or Wally being crippled."

"Don't!" said her father, sharply. "Please God, they'll come out of it without that. And as for the gas—Jim assured us they would be all right, but I'll be glad when I talk to a doctor about them myself."

Inquiries proved disappointing. It was certain that the boys would not be allowed to return directly to them. They would travel in hospital trains and a hospital ship; it was difficult to say where men would be taken, when so many, broken and helpless, were being brought to England every day. The Victorian Agent-General was sympathetic and helpful; he promised to find out all that could be found from the overworked authorities, and to let them know at the earliest possible moment.

"But I fancy that long son of yours will find a way of letting you know himself, Mr. Linton," he said. "I'll do my best—but I wouldn't mind betting he gets ahead of me."

They came out of the building that is a kind of oasis in London to all homesick Victorians, pausing, as they always did, to look at the exhibits in the outer office—wool and wheat and timber, big model gold nuggets, and the shining fruits that spoke of the orchards on the hillsides at home; with pictures of wide pastures where sleek cattle stood in the knee-high grass, or reapers and binders whirred through splendid crops. It was a little patch of Australia, planted in the very heart of London; hard to realize that just outside the swinging glass doors the grey city—history suddenly become a live thing—stretched away eastward, and, to the west, the roaring Strand carried its mighty burden of traffic.

"I'll always be glad I had the chance of seeing London," said Norah. "But whenever I come here I know how glad I'll be to go back!"

"I know that without coming here," said her father, drily. "It would be jolly if we could take those boys home to get strong, Norah."

"To Billabong?" said Norah, wistfully. "Oh-h! But we'll do it some day, daddy."

"I trust so. Won't there be a scene when we get back!"

"Oh, I dream about it!" said Norah. "And I wake up all homesick. Can't you picture Brownie, dad!—she'll have cooked everything any of us ever liked, and the house will be shining from top to bottom, and there won't be a thing different—I know she dusts your old pipes and Jim's stockwhips herself every day! And Murty will have the horses jumping out of their skins with fitness, and Lee Wing's garden will be something marvellous."

"And Billy," said David Linton, laughing. "Can't you see his black face—and his grin!"

"Oh, and the great wide paddocks—the view from the verandah, across the lagoon and looking right over the plains! I don't seem to have looked at anything far away since we came off the ship," said Norah; "all the views are shut in by houses, and the air is so thick one couldn't see far, in any case!"

"They tell me there's clear air in Ireland," said her father.

"Then I want to go there," responded his daughter, promptly.

"Well—we might do worse than that. I've been thinking a good deal, Norah; if the boys don't get well quickly—and I believe few of the gassed men do—we shall have to take them away somewhere for a change."

"Certainly," agreed Norah. "We couldn't keep them in London."

"No, of course not. Country air and not too many people; that is the kind of tonic our boys will want. What would you think of going to Ireland?"

Norah drew a long breath of delight.

"Oh-h!" she said. "You do make the most beautiful plans, daddy! We've always wanted to go there more than anywhere: and war wouldn't seem so near to us there, and we could try to make the boys forget gas and trenches and shells and all sorts of horrors."

"That's just it," said her father. "The wisest doctor I ever knew used to say that change of environment was worth far more than change of air; we might try to manage both for them, Norah. Donegal was your mother's country: I've been meaning to go there. She loved it till the day she died."

In the tumult of the Strand Norah slipped a hand into her father's. Very seldom did he speak of the one who was always in his memory: the little mother who had grown tired, and had slipped out of life when Norah was a baby.

"Let's go there, daddy," she begged.

"We'll consult the boys," said Mr. Linton. "Eh, but it's good to think we shall have them to consult with to-morrow! You know, Norah, since Jim left school, I've become so used to consulting him on all points, that I feel a lost old man without him."

"You'll never be old!" said his daughter, indignantly. "But Jim just loves you to talk to him the way you do,—I know he does, only, of course, he's quite unable to say so."

"Jim has lots of sense," said Jim's father. "So has Wally, for that matter: there is plenty of shrewdness hidden somewhere in that feather-pate of his. They're very reliable boys. I was 'thinking back' the other night, and I don't remember ever having been really angry with Jim in my life."

"I should think not!" said Norah, regarding him with wide eyes of amazement. "Why would you be angry with him?"

"Why, I don't know," said her father rather helplessly. "Jim never was a pattern sort of boy."

"No, but he had sense," said Norah. She began to laugh. "Oh, I don't know how it is," she said. "We've all been mates always: and mates don't get angry with each other, or they wouldn't be mates."

"I suppose that's it," Mr. Linton said, accepting this comprehensive description of a bush family standpoint. "There's a 'bus that will go our way, Norah: I've had enough of elbowing my way through this crowd."

They climbed on top of the motor-'bus, and found the front seat empty; and when Norah was on the front seat of a 'bus she always felt that it was her own private equipage and that she owned London. To their left was the huge yard of Charing Cross Station, crowded with taxis and cabs and private motors, with streams of foot passengers pouring in and out of the gateways. At Charing Cross one may see in five minutes more foreigners than one meets in many hours in other parts of London, and this was especially the case since the outbreak of war. Homesick Belgian refugees were wont to stray there, to watch the stream of passengers from the incoming Continental trains, hoping against hope that they might see some familiar face. There were soldiers of many nations; unfamiliar uniforms were dotted throughout the crowd, besides the khaki that coloured every London street. Even from the 'bus-top could be heard snatches of talk in many languages—save only one often heard in former days: German. A string of recruits, each wearing the King's ribbon, swung into the station under a smart recruiting sergeant: a cheery little band, apparently relieved that the plunge had at last been taken, and that they were about to shoulder their share of the nation's work.

"Not a straight pair of shoulders among the lot," remarked Mr. Linton, surveying them critically. "It's pleasant to think that very soon they will be almost as well set up as that fellow in the lead. War is going to do a big work in straightening English shoulders—morally and physically."

The 'bus gave a violent jerk, after the manner of 'buses in starting, and moved on through the crowded street, threading its way in and out of the traffic in the most amazing fashion—finding room to squeeze its huge bulk through chinks that looked small for a donkey-cart to pass, and showing an agility in dodging that would have done credit to a hare. It rocked on its triumphal way westward: past the crouching stone lions in Trafalgar Square, where the plinth of the Nelson Column blazed with recruiting posters; past the "Orient" offices, with their big pictures of Australian-going steamers—which made Norah sigh; and so up to Piccadilly Circus, where they found themselves packed into a jam of traffic so tight that it seemed that it could never disentangle. But presently it melted away, and they went on round the stately curve of Regent Street, with its glittering shops; and so home to the hotel—where they had lived so long that it really seemed almost home—and to their own sitting-room, gay with daffodils and primroses, and littered with work. Norah's knitting—khaki socks and mufflers—lay here and there, and there was a pile of finished articles awaiting dispatch to the Red Cross headquarters in the morning. Under the window, a big, workmanlike deal table was littered with scraps of wood, curiously fashioned, with tools in a neat rack. It was David Linton's workshop; all the time he could spare from helping with wounded soldiers went to the fashioning of splints and crutches for the hospitals, where so many were needed every day.

A yellow envelope was on the table now, lying across a splint.

"Duke of Clarence Hospital," it said; "to-morrow afternoon.—Jim."

"She put out a hand and clung to her father's coat."

CHAPTER III
WHEN THE BOYS COME HOME

"Oh! the spring is here again, and all the ways are fair.

The wattle-blossom's out again, and do you know it there?"

Margery Ruth Betts.

"THEY'RE doing quite well," the doctor said, patting Norah benevolently on the shoulder. He was a plump little man, always busy, always in a hurry; but David Linton and his daughter had been regular visitors to the hospital for some time, and he had a regard for them. ("Sensible people," he was wont to say, approvingly: "they don't talk too much to patients, and they don't fuss!") Now he knew that war had hit them personally, and he gave them two of his few spare minutes. "They're tired, of course; and you must expect to see them looking queer. Gas isn't a beautifier. But they'll be all right. Don't stay too long. Don't talk war, if you can keep them off it. And above all, don't speak about gas." He smiled at them both. "Buck them up, Miss Norah—buck them up!" Some one called him hurriedly, and he fled. The khaki ambulances had delivered a heavy load at the hospital that day.

In a little room off a quiet corridor, the scent of golden wattle flung a breath of Australia to greet them, as it had greeted the tired boys when the orderlies had carried them in hours before. Jim and Wally smiled at them from their pillows. No one seemed able to say anything. Afterwards, Norah had a dim idea that she had kissed Wally as well as Jim. It did not appear to matter greatly.

They were white-faced boys, with black shadows under their eyes; but the old merriment was there. A great wave of relief swept over Norah and her father. They had feared they knew not what from this evil choking enemy: it was sudden happiness to see that their boys were not so unlike their old selves.

"We had visions of being up to meet you," said Jim, keeping a hand on Norah's, as she perched on his bed. "But the doctor thought otherwise. Doctors are awful tyrants."

"You had a good crossing?" David Linton found words hard—they stuck in his throat as he looked at his son.

"Oh yes. We didn't know much about it. The hospital train runs you almost on to the ship, and the orderlies have you in a swinging cot before you know where you are. Same at the other side: those fellows do know their job," Jim said, admiringly. "Of course, you get a little tired of being handled, towards the finish, and this room—and bed—seemed awfully good."

"And the wattle was ripping," said Wally. "However did you manage to get it?"

"It comes from the South of France," Norah answered. "There's quite a lot of it in London; only they stare at you if you ask for 'wattle', and you have to learn to say 'mimosa.' One gets broken into anything. I've learned to say 'field' quite naturally when I'm talking of a paddock."

"I wish Murty could hear you," said Wally solemnly. Murty O'Toole was head stockman on Billabong, the home in Australia. He was a very great friend.

"Can't you picture his face!" Norah uttered. "It would be interesting to watch Murty's expression if dad told him to bring in the cattle from the field when he wanted the bullocks mustered in the home-paddock!"

"He'd give me notice," said Mr. Linton, firmly. "Neither long service nor affection would keep him!"

"Well, Murty was born in Ireland, though he did come out to Australia when he was a small boy," Norah said. "So he ought not to feel astonished. But the person I do want to import to England is black Billy. It's part of Billy's principles not to show amazement at anything, but I don't think they'd be proof against a block of traffic in Piccadilly!"

"He'd only say, 'Plenty!'" said Jim, laughing—"that is, if he had any speech left. Poor old Billy, he hates everything but horses, and any motor is a 'devil-wagon' to him. A fleet of big red and yellow 'buses would give him nervous prostration."

"There's one thing that would scare him more," Mr. Linton said. "Do you remember the day last winter when we took Norah to Hampton Court, and you chucked a stone at the Round Pond?" He laughed, and every one followed his example.

"And the stone ran along tinkling over the top of the water," said Norah, recovering. "I never was so taken aback in my life. And all the small children and their nursemaids laughed at me. How was I to know water turned to ice like that? The only frozen thing I had ever seen was ice-cream in Melbourne!"

"Billy never saw ice in his life," said her father. "He would have thought it very bad magic."

"He'd have taken to his heels and made for the bush," said Wally, grinning. "Probably he'd have made himself a boomerang and turned into an up-to-date black Robin Hood, living on those tame old Bushy Park deer."

"With his headquarters in the Hampton Court Maze!" added Jim. "Wouldn't it have been an enormous attraction—the halfpenny papers would have called it 'Wild Life in Quiet Places,' and London would have run special motor-bus trips to see our Billy!"

His laugh ended in a fit of coughing, which left him trembling. Norah patted him anxiously, watching him with troubled eyes.

"Don't you talk too much, or we'll get sent away," she warned him. "We'll do the talking—dad and I. We've heaps to tell you: and such jolly plans."

"You have to make haste and get better," said Mr. Linton, looking from one white face to the other. "Then we're going to take possession of you."

"Kitchener will do that, I guess," said Wally.

"No, Kitchener won—not until you're quite fit. You'll be handed over to us, and it will be our job to get you thoroughly well. And Norah and I have agreed that it can't be done in London."

"So we're all going to Ireland," said Norah, happily.

"Ireland!" Jim uttered.

"Yes. You're sure to get leave, so that you can be thoroughly repaired. We're going to find some jolly place in Donegal, where it's quiet and peaceful, and we're all going to buy rods and find out how to catch trout. Brown trout," said Norah, learnedly. "We know all about it, because we bought ever so many guide-books and studied them all last night."

"I say!" ejaculated both patients as one man.

"It sounds rather like Heaven," said Jim, drawing a long breath. "Do you really think it can be managed, dad?"

"I don't see why not," said his father.

"We must get back to our job as soon as we can."

"Certainly you must. But there's no sense in your going back until you are perfectly fit. They wouldn't want you. And though you were not as badly gassed as many—thank goodness!—and your recovery won't be such a trying matter as if you had had a bigger dose, every one agrees that gas takes its time."

"I shouldn't wonder," Jim said, grimly.

"That being so, London does not strike me as a good place for convalescents," said Mr. Linton. "Pure air is what you'll need; and that is not the fine, solid, grey variety of atmosphere you get here. And Zeppelins will be happening along freely, once they feel at home on the track to England. I don't believe they will limit their raids to London. The big manufacturing towns will come in for a share of their attention sooner or later; and they won't spare the country places over which they fly."

"Not they!" said Wally.

"So, all things considered, I think you would be better in Ireland. I believe it's peaceful there, if you don't talk politics. We don't want any adventures."

"We've had quite enough since we left Billabong," said Norah.

"Hear, hear!" said Wally. "I guess the calm peace of a bog in Ireland is just about our form until we're ready to go back and take our turn at strafing."

"Then that's settled—if the doctors will back me up," Mr. Linton said. "Just as soon as they will let you we'll pack up the fewest possible clothes and set out for a sleepy holiday in Ireland: trout-fishing, old ruins, bogs, heather, and no adventures at all."

Later on, they were to recall this peaceful forecast with amazement. At present it seemed a dream of everything the heart could desire; they fell into a happy discussion of ways and means, of the best places to buy fishing-tackle, of the clothes demanded by bogs and heathery mountains; until a nurse arrived with tea, and a warning word that the patients had talked nearly enough. At which the patients waxed indignant, declaring that their visitors had only been with them about ten minutes.

"Ten minutes!" said the nurse, round-eyed. "Over an hour—and doctor's orders were——"

"Never you mind the doctor's orders," Jim said solemnly. "Doctors don't know everything. Why, in Boulogne——" He broke off, assuming an air of meek unconsciousness of debate as the doctor himself appeared suddenly.

"I beg your pardon," said the doctor, transfixing patients with an eagle glance, while the nurse made an unobtrusive escape. "You were saying something about doctors, I think?"

"Nothing, I assure you, sir," said Jim, grinning widely.

"Doctors—and Boulogne," repeated the new-comer, firmly. "Don't let me interrupt you."

"No, sir. Certainly not," said Jim. "The doctors in Boulogne are very hard-worked."

"H'm!" said his medical attendant, receiving this piece of information with the suspicion it merited. "Quite so. We're all hard-worked, these times, chiefly with looking after bad boys who ought to be back at school, getting swished. It's an awful fate for a respectable M.D." He gazed severely at the cheerful faces on the pillows.

"You ought to be asleep; and of course you are not. Is this a hospital ward, or an Australian picnic?"

"Both," said Wally, laughing. "Don't be rough on us, doctor; it isn't every day we kill a pig!"

The doctor stared.

"You put things pleasantly!" he said. "It seems to me that the pigs were trying to kill you: but you're all extraordinarily cheerful about it. Now, where's Miss Norah gone? I never saw such a girl—she moves like quicksilver!"

Norah returned, bearing a spare cup.

"Do have some tea, doctor," she begged.

"I haven't time, but I will," said the doctor, abandoning professional cares, and sitting down. "One's life is all topsy-turvy nowadays. A year ago I would not have dreamed of having tea in a patient's bedroom—let alone two patients—but then, a year ago I was practising in Harley Street, developing a sweet, bedside manner and the figure of an alderman. Today I'm a semi-military hack, with no manner at all, and my patients chaff me—actually chaff me, Miss Norah! It's very distressing to one's inherited notions."

"It must be," said Norah, deeply sympathetic. "The cake is quite good, doctor."

"It is," agreed the doctor, accepting some. "Occasionally I find a pompous old colonel or brigadier among my patients, and we exchange soothing confidences about the terrible future of the medical profession and the Army. That helps; but then I come back to the long procession of the foolish subalterns who go out to Flanders without ever having learned to dodge!" His eye twinkled as he glared at Jim and Wally. Norah, whose visits to wounded soldiers during many weeks had taught her something beyond his reputation as the most skilful and most merciful of surgeons, listened unmoved and offered him more tea.

"It's no good trying to impress you!" said the doctor, surrendering his cup. "Thank you, I will have some more—in pure kindness of heart towards you, Miss Norah, since, when I leave this room, all visitors go with me!"

"Oh!" said Norah. "I'll get some fresh tea, doctor!"

"You will not," said the doctor, severely. "The picnic is nearly at an end: you can have another to-morrow, if you're good."

"When can we remove the patients, doctor?" asked Mr. Linton, who had been sitting in amused silence. A great contentment had settled on his face: already the lines of anxiety were smoothed away. He did not want to talk; it was sufficient to sit and watch Jim, occasionally meeting his eyes with a half-smile.

"Remove the patients—Good gracious!" ejaculated the doctor. "Why they've only just been removed once! Can't you let them settle down a little?"

"We want to take them to Ireland," said Norah, eagerly. "Can we, doctor?"

"H'm," said the doctor, reflectively. "There might be worse plans. We'll see. Ireland: that's the place where the motto is, 'When you see a head, hit it!' isn't it?"

"I don't think it's universal," said Mr. Linton mildly. "It's really much more peaceful than English legends would lead you to believe."

"Between you and me, what the average Englishmen knows of Ireland might, I believe, he put into one's eye without inconvenience," affirmed the doctor. "I'm a Scot, and I don't mind admitting I don't know anything. But no Englishman tells an Irish story without making his speakers say 'Bedad!' and 'Begorra!' in turn: and I've known a heap of Irishmen, and their conversation was singularly free from those remarks. I have an inward conviction that the English-made Irishman doesn't exist; only I never have time to verify any of my inward convictions. And perhaps that's as well, because then they never lose weight! Have I drunk all the tea, Miss Norah?"

"I'm afraid so," said Norah, tilting the teapot regretfully and without success. "Do let me get you some more. I know quite well where they make it."

"Go to!" said the doctor, rising. "Don't tempt an honest man from the path of duty. I'm off—and I give you three minutes. Then the patients are to compose themselves to slumber."

"And Ireland, doctor?"

"Ireland?" said the doctor, pausing in the doorway. "Oh, there's lots of time to think about that distressful country." He relented a little, looking at the eager faces. "Very possibly. We'll re-open the discussion this day week. Three minutes, mind. Good-bye." His quick steps died away along the corridor.

Half an hour later Wally wriggled on his pillow.

"Asleep, Jim?"

"No—not quite."

"D'you know something? Your people were here quite a while. And they never said one word about gas or war or any silly rot like that!"

"No," said Jim, drowsily. "Bricks, weren't they? Go to sleep."

CHAPTER IV
TO IRELAND

"Be it granted me to behold you again in dying,

Hills of home."

R. L. Stevenson.

HOLYHEAD pier was in the state of wild turmoil that seethes between the arrival of the mail and its transhipping to the Dublin boat. Passengers ran hither and thither, distractedly seeking luggage, while stolid English porters lent a deaf ear to their complainings or assured them absent-mindedly that everything would be all right on the other side; an assurance always given light-heartedly by the porter who is comfortably certain of the fact that, whatever happens on the other side, he will not be there. First and third class passengers mingled inextricably in the luggage-hunt, with equal lack of success, and divided into two streams when the whistle blew an impatient summons, seeking their respective gangways under the guiding shouts of officials on the upper deck. Through the crowd ploughed the mail trollies, regarding first and third class travellers alike as mere obstructors of His Majesty's business, and asserting their right-of-way by sheer weight and impetus. Overhead, a grey sky hung darkly, and was reflected in a grey, white-flecked sea.

It was not the usual Ireland-bound crowd of early summer. Comparatively few women were travelling, and except for a few elderly men, there was an entire absence of the knickerbocker-suited, tweed-capped travellers, with golf-clubs and rod-boxes, who make a yearly pilgrimage across the Irish Sea. Most of them were in Flanders or Gallipoli now, and khaki had replaced the rough tweeds; many would never come again. In their stead, khaki sprinkled the crowd thickly. A big detachment of soldiers returning after furlough, crowded the boat for'ard. Officers in heavy great-coats were everywhere; one chubby subaltern in charge of a regimental band, which had been assisting in a recruiting tour in Wales. A small group surrounded a tall old general, whose great-coat showed the crossed sword and baton, while his gold-laced and red-banded cap made him the object of awed glances from junior officers, who forthwith put as much of the ship as possible between themselves and his eagle eye.

Jim Linton and Wally Meadows were among the first out of the train. It was Jim's way to let a crowd disperse a little before he attempted to reach a given point. "You get there just as quickly, and it saves an awful lot of pushing and shoving," he said. But Wally's impatience never brooked any such delay; at all times he found it difficult to sit still, and once movement was permitted him, he was wont, as Jim further said, "to run three ways at once." Therefore, Jim being too peaceably inclined to argue the matter, they made a hurried descent to the platform, collected hand-luggage hastily, discovered a porter, assisted Mr. Linton and Norah to alight, and had marshalled their forces on the upper deck of the steamer while yet the main body of the passengers strove agonizedly to find their belongings. Then Jim made a leisurely inspection, discovered their heavy luggage in perfect safety, duly embarked: and rejoined his party with the calm certainty of all being right with the world.

People were disposing themselves after the varied fashion of 'cross-Channel passengers. Apprehensive ladies and a few men cast a despondent look at the grey sea and the white horses tumbling off-shore, and prudently sought the shelter of the cabins, hoping, by prompt lying down, to cheat the demon of sea-sickness. More seasoned travellers selected chairs on the main decks, pitched them where any gleams of sun might reach them, and settled down, rolled in rugs, to read through the boredom of the passage. On the railings, small boys perched themselves with the fell determination of small boys all the world over, while anxious mothers rent the air with fruitless appeals for them to come down, and wrathful fathers emphasized the commands with blows, or else smoked stolidly in the conviction that a small boy who was meant to fall in the sea would certainly fall there, in spite of his parents. Babies wailed dismally, until borne off to the cabin by mothers and nurses; sirens rent the air with hoarse shrieks; cranes, loading luggage, rattled and banged, and above their din rose the shouts of newsboys hawking London and Dublin papers. Every hand on the ship was working furiously, for the mail has no time to spare, and nothing matters to it but the time-table.

They were off presently, slipping away almost imperceptibly from the wharf, and nosing out to sea through the grey waves. The ship thrust her bow into them doggedly. The mail-boat's line is a straight line, and she takes no account of the foaming billows and the anguish of passengers, thrusting through everything from port to port. Several people who had settled down on deck more in hope than certainty cast sad glances on the sea, and disappeared hurriedly below.

Jim and Wally turned up their coat-collars as the breeze freshened, and stood swaying easily to the motion of the ship. They still bore traces of the ordeal they had undergone in the trenches; each was unnaturally pale and heavy-eyed, and recurring attacks of throat-trouble had kept them from regaining full strength. Wally's eyes, too, were weak: he was under orders to rest them altogether, and was therefore openly jubilant because he could not read war news—which, as he said, was one of the most wearying occupations, only you couldn't cease doing it without a decent excuse. "Vetted" by a Medical Board, the pair had been given six weeks' leave, at the end of which time they were to report progress.

Of the nerve-disorder which so frequently follows in the track of gas-poisoning they were fortunately entirely free. Possibly their dose had not been large enough: or their clean youth and perfect health had helped them to throw off the effects felt heavily by older men. They could joke about it now, and their longing to get "some of their own back" was so keen as almost to discount an Irish holiday. Still, war was likely to last long enough to give them all the fighting they needed: there was, after all, no immediate hurry. And it was glorious to feel strength returning: and the new fishing-rods and tackle bore fascinating promise, while Ireland itself was a country of their dreams.

As for Mr. Linton and Norah, they looked after the boys unceasingly, fed them at alarmingly short intervals, and in general manifested so subservient a desire to run all their errands that the victims revolted, declaring they were patients no longer, and threatening severe measures if they were not restored to independence. Norah and her father submitted unwillingly. To nurse trench-worn warriors had the double effect of being in itself comforting, while, so long as the nursing lasted, the warriors could not possibly consider returning to the trenches.

They looked about them as the swift steamer raced westward. Soldiers, soldiers everywhere; every likely youngster was in uniform, and there were many older men whose keen, quiet faces bore the ineffaceable stamp of the regular officer of the old Army—the old Army that was gone for ever, only a fragment left after the first fierce onslaught of war. The men for'ard were laughing and singing, just as they laughed and sang in the trenches; a cornet-player belonging to the band had found his instrument and was leading the tune. Near Norah, three or four nuns, sweet-faced and grave, were seated, evidently enjoying the keen wind that swept into their faces. There was the usual sprinkling of passengers, some mere heaps of rugs in deck-chairs, others walking briskly up and down. Somewhat apart, a tall old priest stood by the rail, looking ahead: a gaunt old man with burning, dark eyes, that searched the grey sea and sky wistfully, as if looking for the land to which they were hastening. Jim, strolling backwards and forwards, came presently to a standstill near him, and asked a question.

"Do you know what time we get in, sir?"

" 'Tis about three hours, I believe—that or less," said the old man, courteously. He turned a steady glance on Jim, and apparently approved of him, for he smiled. "Do you not know Ireland, then?"

Jim shook his head. "It's my first visit."

"So?" The old eyes looked ahead once more. "They take under three hours now to cross; 'twas many more last time I came away—the bitter day!" he added, half under his breath. "And that's three-and-forty years ago, my son!"

"What! and you've never been back, sir?"

"Never. I've been in America. A good country; but it never lets you go, and it never gets to be home. All that three-and-forty years I've been thinking of the day I'd be going back again."

"And it's come," said Jim, his smile suddenly lighting his grey eyes. The old man smiled back

"If you weren't so young I'd say you knew what it was to be homesick," said he.

"I come from Australia," said Jim, briefly.

"Well, well, well!" the priest said. "There's another great country—only so far away. There's many a good Irishman there, they tell me."

"Any number of them," said Jim. "We've got one of the best on our place—Murty O'Toole. He taught me to ride."

"Did he so? There were O'Tooles in Wicklow when I was a boy; but sure and they're all over the world. You'll be glad to go back, when the time comes?"

"Glad!" said Jim, explosively. He laughed. "It's very jolly, of course, to visit other places. But home's home, isn't it, sir?"

"Aye," said the old man. He looked ahead, his eyes misty. "Three-and-forty years I've dreamed of it; and now I'm waiting to see the hills of Ireland coming out of the sea, and this last hour seems longer than all the years. Well, well; and they're all dead, all the people I knew; and I going home to die, like a wornout old dog."

"You'll live in Ireland many a year yet, sir," Jim told him, quickly.

"No, no; I'm done. 'Tis my heart, and it finished—sure, wouldn't forty years of work in New York finish any heart!" said the old man, laughing. "But I'm lucky to be getting back to Ireland to die. Did you ever hear, now, of the Sons of Tuireann?"

Jim shook his head. "I'm afraid not, sir."

"They were great fighting men, and they had great hardship," said the priest: "and at the end of all things they were on the sea coming home, dying. And one of them cried out that he saw the hills of home. And the others said, 'Raise up our heads on your breast till we see Ireland again: and life or death will be the same to us after that.' So they died. That was a good ending. A man wouldn't ask better. 'Tis a hard thing, dying in a strange country, but you'd go very easy, once you got home." He spoke half to himself, so low that the boy hardly caught the words. They stood silently for awhile, looking ahead across the tumbling sea.

"I had no right to be talking to you about dying," the old priest said presently, turning to Jim with a smile that made his face extraordinarily child-like. "Old men get foolish; and my heart's too big for my body this day, and I getting home. Tell me now—are ye Irish, at all?"

"My mother was Irish," Jim answered.

"I'd have said so. What part might she have come from?—and is she with you?"

"She died when I was a kiddie," Jim answered. "She came from Donegal. Father says she always loved it."

"Well, well! Wherever you're born, you love that place. But I think the love for Ireland is beyond most things. The people leave it because there's no room for them and no money; but no matter where they go they leave the half of their hearts behind. And they put something of the love into their children no matter where they're born, so that they always want to come and see Ireland: and when they come, 'tis no strange place to them; they feel they've come home. You'll feel it—for all that you love that big young country of yours, and want to get back to her. But every old ruin, and every bit of brown bog and heathery mountain, and every little stony field, will say something to you that you will not be able to put into words: and when you go back you will not forget. There, there! I'm talking again!" said the old man; "and to a boy with business of his own. Tell me, now, have you been out across yonder yet?" He nodded in the direction of Flanders.

They talked of war, the priest nodding vehemently and punctuating Jim's brief sentences with exclamations of "Well, well!" The wistfulness dropped from him suddenly; he was a fighting man, a Crusader—with a young man's burning desire to be out in the trenches, and a young man's keenness to hear details of battle. "There's fifty thousand French priests fighting for France," he said, enviously: "none the worse soldiers for being priests, I'll vow, and they'll be all the better priests afterwards for having been soldiers! If I were young! if I were young!" He laughed at his own vehemence. "It's your day," he said; "a great world just now for young men. And they tell me there's any number of them out of khaki yet—standing behind counters and selling lace and ribbons; and some of them doing women's hair! More shame for the women that let them!"

"If a man wants to stay out of the game and do women's work, well that's all he's fit for," said Jim, slowly. "He's not wanted where there's work going. But he ought to have some sort of a brand put on him, so that people will be able to tell him from a man in future!"

The priest chuckled appreciatively.

"Petticoats are the brand he wants," said he. "And an extra tax put on him, to support the widows and children of the men who were men—who went and fought to save his worthless hide. 'Tis a shame, now, they wouldn't make him pay some way. Well, they wouldn't have me in the trenches—and it's good sense they have; but for all I'm a broken-down old ruin I'm going fighting—fighting with my tongue against the boys that stay at home. Perhaps they don't realize—the young ones: they might listen to an old man that was a priest. Just a few days to rest and feel I'm home at last, and I'm going to do my bit as a recruiting sergeant!"

"Good luck!" Jim said, heartily. "Only don't get knocked up, sir."

The old man laughed.

" 'Tis only once a man can die," he said, cheerfully. "I'd die easier knowing I'd done my bit, as you boys say. But I'm in dread I'll lose my temper with them, especially if I meet the lads that dress heads of hair! They wash them too, I'm told. Well, well, it's a queer world!"

Wally came up, faintly indignant at Jim's lengthy absence, and joined in the talk: and presently Mr. Linton and Norah followed, and made friends with the old man. He was such a simple, cheery old man: it was easy to be friends with him. They grew merry over queer stories from many countries, and often the priest's laugh rang out like a boy's, while his own stories brought peals of mirth from his new friends. But through it all his dark eyes kept searching ahead: ever looking, looking till the hills of Ireland should lift from the sea.

"They tell me you have big trees in that Australia of yours," he said. "Tell me now, are they as big as the Californian redwoods?"

"I don't know the redwoods," Wally answered solemnly. "But ours are big. There's a story of twelve men who started with axes and cross-cut saws to get a gum-tree down. They worked on one side for nine months and then they got bored with that, and they packed up and made a journey round to the other side. And there they found a party of fifteen men who'd been working at that side for a year, and they were very surprised——" Laughter overcame him suddenly at the sight of the priest's amazed face.

"You young rascal!" said he, joining in the laugh against himself. "And I taking it all in so meekly!"

"I might go on, if you liked, sir, and tell you the story of the man who was out in the bush bringing home some calves," said Wally.

"Don't spare me," begged his hearer.

"Well, he found his way blocked by a fallen tree, too big to get the calves over. So he started to drive them along it, to get round. When he didn't come home they came to the conclusion that he had stolen the calves; and so they had to apologize to him, later on, when he turned up with a nice lot of bullocks. He said proudly that he hadn't lost one, only they had grown up while they were on the journey!"

"That was a long tree!" said the priest, between chuckles. "Well, well, it must be a great country that will grow such timber—and such stories, and the boys to tell them!"

Wally laughed.

"I ought to beg your pardon, sir," he said. "Only no good Australian can resist telling tall stories about his tall trees. But I can tell you a true one of a tree I knew where seven men camped in the hollow butt. They had bunks built inside, all round it, and a table in the middle, and of course, space for a doorway. That tree was over fifty-five feet inside, and goodness only knows what it was outside, buttresses and all."

"And it's true, I suppose, that you could drive a coach-and-four through a tree?" the priest asked.

"Driving a coach-and-four through the hollowed-out stump of a tree used to be common enough with us," said Jim. "Not that the four horses mattered: you might as well say 'and twelve'; it was the width high enough up to take the top of the coach that meant a really big tree. It was easier to make a hollow shell fit for the passage of the coach than to get the whole tree cut down."

"Quite so—quite so," said the priest. "And I've read of church services being held in a hollow tree, in your country."

"Rather. We know one that held twenty-two people. It was in a wild part of the bush, and whatever clergyman came along used to use it—Roman Catholic, Protestant, Presbyterian or Baptist; it didn't matter. Every one used to roll up, for it wasn't often there was a chance of a church service. There were lots of jobs for the travelling parson, too: all the accumulated weddings and christenings."

"Do you tell me!" said the priest.

"My mother had three children before ever a chance came of a baptism," said Mr. Linton. "Then the three were done together. I was the eldest, and I remember being extremely indignant about it—I was four years old, and it was winter, and the water was cold! It was a standing joke against me afterwards that I had behaved so much worse than my small brother and sister." He laughed, and then grew grave. "Poor bush mothers! they didn't have an easy time. Two of my mother's babies died without ever having seen a clergyman; to the end of her life she worried about the little souls that had gone out unbaptized."

"It was themselves needed great hearts—those pioneer women," said the priest.

"They did; and mostly they had great hearts. But then I think most women have, if the need really comes," Mr. Linton said. "Thousands of them were delicate, tenderly-reared women, with no experience of bush conditions in a new country; but they made good. Women have a curious way of finding themselves able to tackle any conditions with which they are actually faced. My mother never was strong, and she had no training for work; I expect she was something of a butterfly until she married my father and went off into the Never-Never. She ended by being a kind of oracle for fifty miles round; people used to send for her at all hours of the day or night, in sickness, and she developed a business capacity better than my father's. I remember her as a little, merry thing: always tired, but never too tired to work for other people. She was only one of thousands of women doing the same thing."

"But the process of learning must have been hard," said the old priest, pityingly.

"Yes. It must have been a tough apprenticeship. My mother told me she used to sit down and cry often at the loneliness and strangeness of it all—in the long days when all the men were miles away from the homestead, and she was alone, with the chance of bush fires and bushrangers and wild blacks. That was until the babies came. After that there was no time to cry—which, she said, was a very good thing for her. Poor little mother!"

He sighed; and in the silence that followed a slight commotion was audible on the bridge. The priest glanced up sharply.

"Nothing—but that cruel business of the Lusitania makes everyone suspicious at sea, nowadays," he said. "Still, the Germans may be active enough in the south, but I don't fancy they'll come into these landlocked waters. Too much risk from our destroyers."

Norah was leaning over the rail.

"What's that thing?" she said, slowly.

Their eyes followed the direction of her pointing finger. Nearly astern, a slender grey object bobbed among the waves: so small a thing that an idle glance might easily have passed it by unnoticed. A shadowy, grey bar, bearing aloft what looked like a nut.

Jim uttered a shout.

"By Jove, it's a submarine!"

Even as he shouted, a long grey shadow came into view under the bar. Simultaneously, the engine-telegraph clanged from the bridge, and following the signal, the steamer altered her course with a jerk that sent most of the standing passengers headlong to the deck. They picked themselves up, unconscious of bruises, rushing again to the rail.

The submarine was well in view—a slender, vicious, grey boat, with a little cluster of men visible on her tiny deck, round the shaft of the periscope. She was terribly near. Suddenly a volume of black smoke gushed from the steamer's funnels; the firemen were flinging themselves at their work below, since on speed alone hung their slender hope of safety. Again she altered her course. Sharp orders came from the bridge; sailors were running to and fro, and an officer was serving out life-belts frantically.

Something shot from the submarine—something that made a long, glistening streak across the water, coming straight towards them like a flash; and David Linton flung his arm round Norah muttering, "My God!" A strained, high voice cried, "A torpedo!" and then silence fell upon the ship, broken only by the smothered gasps of women. Straight and swift the streak came; unimaginably swift, and yet the watching seemed a lifetime.

"Hold tight to the rail," Jim's voice said in Norah's ear. She gripped mechanically; and as she did so, the steamer jerked again, plunging to one side like a frightened horse that sees danger. It was just in time. The torpedo shot past, missing the bow by a fraction—a space so small that it was almost impossible to believe that it had indeed missed. Then came relief, finding vent in an irrepressible shout.

"It's too soon to shout," some one said. "She'll make better shooting next time."

Stewards and sailors were hurrying round, distributing life-belts; it was no easy matter to put them on, for the ship was zigzagging wildly, dodging in a desperate effort to elude her pursuer, and balance was impossible without a firm hold on some fixed object.

"Sit on the deck—it's safest," said Mr. Linton. He fastened Norah's life-belt, while Jim performed a similar office for him, and Wally put one on the old priest, who was so wild with excitement as to be quite oblivious of any such precaution. His face was deadly white, his dark eyes blazing. In his first fall he had lost his black felt hat, and his silver hair waved in the wind.

"The murdering villains—the assassins!" he said. "Yerra, if I could fight!"

An officer called for helpers to bring the women and children from below. Jim and Wally sprang in answer, and a crowd of soldiers came tumbling up from for'ard, elbowing their officers in mad excitement and the rush to be first. Quick and strong hands were needed on the companion ladders with their burdens, as the ship plunged hither and thither, racing in zig-zags at top speed. Many of the women were helpless between fear and the aftermath of sea-sickness; but they came without outcry, with set white faces, determined, if this were indeed Death, to die decently. The babies howled with a lusty disregard of the world common to babies, while the soldiers patted them with far more concern than they showed for the submarine. In a very few minutes not a soul was left below.

"Why do we zigzag?" Norah asked, clinging to the rail as a fresh jerk shook the ship.

"It's our only chance," Jim answered. "I don't think the submarines can beat these boats for speed, or else she'd just come up and sink us at her leisure; and she can't take aim accurately if we're dodging. Of course we cut down our speed by not going straight; but we can't afford the risk of letting her train her torpedo-tube carefully on us. Jove, can't the skipper handle this ship! She answers the helm like a motor-car."

"And can't she go!" uttered Wally.

"Oh, the mail-boats are built for speed and not much else—thank goodness!" Jim said. "Look!—she's firing again!"

Again the streak shot from the pursuing submarine and darted towards them. They held their breath.

It was a very close shave—only a lightning swerve saved the mail-boat. The old priest uttered a sudden shout of triumph. "Whirroo!" he cried—for a moment just the boy who had left Wicklow more than forty years ago. He shook as he gripped the rail, laughing at the racing grey shadow that followed them.

Jim Linton's eyes were on his little sister: and Norah, feeling them, slipped a hand into his.

"If it hadn't been for us you wouldn't be in this," he said, miserably.

Norah opened her eyes in amazement.

"But that just makes it not matter so much," she said. "Just fancy if we weren't all together! Don't you worry, Jimmy." She smiled at him very cheerfully.

"If she hits us and we begin to sink, don't wait for the ship to go over," Mr. Linton said. "Half the boats on the Lusitania were death-traps. Let us all jump in and keep together if we can; we would have more chance of being picked up, and less of being taken down in the suction as she sank. Can you swim, Father?"—to the priest.

"I can. But it's years since I tried, and I don't know would I keep afloat at all," said the old man, with unimpaired cheerfulness. "Let you take your own course, and not trouble about me. I'm too old to try jumping, and there'll be some poor souls I could maybe help. And we're not beaten yet." He gave a quick laugh, his grey head well up. "We're running away, but it's a good fight we're putting up, all the same: something to see, after forty years in a New York slum!"

"I believe he likes it!" said Wally, under his breath. But the old man caught the words.

"Like it! I used to dream of adventures when I was a boy, and it was all the sea—clean winds and waves, and ships that were always magic to me. And it ended in a slum: forty years of it, doing my work in the midst of filth and wretchedness. Well, every man has his work, and mine lay there. And now, at the end, this! I always knew 'twas luck I'd have if I got back to Ireland!"

They had raced away in a straight course after the second torpedo, increasing the distance from their pursuer. Now, however, a shot hummed past them, and the captain dared no longer risk a hit—again the ship swerved from side to side, in short, irregular tacks, and the submarine drew nearer once more. On and on—leaping like a hare when the greyhound is behind her: engines throbbing, smoke blackening the sky in her wake. Some of the firemen had staggered up, exhausted, their places taken by volunteers. Ahead, a dim line lay upon the sea: the Irish coast, where lay safety. Would they ever reach it?

Then, from the north, came rescue: a patrol-boat, racing down upon them with threatening guns ready to speak in their defence. She came out of a light haze, which, blowing away, revealed her dogged grey shape, with the white water churning and parting at her bow. Presently one of her guns spoke, and a shell buried itself in the sea not far from the submarine.

"So long, Brother Boche!" said an officer; and suddenly, as if in answer, the submarine disappeared, submerging to the safety of the underworld. The mail-boat ceased to zigzag, running a straight course until near the destroyer, as a child runs to a protector.

The tension relaxed. Voices broke out in quick clamour: and then cheer after cheer came from the pent-up passengers, redoubling as the captain's face showed over the railings of the bridge. The captain grinned, saluted, and looked at his watch all at once: the danger was over, and now the pressing business of his ordinary life reasserted itself—the landing in time at Kingstown Pier of His Majesty's mails.

People were laughing and talking nervously, keeping an anxious look-out towards the spot where the submarine had disappeared; scarcely realizing that their peril was past, and that the grey hunter would not again reveal itself, hurrying upon their track. The destroyer shot past them, seeking the enemy, with signal flags talking busily to the mail-boat. A comforting sense of security was in her wake.

"Well!" said Jim. "We left England to find peace and quiet; but if this is a specimen of what Ireland means to give us———"

"We'd better get back to the peaceful marshes of Flanders," finished Wally.

"I used to think when I was at home—at Billabong—that excitement would be nice," said Norah. "But it isn't—not a bit: or else I've had an overdose. At any rate, I don't want any more as long as I live."

A little sigh came from behind her, and her father made a sudden movement, springing to the side of the priest. The old man was swaying backwards and forwards. They caught him, and laid him gently on the deck. His lips parted, and he tried to speak, but no sound came.

"Go and look for a doctor," said Mr. Linton to Wally. "Quick!"

He tore at the old man's collar, while Norah rubbed his hands desperately. It seemed the only thing she could do. A little life came into the white face, and his voice came faintly.

" 'Tis the finish for me—don't worry . . . my heart." He smiled at them. "And the doctor after telling me not to get excited."

"Don't talk," Norah begged.

"It can't hurt me. Don't mind, little one." He saw the tears in her eyes, and tightened his hand on her fingers. " 'Tis a good ending. I wouldn't ask for a better."

Wally came back, a young man in uniform, with the R.A.M.C. badge on his collar, at his heels. The doctor bent over the old priest. Presently he rose, shaking his head as he met David Linton's eyes.

"There's nothing to be done," he said, softly.

The old man's hearing was no less acute.

" 'Tis myself could have told you that," he said. "I knew . . . next time it came. And . . . when a man's ready . . ."

His voice became almost inaudible, murmuring broken words of prayer. Behind them Jim had formed a line of soldiers, keeping off the curious crowd. Presently he spoke again.

"It's easy, dying. Only it would be easier if I'd seen it again . . . Ireland."

"We're very near," Norah told him, pityingly.

"Near! And not to see it!" He tried to rise, helplessly. "Ah, but let me look—let me look!"

David Linton's eyes met the doctor's.

"It can't hurt him," whispered the doctor. "Nothing can do that now."

They lifted him, very gently. Ahead, the hills of Wicklow were green and near. The grey sky had broken, and a little shaft of sunlight stole out and lay upon the coast. It was as though Ireland smiled to welcome back her son.

The dark eyes looked long and wistfully. Once he smiled at Norah; and then looked back quickly, as though to lose no instant of home. Presently his lips parted in broken words.

"Till we see . . . till we see Ireland again; and life or death will be the same to us after that." Then no more words came. But when the doctor signed to them to lay him down he was still smiling.

CHAPTER V
INTO DONEGAL
"A homely-looking folk they are, these people of my kin;

Their hands are hard as horse-shoes, but their hearts come through the skin.

Old Michael Clancy said to me (his age is eighty-seven),

'There's no place like Australia—barring Ireland and Heaven!' "

V. J. Daley.

"WE ought to be nearly there," said Jim.

" 'Ought' seems to be the last argument that counts on this railway line," his father answered. "What grounds have you for your fond belief?"

"It's not time-tables," his son admitted. "They wore out long ago; I scrapped them when they got to the stage when reading them only led to despair. Partly I'm hoping that the guard wasn't merely trying to keep up my spirits when he told me we'd get to Killard at three o'clock if Jamesy Doyle wasn't late with his milk-cans at Ballymoe; only he added that 'twas the bad little ass Jamesy had, and if it lay down in the cart how would the poor man be in time?"

"And will they wait for Jamesy and his cans?" queried Wally.

"Most certainly, I should think. Passengers are just odd happenings, to the guard; but Jamesy is married to a woman that's the cousin of his wife's aunt, and the guard evidently has a strong family sense. This train exists as much to carry Jamesy's cans as anything else. However, there's Ballymoe, and the gentleman on the platform looks as if he might be Jamesy. And there's the ass in the cart outside, standing up. I expect it's all right."

The little train drew slowly into the wayside station, and the guard, descending, wrung the hand of the somnolent gentleman enthroned upon the milk-cans. Together they proceeded to load them into the van, but being overcome by argument in the middle of the operation, relinquished work, sat down on the cans, and gave themselves up to the delights of conversation. The Linton family got out, and walked along the platform. They had been travelling from early morning into the wilds of Donegal, and, since leaving the main line for a succession of local trains, had grown well accustomed to these sociable delays. Presently the engine-driver and his fireman left their engine and joined the discussion on the milk-cans. Norah strolled to the road and scratched the ass gently, a proceeding accepted by the ass without resentment, but without enthusiasm. Time went by.

The gathering on the platform dissolved itself after a while, the first move being made by Mr. Jamesy Doyle, who remarked that his wife'd be tearing the hair off of him, and she waiting for him for dinner.

"She'll not wait long on ye; I know that one!" said the guard.

"She will, then; sure, haven't I it bought in the little cart yonder?" said Jamesy, with the calmness of certainty. He assisted to place the remainder of his property in the van, and the guard, addressing Norah with enormous politeness, mentioned that when she was quite ready the train would go on. "Let you not be hurrying yourself—sure we're that late already as makes no difference," he added, pleasantly. They climbed in, and the little train clanged and rattled on its way.

At the next station two energetic men in tweed suits descended hurriedly from the one first-class smoking-carriage and demanded their bicycles, which had been put in an empty truck—the train being of the type known as a "mixed goods." Thereafter arose sounds of wrath and vituperation.

"Something's up; I'm going to see," said Wally.

They all went to see. The two cyclists, visions of helpless rage, confronted a scene of desolation. The truck, being opened, disclosed upon the floor a mingled heap of scrap-iron and twisted metal, which had once been two fair bicycles: in the midst of which, firmly caught among the battered spokes, a couple of fat wethers stood and bleated a woe almost equal to that of the cyclists. A dozen more sheep, most of them bearing traces of conflict with the defunct machines, in the shape of scarred legs, pressed about the doorway, while the guard, distraught to incoherence, endeavoured to restrain them from escaping while attempting to justify himself before the outraged owners. Totally unsuccessful in the second endeavour, he was only partially fortunate in the first: a black-faced sheep, bearing a mudguard wedged upon his horns, made a dash for freedom and fled wildly down the platform, apparently maddened by his unfamiliar adornment.

"And I after putting them in at one end of the truck!" lamented the guard—"and them bikes standing against the other end! Wasn't there room for them all—how would I know they'd mix up on me! Get back there, bad luck to ye, ye vilyun!"—to another black-faced aspirant for liberty.

Helpers, divided in their sympathies, but with the preponderance of feeling on the side of the guard, appeared mysteriously from an apparently empty landscape and disentangled the sheep from the ruins. The engine-driver, cutting the Gordian knot of debate, discovered that the time-table demanded that the train should proceed forthwith; and the cyclists were left foaming over a twisted heap on the platform, threatening immediate telegrams to headquarters, and, if necessary, murder. As the train slid away from the sound of their lamentations, the fugitive sheep could be descried standing on a bank, his black visage melancholy beneath the mudguard.

At the next station, the guard, with a chastened face, appeared at the window.

"Killard, sir," he stated. "And Patsy Burke, he have the outside car and an ass-cart for ye."

Mr. Linton and his party obeyed the summons gladly. They found themselves on a grass-grown platform, boasting very rudimentary station-buildings. Beyond, a road ran east and west, bordered by high banks, while on either side were small fields and wide, flat stretches of bog. A long, thin man advanced to meet them. No one else had left the train, and he accepted them, without introduction, as his responsibility.

"The car is below in the road," he said. "The little horse, he have an objection to the train; he'd lep a ditch sooner than face it. I'll throw the luggage on the ass-cart, sir, before I take you up."

The guard, still subdued in spirit, was diligently hauling out boxes from his van. A suit-case and the rod-box, failing to appear, were made the objects of fevered search, despaired of, promised by the next train, and finally discovered in an empty third class carriage, all within the space of five minutes. The ass-cart, drawn by a dispirited donkey without energy to disapprove of trains, was backed on to the platform, and the luggage piled upon it in a tottery heap, secured—more or less—by an assortment of knotted string and old rope. Then the guard and engine-driver, both of whom had assisted enthusiastically, bade an affectionate farewell, and the train disappeared slowly, while the Australians followed Patsy Burke meekly to the outside car.

Dublin had already introduced them to the jaunting-car of Ireland, and they had fallen instant victims to the fascination of that most irresponsible vehicle. English tourists are wont to regard it with fear and trembling until familiar with its ways: to hold on desperately, to sit stiffly, and, very frequently, to fall off when rounding corners. That the Linton party did none of these things was not due to any superior intelligence on their parts, but merely to the fact that the back-to-back position on the open-air cars of the Melbourne tramways proved an excellent introduction to the Irish vehicle—insomuch that the force of habit was so strong in Wally that the Melbourne gripman's habitual ejaculation, "Hold tight round the curve!" sprang unbidden to his lips every time the jarveys took a corner on one wheel. The Dublin jarveys had liked the cheery Australians, who paid well and frankly averred that there was never any conveyance like the jingling cars with their merry little bells, and their good horses; and the jarveys of Dublin are a critical race, with quick tongues and quicker wits. They had confided to them their woes, which centred round the introduction of motor-cars and the complete indifference of pedestrians to the rule of the road—an indifference universal throughout Ireland, where the unseasoned traveller is perpetually a-shiver with dread at threatened street tragedies, perpetually averted by good luck that amounts to a miracle.

"I never seen the equal of these people," one of their drivers had said, emitting a roar like a bull of Bashan, which barely saved an elderly woman from what looked like deliberate suicide under his horse's hoofs. "Yerra, ma'am, is it owning the road you are?"—to the lady, who pursued her leisurely way with the calmness born of many such episodes. "Young or old, 'tis all the same; they do be strolling the streets for all the world as if they was picking mushrooms, and taking no notice of you till you'd be knocking them down—and then they do be annoyed! There's only one way, and that is to let a roar out of you at them—and then the look they give you is worse than a curse!"

"I suppose you get into trouble if you kill more than six a day," Wally had said.

The jarvey grinned.

"Trouble, is it? Sure, some of them makes a trade of it; there's them old wasters in this town that'd ask nothing better than that you'd knock 'em down—not to kill them, but to knock a small piece off them, the way you'd have to support them afterwards. There's one man I but tipped with the end of a shaft, and he strolling at his aise in a crowd. Crawling at a slow walk I was; and what did he do but rowl on the ground before me, letting on that he was kilt. There was none of the polis about, so I left him rowling and calling murder!"

"Did you hear any more of him?"

"I did. Didn't he come to me that evening and say he had his witnesses ready, and he'd be making a polis-court matter of it if I didn't give him five pounds? 'I do be making twenty-eight shillings a week,' says he, 'in me health,' says he, and now 'tis the way I cannot lift me hand to me head,' he says. Him, that never earned five shillings in a week in his life, and not that, if he could steal it! I towld him to bring his polis-court and his dirty witnesses, and that if he did, I'd pay the five pounds for the pleasure I'd have in belting the life out of him."

"And did he bring it?"

"He did not. I seen him a week after that, and he cleaning steps. 'I'm glad to see you looking so well and hearty, me poor man!' says I to him; and he thrun a look at me fit to kill. Sure I knew that one'd be more anxious to keep out of the way of the polis than to be dandhering about them with his cases!"

The Dublin cars had been smart affairs, spick-and-span with bright paint and clean upholstering, every buckle on their harness polished brightly. Their rubber tyres strove to soften the asperities of cobbled streets. But the car to which Patsy Burke led the Australians was of a different aspect: small and forbidding, with straight up-and-down seats whereon reposed cushions from which the stuffing had chiefly escaped, the insignificant remnant remaining in hard knobs in the corners. The original wood peeped out through faint streaks of the original paint, while here and there patches of deal and hoop-iron lent variety to the exterior. Many different sets had contributed towards the composition of the harness, wherein nothing matched except in age and decrepitude. A tattered urchin stood at the head of the little horse which had an objection to trains. The horse was asleep.

"If I were asked," murmured Norah, surveying him, "I would say he had an objection to moving at all."

"He looks as if he would like to lean up against a tree and dream," said Wally, "and good gracious! is he going to drag the lot of us!"

"Why wouldn't he?" asked Mr. Burke, with some asperity. "Git along with ye to the ass, John Conolly,"—to the boy—"and lend a hand to the big thrunk when the road does be rough, or it will fall off on ye. Will ye get up, miss?"

"Is it far?" asked Norah, regarding the somnolent horse with troubled eyes.

" 'Tis five Irish miles, miss."

"But can he take us all? There's—there's so much of us," said Norah, her glance roving over her tall menfolk, and dwelling finally on Mr. Burke, who was not less tall.

"Him!" said Mr. Burke. "But isn't the luggage on the ass-cart? Sure it'll only be a luxury for him—many's the time I've known that one with seven or eight behind him, going to a funeral, and he that full of courage, I'd me own throubles to keep him from bolting? Let ye get up, and 'tis little he'll be making of ye."

They got up, unhappily, and Mr. Burke hopped into the driver's seat—which is occupied only in time of stress, the jarvey greatly preferring to drive from the side. He said, "G'wan, now!" to the little horse, and that animal awoke and took the road gallantly, while a cracked bell on his collar rattled a discordant accompaniment to his hoof-beats.

They jogged on between the high banks. The scent of the whitethorn that made snow upon their crests flooded the air, and mingled with deep wafts of odour from clumps of furze lying golden in the fields. There were other flowers starring the hedges; honeysuckle, waving long arms of sweetness, and, nestling closely in the grass-grown banks, clusters of wild violets, starry celandines and even a few late primroses. There were many houses in sight; little whitewashed cabins scattered over the hills, approached by narrow boreens or tiny lanes, so narrow that it seemed that even an ass-cart could scarcely manage to squeeze in between their towering banks.

"Did you ever see such little paddocks—fields, I ought to say?" uttered Wally. "And the great fat banks and hedges between them! Why, they must cover as much ground as there is in many of the fields!"

"We'd put wire-fences, in Australia," said Mr. Linton, laughing. "It's queer, when you come to think of it: we're supposed to have land to spare, but we put the narrowest fences that can be made; and here, there isn't enough to go round, and they cover up ever so much of it with their banks."

"Oh, but aren't you glad they don't make wire-fences!" Norah broke out. "They're so hideous: and these hedges are just exquisite."

"Not being a landholder, I am, indeed," said her father. "The idea of this landscape given up to wire-fences is depressing—long may they stick to their banks! And their shelter must be valuable in this country; they don't seem to have many trees." His eye ran over the bare little fields. "Don't you grow trees, in Donegal?" he asked of the back of Mr. Burke.

That gentleman, feeling himself addressed, swung round.

"There do be plenty in the woods and in gentlemen's grounds, sir. I never seen any in the fields. They do say there was any amount in the ould ancient days, or how would the bogs be there? Forests, no less; and quare beasts in them. I've seen ould heads of deer with horns that wide you'd never get them up a boreen. There were no fields and no fences in those days, and people lived by hunting—great hunting those big deer would give them, to be sure. If you'd kill a rabbit nowadays it'd be as much as you'd do to ate it before the polis had you!"

"If killing rabbits is what you care for, you might come to Australia," said Jim, laughing. "You would certainly be welcome there. Only after a little while, you wouldn't eat any."

"There was a lad I knew in Derry went out to them parts," said Mr. Burke, "and he sent home letters with such tales of his doings you wouldn't believe them. He said there were beasts that hopped on their tails faster than a horse 'ud gallop, and rabbits that had the face ate off the country. Like a carpet on the floor, he says. But sure he was always the boy that'd spin you a yarn."

"It was a true yarn, anyhow," Jim remarked.

"Do ye tell me, now?" The long face of Patsy Burke was respectful, but incredulous, "And another thing he said, that a man couldn't believe: that the genthry'd go out and poison foxes!"

"They would," said Mr. Linton. "Gladly."

"But———" Words failed Mr. Burke. He gaped at his passengers. The horse dropped to a walk, unheeded.

"Poison them, or shoot them, or get rid of them in any way possible," said Jim, enjoying the mounting agony of Mr. Burke. "We can't do much hunting, you see, when we live on big places, with the nearest neighbour perhaps twenty miles off; and often the hills are so steep and rough, and so thick with fallen timber, that horses and hounds would want wings to hunt through them. But a man may have thousands of sheep on hills like that."

"Do ye tell me? Thousands, is it?"

"Rather. And the foxes breed like rabbits in those hills, and there's nothing they like so well as young lambs. You can go out in the morning and find forty or fifty dead lambs—the cruel brutes of foxes just eat their noses and go on to the next. When you see that number of little lambs killed, in that fashion, you're ready to start poisoning foxes."

"Ye would so," said Mr. Burke, explosively. "And no one interferes with ye?"

"Why, you get paid for it," Jim said. To which Mr. Burke replied by a gasp of "God help us!" and relieved his feelings by lashing the horse with a shout of "G'wan, now!" The horse broke into a surprised canter, and they rocked down a little hill. At its foot a wide expanse of bog stretched westward, looking like a great grassy plain. Here and there, near the road, men were working at cutting turf, armed with the loy or narrow, sharp spade, which takes out a sod of turf, the size of a brick, to be stacked to dry in the sun. A great corner had already been cut away, and lay bleak and desolate. Above its level the wall of turf rose three or four feet, a dark-brown glutinous-looking mass, smoothly marked with the scars of the loy. There were deep pools of water here and there: the brown bog-water that scares the English tourists who finds it in a bedroom jug in a hotel, and gives foundation for future scathing comments on the dirty ways of Ireland: the fact being that if its exquisite velvet-softness could be taken to London, most of the Bond Street complexion specialists would go out of business for lack of customers.

"So that's turf," commented Wally, looking curiously at the rough stacks of sods, which the sun was drying to a lighter colour than the deep brown of the bog-face. "It doesn't look the sort of stuff you'd make fires of—wherein I expect I show my hideous ignorance."

Mr. Burke had begun with a snort at the first part of this remark, but checked it in its birth at the frank avowal of the conclusion.

"Wait till ye see it burn, sir," he said. "Ye'd not want a better fire, barring ye could get a bit of bog-wood to mix with it. Then ye'd not get its aiqual if ye were walking the world all your life."

"Are those pools deep?" Norah asked, looking at the still brown water, fringed with reeds and sedges.

"Some of 'em's no depth at all; and there's some that deep that no man knows the bottom of 'em. They'd take anyone and swallow him entirely, the way he'd never be heard of again; and they do say the bog keeps 'em fresh as if they'd just fallen in, only I dunno would it be true: I never seen anybody that had come out. It's one of the old stories that do be going in the country."

"When we talk about a bog, we mean something that looks—well, boggy," Norah said. "I never thought an Irish bog looked so pretty; all grass and rushes, like a big plain. Why do they call it a bog?"

"You'd know if you got into it," said Mr. Burke, bearing patiently with the ignorance of the foreigner. "There's parts of it firm enough to gallop a horse over; but you'd want to know where you were going, it's that treacherous—it'd let you down as deep as your waist in a second, and it looking safe as a street. Some of the mosses that do be growing on it 'ud warn you: there's one or two kinds that only grow where it's deep and quaking. As for pretty—it's airly yet for flowers; but you'd see it like a garden, in the autumn, with meadowsweet and loosestrife and canavan, that they call the bog-cotton, like snow lying on it. There's no end to the quare things that do be growing in a bog."

They passed ass-carts, built up with basket work to form creels, piled high with turf,—generally in the charge of a barefooted urchin, dark-eyed and graceful in his rags, who would fling a cheery "Good-day" at the car rattling by, touching his cap to "the genthry."

" 'Tis a great year for saving turf," Mr. Burke told them. "There's no knowing what the war'll be doing with prices; they say the poor people'll be hard put to it to go on living at all. So everyone's getting turf; sure, it's easier to be hungry if you're warm. I dunno, at all, why would they make a war: didn't we have enough and too much to pay for tea and tobacco as it was without the ould Kaiser poking in his nose?" Thus adjusting satisfactorily the responsibility for his financial troubles, Mr. Burke addressed the horse angrily, and drove on in silence.

They came to a little river, brawling merrily under a bridge of grey stone. A turn in the road brought trees in view, fringing a lough that lay tranquil in the sunlight; a placid sheet of blue water broken here and there by tiny islands. Towards the end that was nearest, the trees were thickly planted. Between them they caught glimpses of an old stone house nestling in a wilderness of a garden that ran down almost to the edge of the lough.

Patsy Burke swung the little horse in through a gateway, the iron gates of which stood invitingly open. They jogged up a winding avenue, overhung with lofty beech-trees. It ended suddenly in front of the house. Through a wide doorway they could see a dim hall, where a bewildering collection of old guns and blunderbusses was ranged over a massive mahogany table, the legs of which ended in claw-feet that would have drawn a connoisseur like a magnet. Honeysuckle and roses climbed together up the old walls, framing the doorway in blossom.

"Are ye there, ma'am?" bawled Patsy.

A pleasant-faced woman came through the hall quickly.

"I'd have given up expecting you, if that old train was ever in time," she said, giving a hand to Norah as that damsel hopped from the car. "Aren't you all tired out, and you travelling since early morning? Come in then—there's hot water waiting in your rooms, and tea will be ready in ten minutes. Is the luggage coming, Patsy?"

"It is, ma'am," responded Mr. Burke. "Lasteways, if that image of a John Conolly doesn't play any of his thricks with the ass."

"Perhaps, now, you'd be better going back to meet him when you have the horse stabled," suggested his mistress. "I wouldn't have the luggage delayed."

"Ah, sure, it will be all right," said Mr. Burke, hastily, "John Conolly's not that bad; he'll get it here sometime, but where'd be the use of hurrying the ass? Well, I'll throw a look down the road when I'm after putting the car by, ma'am."

"And that makes sure of me poor Brownie getting a good grooming," murmured the landlady, ushering her guests into the house as the car jogged stablewards. "Patsy's not that fond of a walk that he'd scamp his job to be travelling the road after John Conolly. Are you there, Bridget?"

"I am, ma'am," said a pretty girl, appearing from the back of the hall with such swiftness as to compel the belief that she had been surreptitiously observing the new-comers.

"Take the gentlemen to their rooms," commanded the landlady. "Will you come with me, Miss Linton?"

Norah followed her up the broad staircase. A wide corridor led through mouldering archways, whence passages branched off to right and left. The walls bore signs of decorations of a bygone day, now faint and faded with age. The landlady threw open the door of a large room, with two windows looking over the lough. A huge bed occupied an alcove: bare acreages of floor intervened between isolated pieces of furniture, with rugs lying, like islands, on the stained boards.

"I took up the carpet—'twas old and there were holes in it you'd fall through," said the landlady. "But I could put you in a smaller room if you'd rather have a carpet."

"I like this," Norah said, looking round the clean bareness of the room. "But can't I have the windows open?"

"You'll have to fight Bridget over them," replied the landlady, flinging both windows wide. "I opened them twice this morning, but she shut them again; and the second time she was so anxious about all the deaths you'd be dying with the dint of the cold blast sweeping in, that I let them stay."

"I didn't think there was any cold blast," Norah said laughing.

"There wasn't; but Bridget thinks that any air that comes in through an open window is a blast, even if it's the middle of summer. Have you everything you want, Miss Linton? I'm sure you'll all be famished for your tea, and I'll run and see to it."

"I think this is a jolly place," Norah said, as they gathered, ten minutes later, round a table that might certainly have groaned under its load of good things, had it not been made of exceedingly solid old mahogany. "It's not a bit like a boarding-house, is it? There's such a home-y feel about it."

"There's a home-y look about this table," Jim averred. "I haven't seen anything like it since we left Billabong."

There were crusty loaves of Irish soda-bread, which is better than anything else except the home-made bread of Australia, heaps of brown, crisp scones, buttered hot-cakes, and glass dishes with ruby-coloured jams. A bowl of cream was in the middle, and a dish of rich dark honey in the comb—not like the anæmic honey one buys in London, which is made by fat and lazy bees out of dishes of sugar and water, and tastes like it. The Irish bees had worked over miles of heathery moorland, and their honey held something of the heather's fresh sweetness.

"Think of the trenches—and bully beef!" ejaculated Wally. "I say, what's this?"

He had uncovered a smoking plateful of a queer flat substance, on which attention was immediately focussed.

"Does one eat it?" Norah queried.

"Blessed if I know," Jim answered. "It looks a bit queer."

Light suddenly illumined Mr. Linton.

"Bless us, that's potato-cake!" he exclaimed. "I haven't tasted it for many a year, and it's one of the best things going. It ought to be eaten so hot that it burns the mouth, so I advise you not to lose time.' He helped himself, declaring that no considerations of etiquette were to stand in the way of the proper temperature of a potato-cake, and the others somewhat doubtfully followed his example. In a very short time the plate was empty.

"That's a recipe I'll take back to Brownie!" was Norah's significant comment. "Do you think Mrs. Moroney would let me have a lesson on it in the kitchen?"

"Mrs. Moroney seems inclined to eat from one's hand," said Mr. Linton. "She's desperately anxious for us to be comfortable. You know, we were told in London that she had only begun this business since the war—her husband is at the front—so time hasn't soured her as it sours most landladies. We're lucky in catching her in the fluid state: later on she'll solidify into the adamantine condition that is truly landladylike."

"Meanwhile, she's rather an old duck," said Wally. "Hallo, who's that?"

A small rosy face, crowned with a tangle of yellow curls, was peeping round the doorway. Finding itself observed, it hastily disappeared. Norah snatched a sponge-cake and went in swift pursuit, returning, a moment later, with a very small boy clad in a blue shirt and ridiculously diminutive knickerbockers, who greeted the company with a friendly smile somewhat complicated by a large mouthful of cake.

"Well, you're a cheerful person," Jim said. "What's your name?"

"Timsy," said the new-comer. "And I'm eight."

"I call that genius," said Wally. "He knew you'd ask him that next, so he saved you the trouble. Do you live here, Timsy?"

The small boy nodded vigorously.

"Me daddy's gorn," he volunteered.

"Where?"

"Fightin' the Gair-mins. They's bad—they's after hurtin' him in the laig."

"Did they?" said Wally, sympathetically. "Poor daddy! Is he better?"

"He is. He's goin' to shoot me some."

"Is he, now? Will he bring them home?"

"I dunno will he. I asked the postman, an' he said daddy couldn't post 'em."

"That wasn't nice of the postman," said Jim. "What would you do with them if you got them?"

"Frow fings at 'em," said Timsy, valiantly.

"Good man!" said Jim. "We'll have you in the trenches before the war's over, I expect. Another cake, old chap?"

Timsy accepted the cake graciously, digging his white teeth into it with appreciation.

"I'm after having me tea," he confided. "An' Bridget said there wasn't any cake. But there's lots." His eye swept the table.

"There is, indeed," said Jim, guiltily. "Just you have as much as you feel like."

"Are you a soldier?" demanded Timsy, his eyes on Jim's uniform.

The boy nodded.

"Like me daddy?"

"Not as good, I expect," said Jim.

"Me daddy's the finest soldier ever went out of Ireland—old Nanny told me he was. And she said if once he met that old Kaiser he'd be sorry he ever got borned. An' he would, too, if me daddy cot him. An he's a sergeant, 'cause he's got free stripes on his arm. Why hasn't you got any?"

"I don't know as much as your daddy," said Jim, probably with perfect truth. "When I get bigger they may give me some."

"You're bigger than me daddy, now," said Timsy, surveying him. "Only you haven't got any whiskers. I 'spect you have to have whiskers before you get free stripes."

"I expect so," Jim agreed. "I'll grow some the first minute I get time. What have you done with your legs, Timsy?"

"Scratched 'em, I 'spect," said Timsy, indifferently, casting a fleeting glance at his bare brown legs, which bore many marks of warfare. "They's bwambles in the wood. Why is your buttons dif-runt to me daddy's?"

"What are your daddy's like?"

Timsy fished laboriously in the pocket of his shirt.

"I got one here," he said. "It came uncottoned, an' fell off, an' daddy said I could have it. Look—it's nicer than yours."

"Of course it is—isn't your daddy a sergeant?" said Jim, gravely. Timsy looked up sharply, and was seized with compunction.

"Don't you mind," he said, hastily putting away his cherished button, lest dangling it before the eyes of his new friend should excite vain longings in his soul. He slipped a grimy little paw into Jim's. " 'Twill not be long at all before they make a sergeant of you. Can you hurry up an' grow whiskers?"

"I'll do my best," returned Jim, laughing. "You're a good old sportsman, Timsy. Have another cake."

Timsy's head was bent over the dish in the tremendous effort of selection, when a slight commotion was heard in the hall.

"I was without in the scullery," said a high-pitched voice, "and I after giving him his tea. 'Let you sit quiet there till I have a minute to put a decent appearance on you,' says I. ' 'Tis not in them ould rags you'd be having the genthry see you,' I says. With that I wint back, an' the kitchen was as bare as the palm of me hand. I've called him till me throat's cracking——"

"Is that you, Timsy?" whispered Norah. The dancing eyes of the culprit were sufficient answer.

"Blessed Hour!" said the voice of Mrs. Moroney, torn between relief and wrath. Her good-natured face hung in the doorway, presently followed by her ample form. "Is it you, then, Timsy Moroney, disgracing me and annoying the gentleman! Why would you have him on your knee, sir, and he the ragamuffin of the world? I'd not have you troubled with him."

"He's not troubling me at all, Mrs. Moroney," Jim assured her. "He's an awfully friendly little chap. Does it matter if he has cakes?"

The question savoured of shutting the stable-door after the stealing of the steed. Timsy ate his cake hurriedly, lest disaster await him in the answer.

"There's nothing he doesn't eat," said his mother resignedly. "But I'd not let him annoy you, sir."

"There was no cake in the kitchen!" said Timsy, fixing reproachful eyes on his parent. "How would I have me tea, an' no cake?"

"Cock you up with cake!" returned Mrs. Moroney, spiritedly. "Well able to go without it you are, for once in a while." She relented before her son's appealing gaze. "Come away, then, and let Bridget wash you: sure, she's screaming all over the place after you."

Timsy hesitated, regarding Jim with affection.

"Can I come back some time?" he demanded.

"Of course you can," said Jim.

The small boy climbed down slowly.

"I'm destroyed with washin'," he complained. " 'Tis only at dinner-time she had me all soaped. An' I hate shoes . . ." The voice of his lamentations died away as his mother swept him from the room.

"Nice kid," said Jim, getting up. "Let's go out and reconnoitre."

The shadows were lengthening across the strip of tree-fringed grass leading to the gate. Near the house, the garden was a wilderness of colour and fragrance. Roses and sweet-peas, stocks and asters, nasturtiums and clematis, in a bewildering tangle, jostled each other in the untidy beds and on the old stone walls. Here and there was a mouldering summer-house, its entrance almost blocked with hanging creepers, while in shady nooks in the winding walks were seats with an appearance of old age that suggested prudence in sitting down.

Presently they came upon a path leading abruptly down-hill to the lough. They followed it, passing out of the garden into a little field where small black Kerry cattle looked inquisitively at them, and through a rickety gate on to the shore, where grey pebbles made a rough beach. A disconsolate donkey, attached to a windlass, walked round and round in a weary circle, pumping water up to the house—a spectacle which promptly set Norah to hunting for a thistle for him, which the donkey received coldly.

"It would take more than a thistle to sweeten that job," said Wally. "Come and look at the boat."

Mr. Patsy Burke was rather feverishly busy with the boat—it had apparently occurred to him that since the new-comers would assuredly want her it might be as well to make certain that she was sound. She was not sound—to rectify which obvious condition Mr. Burke laboured mightily.

"She's seen better days," remarked Mr. Linton, looking at the ancient vessel with critical eyes. Already she had been extensively patched: her paint was merely a memory, and she bore "a general flavour of mild decay." The oars, which lay near, had also been mended many times. They did not match: a fact which the Australians were to discover later.

"Ah, sure, she's a good boat," said Mr. Burke. " 'Tis only the thrifle of a leak she have in her. You wouldn't ask an aisier or a kinder boat to pull than that one—begob, she's the best boat to be found on any lough hereabouts." This assertion also was to be verified by time. "In the ould times, when the family was here, many's the day I've seen her, full of red cushions and fine ladies, and she tearing up the lough like a racehorse!" The poetic nature of Mr. Burke's memories moved him to a sigh.

"Who was the family?" queried Mr. Linton.

"The O'Donnells, to be sure," answered Mr. Burke, his long face expressing faint surprise at ignorance so vast. "They owned all this country, from the ould ancient times—but there's none of them left now. Me gran'father, and his gran'father before him, was tenants under them. I'm told they were kings, one time. But there's nothing left of any of the ould stock now—all their houses is sold, or falling to pieces, an' they at the ends of the earth, seeking their fortune."

"The house is very old, isn't it?" Norah asked.

" 'Tis ould, and 'tis falling to decay—it 'ud take a power of money to put it right. Ah, the good days is gone from Ireland—what with the land war and the famine, all the money was swept from her." Mr. Burke stopped abruptly. He pulled his battered felt hat over his eyes and hammered vigorously at the old boat.

They went up through the fragrant garden, now heavy with evening shadows. Above them the gaunt old house towered, bosomed in its trees, dim with the night mist from the lough. Lights were beginning to twinkle from the windows, and the faint acrid smell of turf fires stole upon the still air. To Norah's fancy the silent garden was peopled with shadowy forms—tall gallants and exquisite ladies of a bygone day, and little children who ran, laughing, along paths that had no tangle of neglected growth. It was theirs; the dream visions made her feel an interloper as she crossed the threshold into the lit hall.

CHAPTER VI
OF LITTLE BROWN TROUT

"Loughareema! Loughareema!

    Lies so high among the heather,

A little lough, a dark lough,

    The wather's black an' deep:

Ould herons go a-fishing there,

    An' sea-gulls all together

Float roun' the one green island

    On the fairy lough asleep."

Moira O'Neil.

A WEEK went by with the mysterious swiftness of holiday weeks, especially in Ireland. No one quite knew what became of the long June days; they dawned in light mists that lay on the surface of Lough Aniller, reddened with the sunrise, only to vanish as the sun mounted; they widened to warm brightness, with clear blue skies flecked with the tiniest cloudlets; and sank to long, delicious twilights, with just enough chill in the air to make light coats necessary. No one was inclined for strenuous exertion. Jim and Wally, under orders to take life very easily for the present, were content to lie about in the fragrant grass, to go for short walks along the borders of the lough, or to let Patsy Burke row them slowly up its placid waters, where scarcely a ripple marked the rising of a trout. To Norah and her father it was sufficient happiness to watch their boys gradually winning back strength. Each day that went by and brought no recurrence of throat-trouble was something achieved; and the long, golden days smoothed the weary lines from the boyish faces, and brought something of the old tan into their cheeks. There was no doubt that as a sanatorium Donegal merited all that had been claimed of her.

They were the only guests in the old stone house. Later on, Mrs. Moroney told them, people were coming from Dublin and Belfast: but the war had temporarily killed the tourist traffic from England, and Irish fishing was having a much-needed rest.

"But for the fowl I have, indeed, I'd be hard put to it," said Mrs. Moroney. She reared innumerable ducks and chickens, and carried on a thriving trade, sending them ready dressed to England—aided by a parcels post system which, unlike that of Australia, does not appear to regard the senders and receivers of parcels as wealthy eccentrics, to be heavily charged, but otherwise unworthy of consideration. At all times Mrs. Moroney was to be found plucking and dressing her wares—keeping, nevertheless, an eagle eye upon her household, and always ready to take interest in the doings of her guests. Good nature beamed from her countenance, and chicken-fluff always ornamented her hair.

Timsy had constituted himself Jim's shadow, and courier-in-chief to the party. He knew all the country with a boy's knowledge, had an acquaintance with the ways of trout which seemed miraculous in one of his years, and cherished a feud of long standing with John Conolly, whose treatment of the little ass did not come up to the standard instilled into Timsy by the sergeant, now in France. All these matters he placed at the absolute disposal of Jim. The rest of the party he treated politely: they were well enough. But the big boy in khaki was somehow different, and Timsy gave him all his warm little heart.

It was a shock to him that Jim and Wally appeared in rough tweeds on the morning after their arrival.

"Where's you uny-forms?" demanded Timsy, hopping on one foot on the mossy path, rather like an impertinent sparrow.

"Upstairs," Jim said, solemnly.

"Why for don't you put 'em on?"

"Didn't want to."

Timsy surveyed him with a pained air.

"Me daddy says uny-form had a right to be wore all the time," he said. "He didn't have no uvver clothes when he came home."

Jim relented at the small, worried face.

"Tell you how it is, old man," he said. "The old Germans laid us out; and we're going to get better as quick as we can, to go and lick them."

"Yes?" said Timsy, digging his heel into the earth, in bloodthirsty ecstasy. "That's what me daddy's after doing."

"Of course he is. Well, we'll get better quicker if we haven't got to wear heavy uniforms all the time, don't you see? So we asked leave; and a big general said we could put on other clothes. He was a very big general, so it's all right, isn't it?"

"Was he very big?"

"Enormous," said Jim, gravely.

"If he was very 'normous, I 'spect it's all right," Timsy said, relinquishing his point with reluctance. "Only I likes you best in uny-forms." His eye suddenly lit with new hope. "Do you think you'd wear 'em on Sunday, an' you goin' to church?"

"I would," Jim said. "There, it's a bargain, Timsy." So Timsy accepted the tweed knickerbockers as necessary evils, and peace reigned.

As for the trout, they had remained in peace. Patsy Burke had given the Australians a few lessons in throwing a fly, a gentle art to which they did not take very kindly, though they proved apt enough pupils. But the trout were not rising, and they found it dull. Their previous experience had been either the primitive method of a stick, a string, and a worm, in the creeks at home, or a deep-sea hand-line with a substantial bait and a heavy sinker. They liked these peaceful ways, and to them the incessant business of casting seemed, in the Australian phrase, "too much like hard work." They endeavoured, however, to keep this view from the scandalized Mr. Burke, whose scorn at the mere mention of a hand-line was almost painful to witness.

In defence of their apathy, it must be admitted that the sport was poor. The weather had been unfavourable, and the brown trout declined to rise; but even in the best of years Lough Aniller, the big lough by the house, was not a good fishing lake. A few rises came to them, which they missed: and they had the poor satisfaction of beholding Mr. Burke land a specimen which weighed not quite a quarter of a pound. It did not seem, to untutored eyes quite worth the candle.

" 'Tis a poor lake, anyways," Mr. Burke said. They were paddling home in the setting sun, the water full of bright reflections. "I dunno why the trout wouldn't be in it: it's the biggest hereabouts, but they don't seem wishful for it at all. There's Lough Nacurra and Lough Anoor—they're little enough, but you'd get finer fishing in them in a day than in a week of Lough Aniller."

"Why don't we go there?" spoke Wally, lazily.

"There's no reason in the world why you shouldn't. Sure, they're no distance, and the fishing belongs to the house; there'll not be a rod on them, barring your own."

"What do they mean, Patsy?" Norah asked. Mr. Burke was her instructor in the Irish language, and she thirsted for translations of each unknown word.

"Lough Anoor's the lough of the gold, miss, and Lough Nacurra's the lough of the Champions. I dunno why they have those names on them; there's a lot of ould stories goin'. Whatever reason anybody was to give, no one could say it was wrong."

"Well, Lough Aniller means the lough of the Eagle, you said, Patsy, but there don't seem any eagles about."

"Thrue for ye," agreed Mr. Burke; "they do not. But I wouldn't wonder if there was any amount of them here in the ould ancient times." He scanned the placid waters with disfavour. "There's one thing they couldn't call it, and that's Nabrack—the lough of the Trout!"

"They certainly couldn't—whoever 'they' may be," said Wally, laughing. "There are just about as many trout in this lough as there are in the front garden, I believe. Who'll come to one of the others to-morrow?—I'll have to learn their names before I say them in public. I vote for the one that belongs to the Champions!"

"Lough Nacurra—ye might do worse," said Patsy. " 'Tis a good little lough, and there's a small little island in it, that 'ud be a good place for you to be taking your dinners. The boat's no great thing at all—but she's better than the one on Lough Anoor."

"What!" exclaimed Mr. Linton. "Is she worse than this one?" The boat on Lough Aniller had not struck the party as an up-to-date craft.

"She is," said Mr. Burke. "But there's no distance to be pulling her: sure, the lough's not big enough to go any ways far. If 'twas Lough Anoor, now, there'd be no good in me comin' with you, for five couldn't sit in her. Four'll be all she'll hold."

"Is she safe?" asked Mr. Linton.

"Is it safe? Sure, you wouldn't sink that one, not if you danced in her," said Patsy.

They had drifted almost to the end of the lough. Above them the high road crossed the stone bridge. The whir of a motor hummed across it, and, looking up, they saw a grey runabout car, driven by a man of whose face little could be seen, since goggles hid his eyes and his cap was pulled low. Patsy touched his cap hastily as the car vanished in its own dust.

" 'Tis the young masther," he said; and added, as if in further explanation, "Sir John, I mean—Sir John O'Neill."

"Does he live here?" Norah asked.

"He do, miss. But a lot of his time he's somewhere else—London or foreign parts."

"I thought every landowner about here had gone to the war," Mr. Linton said.

"Begob, Sir John 'ud give the two eyes out of his head to be gone, too," said Patsy, shortly. "But they won't take him. 'Tis—'tis weakly he is. He have the spirit of ten men in him; them ould German's 'ud find their hands full, and they to be tackling him in a tight place. Well, well—some people don't get much luck." He stopped short, and rowed violently for some time.

"Do you get many salmon here?" Jim asked, idly. It was evident that Mr. Burke did not wish to pursue the subject of Sir John O'Neill.

"In the river—but only a few," replied the boatman. " 'Twouldn't be worth your while getting a licence, sir. Sure it's them 'ud give you a different idea of fishing. I got one in Lough Illion, in Kerry, one time when I was staying in them parts. That was the fish! He tuk me four and a half hours to kill."

"Whew—w!" said Jim, respectfully. "He must have been a big fellow."

"Well, he was not that big at all; but he tuk the fly as if he meant it, and down he went to the bottom like a shtone. An' there he lay, and I going round and round him in the boat, trying any ways to shift him, and he sulking in the weeds. Banging my rod I was, and pelting at him all the bits of rock I had in the boat, and I couldn't shtir him. I was famished out, for it was pegging hailshtones and sleet. At last he come up; and then he thought better of it, when he saw the sky above him, and he was going down again, and I let a dhrive at him with the gaff, and got him just near the tail—great luck I had with him, to be sure."

"It was about time you did have some luck," Jim remarked.

"There's not many of them 'ud sulk like that," said Patsy. "Generally they'd be tiring themselves with the runs they's take at the first. And if they thrun a lep or two—'tis the lep takes most out of them: it breaks their courage. There's nothing like a salmon, to my way of thinking, though there's a lot of the gentry do be sticking to the little brown trout. Will ye be for Lough Nacurra in the morning, sir?"

"We will—if you'll promise us fish," Jim responded.

"It 'ud be a bold man to promise anything this weather," said Patsy, looking with disfavour at the clear sky and the placid lough. "Still-an'-all, 'tis a good lough; if they're rising anywhere it'll be on Nacurra."

Morning came with a haze lying on the blue hills, and a fitful breeze: the best fishing day yet, Patsy pronounced it, as he shouldered a gigantic luncheon-basket and led the way down the avenue and along the dusty high road. They struck across the bog presently, following a path that led through a tangle of the sweet bog-myrtle; and, in a little harbour of smooth grey stones at the western end of Lough Nacurra, came upon their boat, half-concealed among the rushes fringing the water's edge. The lough was a long narrow sheet of water, widening a little at the far end, where a thickly-wooded island showed dimly through the haze.

"Have you been storing water in the boat?" Jim inquired, gravely, surveying the ancient craft among the rushes. Its bottom timbers bore evidence of long soaking.

"Tis a thrifle of dampness she have in her," admitted Mr. Burke, stepping in carefully and getting to work with a baling-tin. "I'm after sending John Conolly up only this morning to bale her out, but he's the champion at scamping a job. Ah, she'll dry out beautifully in the sun, sir, once I have her emptied. There now—let you get in gently, sir."

"I will," said Mr. Linton, placing his feet with extreme caution, and coming to rest thankfully in the stern. "I don't want to begin the day with a ducking, and those bottom boards look as if they would crumble under my weight. Take care, Wally—this is a craft to be treated with respect."

"Have you drowned many in this one?" queried Jim.

Mr. Burke emitted a deep chuckle.

"Yerra, you will have your joke, sir!" he said, making hasty repairs to a rowlock that chiefly consisted of rusty wire, of which more than one strand had broken away. "There's many a good fish killed in worse boats than this. A lick of paint, now, and you wouldn't know her."

"I wouldn't call her a boat at all," retorted Jim, disposing his long legs so as to avoid, as far as possible, the steadily increasing dampness in the bottom. "She's a hoary antique, and she ought to be in a museum; but if you say she'll stay afloat, Patsy, we're game. Lend me that baling-tin while you're rowing, and I'll try to discourage the lough from entering."

Mr. Linton declined to fish, remarking that he preferred to be ready to swim when necessary, and would meanwhile officiate as baler as soon as Jim was ready to get to work with his rod. Patsy pulled out gently, until they were clear of rushes. A light wind rippled the water, sending tiny wavelets lapping against the sides of the boat; overhead, clouds drifted across a soft blue sky and now and then blotted out the sun. The hills sloping down to the lough on three sides were half shrouded in haze.

" 'Tis a perfect fishing-day," Patsy pronounced, shipping his oars and letting the boat drift gently. "If there was a little more wind itself ye'd soon have a tremenjious basket of fish."

Patsy's predictions were by this time well known to the Australians. He suffered, as Wally said, from enthusiasms, and all his geese were swans; so that his cheerful forecast raised no throb of hope in their hearts. He had been as cheerful on other mornings, when they had fished in vain.

"I don't quite see the fascination of it," Wally commented, after ten minutes of steady whipping the water. "It's so continuous; and you get nothing for it."

"Give me a good sinker and a plump slab of clam for a bait—and the schnapper on the bite," Jim responded. "I don't believe these trout know how to bite at all."

"You don't say bite—it's 'rise,'" said Norah, gloomily.

"Why?"

"I don't know. Perhaps because they don't bite. They certainly don't."

"They do not," Wally agreed. "Perhaps they rise and saunter past this queer collection of sham insects that we dangle on the face of the waters: and if you have luck you hook them as they go by. Only we don't have luck."

They fished on, sadly, casting with a precision that won commendation from Mr. Burke, and to which long practice with a stock whip had probably contributed. Nothing occurred, except the end of the lough: whereupon Patsy resumed the oars, rowed to the end whence they had started, and began up drift again.

"Do people do this all day—for weeks?" Norah demanded.

"Yerra, they do, miss."

"Well, what do they do it for?" Norah said, desperately. "I don't see any fun at all. I'm going to take the oars presently, Patsy, and you can have my rod."

"If ever I put hard-earned pay into contraptions like this again!" Jim uttered, gazing despondently on the dainty ten feet green-heart rods, new and workmanlike with their fresh tackle. "They looked just top-hole in the shop, and they do still; but that's all there is about them. I vote we go and scramble over a heathery mountain or two, and stop whipping this old lough."

"Hear, hear!" said Wally. "Let's get Patsy to put us ashore at the lower end, and we'll leave the trout to some one else. I'm blessed if I fish again until we get back to the creek at Billabong—with a worm and a sinker, and a nice little cork bobbing on the top of the water. No science, but you get fish. These old Irish trout—my aunt!"

His reel whirred suddenly under his hand, and his rod bent double. There was a swirl in the water. The line ran out sharply, and something that was living gold in the sunlight leaped, flashed for an instant, and was gone again. Patsy uttered a howl.

"Leave him run, sir!—give and take! Reel in when the strain is off him. Aisy now, sir!"

"Off him!" gasped Wally. "Why, he pulls like a working bullock! Won't the rod break?"

"It will not," said Patsy. "Drop the point, sir, if he leps. Yerra, sure that's a fine grand trout ye have—did ye see the great splashing rise he made to ye? Howld him, sir—he'll get off on ye if ye slacken too much. Wind in when ye get a chanst, and bring him nice and aisy to the boat—I have the net ready."

"Bring him to the boat!—it's himself that's doing all the bringing!" uttered Wally. "Tell me if I'm messing it up, Patsy."

"Begob, you're doing fine!" said Patsy—"ye're playing him beautiful. Give and take, and his head'll come up presently—don't be afraid if he do run from ye. Oh, murder, there's the little mistress got one too!"

Norah's reel sang suddenly, and a fish went off astern. The owner of the rod made a wild effort to play him sitting down, and then stood up, her rod describing erratic circles while Mr. Linton grasped her skirt in a desperate effort to steady her.

"I'm all right, daddy!" she gasped. "Oh, such a beauty—I know he weighs a ton!"

"Let him go, miss!" shouted Patsy, rendered desperate by the hopelessness of coaching two novices at once. "Give him his head—he'll come back to ye. There y'are, sir—did ye see his head come up?—wind him in! No, not you, miss—let him have his run: sure that one won't be tired this long while, by the looks of him. Oh, murder, sir, is he gone from you?"—as the trout made a fresh dash for freedom and fled under the boat. "No,—howld on to the vilyun an' he'll be back. Kape a nice, steady strain on him, miss—give and take." He hovered over the side, feverishly grasping the handle of the landing-net. "Ye have him bet, sir—here he comes. Nice and aisy does it—don't hurry him—kape your point up. Back a little—ah, I have him!"

The net slipped under Wally's fish deftly. Simultaneously, Norah's trout executed a wild leap, and Norah reeled him, quite involuntarily, near the boat. Patsy, responding gallantly to her cry for help, dropped the first trout hastily, and turned just in time to net the second, by sheer good luck. The excitement of the moment overcame him, and Norah's fish, falling upon Wally's, entangled both casts and lines by a few frantic leaps, before Patsy could collect himself sufficiently to pounce upon them. The boat rocked with enthusiasm. Jim had prudently reeled in, to be out of the way of possible happenings, and stood, beaming, while the victorious anglers looked at each other with parted lips and shining eyes, and Mr. Burke wailed and triumphed alternately.

"Wirra, but them lines is destroyed on us! Oh, the grand fish, entirely!—would ye get as good now, sir, with your sinkers and your big lump of bait! An' you played 'em fine, both of ye! Lave off flopping, will ye, and let me get a howlt of the fly— begob, he have it ate, no less!" Norah's trout was put out of its misery by a quick blow on a thwart, and the fly rescued. "There you are, miss, and he well over a pound if he's an ounce!"

"Oh, daddy, isn't he a beauty!"

"He is, indeed," Mr. Linton said, looking at the golden-brown fish, with his splendid spots. "I never saw a handsomer fellow. Is yours as good Wally?"

"Betther, I believe," boomed Patsy, a vision of triumph. "They might be mates—but Mr. Wally's is bigger. Have ye the little spring-balance, sir? Ye'd ought to weigh them."

"I have it," Wally said. "Eighteen ounces, Nor,—and mine's a pound and a half. Well-l!" He drew a long breath. "If ever I say a word against my little rod again!"

"Oh, wasn't it glorious!" Norah uttered. "Will those lines ever come clear, Patsy?"

"Yerra, they will. Have patience, miss, and I'll get them undone in no time. Cast away now, Mr. Jim—and heaven send he do not land his on the top of this tangle!" added Mr. Burke, in pious hope.

"Hurry up, Jim—it's the best fun since we went bombing!" said Wally. "Gives you a feeling like nothing on earth, and the little rod's just a live thing in your hands. Glory! there's one at you—ah, the brute!" as a big trout rose at Jim's fly, missed, and went down, giving a full view of his beautiful speckled side.

"Cast over him again, Mr. Jim—that one'll come back," Patsy whispered. "Gently—ah, that's the lovely throw!" The flies settled gently on the water, but the trout failed to respond. "Thry him again, sir—that's it; dhraw them back quiet, now. Begob, he have him—howld him, sir! Hark at the little wheel singing: isn't that the fine run he made! Wind him in—don't check him sudden." Mr. Burke babbled on happily until the third big trout lay gasping in the landing-net.

"Didn't I tell you there'd be trout in Lough Nacurra?" he demanded. "Oh, the beauties! them's the grand fish, entirely, no matter where you'd be fishing. Let ye cast out again, sir. Aisy, Miss Norah, let be—sure I'll have it for ye quicker than ye would yourself. There's the terrible tangle now; ye'd not get it in a knot like that, not if ye tried for a week. And is it in Australia you'd get them like that, with a stick and a sinker and a lump of bait? and play them too, same as ye did them there? Well, well, that must be the fine country!"

Mr. Linton laughed.

"Oh there's plenty of good trout-fishing in Australia, Patsy, and plenty of people who use the proper tackle. But it doesn't happen to be in our part of the country."

"Ye'll not beat Irish trout, anywheres in the world," said Mr. Burke, shortly. "Them new countries is all very well in their way, but give me the ould places I'm after knowing all my life." He drew a long breath. "There—I have them untwisted at last: and more by token, here we are at the end of the lough." He fixed Wally with an inquiring gaze. "It was here you wanted to be landed, sir, wasn't it? Will I take down the rod and put you ashore?"

Wally grinned in appreciation.

"It's your game, Patsy," he admitted, cheerfully. "I take it all back. If you'll just hand me that rod again, you won't get me off this lough before dark!"

CHAPTER VII
LOUGH ANOOR
"A capital ship for an ocean trip

Was the Walloping Window-Blind."

Students' Song.

FROM that day the spell of the little brown trout laid itself upon the Australians. The basket of fish which they carried home with pride in the evening, and which caused Mrs. Moroney to call upon the saints to protect her, was the forerunner of many, since the weather was kind and Lough Nacurra had profited by its war-time rest to become the happiest of hunting grounds. Day after day, with and without Mr. Burke, whose multifarious duties often called him elsewhere, they visited the little lough in the bog, until they knew all its best spots as well as Patsy himself, and were familiar with every inch of the wooded island where they generally landed for lunch. With the fever of fishing came to them the patience which—curiously enough—accompanies it, making them content to sit hour after hour if rewarded with an occasional rise: since no lough on this side of Paradise could be expected to live up to the first spectacular minutes in which Lough Nacurra had claimed them for its own. Nevertheless, the little lough held well; and trout figured largely on the table for breakfast and dinner, insomuch that Mrs. Moroney confided to Bridget that 'twas the grand guests they were to be keeping down the expense—a remark retailed to Jim by Timsy, in such innocent certainty that his friend would be pleased, that Jim could not find it in his heart to rebuke him for repeating what he was not meant to hear.

Day by day the air of moorland and mountain worked the boys' cure. Strength came back to them quickly, with long days in the open and long nights of quiet sleep. War seemed very far away. Papers came irregularly, and the younger members of the party were very willing to let Mr. Linton read them and tell them anything startling, without troubling about details. Little by little, the horror of the gas faded; they ceased to dream about it, a nightly torment which had kept them back for the first weeks. The regiment was having a much-needed rest in billets: Anstruther, Garrett, and their other chums were fit and well, and longing for another chance of coming to grips with the enemy. Much of the horror of Gallipoli Mr. Linton succeeded in keeping from them: too many of their school-fellows lay dead upon that most cruel of battlefields, and he suppressed the papers that gave details of the losses. The fog of war always hangs closely: it was easy to make it hide from his boys details of the news that had plunged Australia alike into mourning and into deeper resolve to see the thing through.

For Norah and her father the time was an oasis of peace in a desert of anxiety. Too soon they must send Jim and Wally back, and themselves return to work and wait in London. Now, nothing mattered greatly, and they could try to forget. It was not the least of David Linton's happiness that each day brought back light to Norah's eyes and colour to her cheeks.

So they played about Ireland as they had played all their lives in Australia. The Irish blood that was in them made them curiously at home; they liked the simple, kindly country-folk, and found a ready welcome in the scattered cottages, where already Norah had made friends with at least half a dozen babies. Her education developed on new lines: she picked up a good deal of Irish, and became steeped in the innumerable legends of the country, not in the least realizing that in being told the "ould ancient" stories she was being paid a compliment for which the average tourist might sigh in vain,—for the Irish peasant is jealous of his folk-stories, and seldom tells them to anyone not of the country. In the great stone kitchen Mrs. Moroney gave her lessons in the manufacture of potato-cakes, colcannon, soda-bread, and other national delicacies, and, with old Nanny the cook, listened to stories of Australia with frequent ejaculations of "God help us!" while Jim and Wally talked much to Patsy Burke and John Conolly, and to the men in the villages, doing a little recruiting work as occasion offered. They also talked of Australia, since they could not help it, and became at times slightly confused as to the number of men for whom they had promised to find work after the war, on Billabong, if possible. However, as Jim said resignedly if Billabong overflowed with men, there were other places—Australia was large and empty. They could all come.

"Are you there, Norah? Coo-ee!"

An answering "Coo-ee!" came from one of the mouldering summer-houses in the garden, and Wally plunged down the overgrown walk in its direction. Norah was not in the summer-house, which she described as an insecty place, but cross-legged on a sunny patch of grass behind it, surrounded by innumerable letters. The Australian mail had arrived that morning; and, since mails in war time were apt to be "hung up" until a ship could be found to take them, letters were wont to accumulate in alarming quantities.

"Good gracious, are you still reading?" inquired Wally. "I finished all mine ages ago: not that I ever get such awful bundles as you do. Jim and your father are plunged in business letters, and I'm like Mary's little lamb, or Bo-Peep's sheep, or whichever mutton it was that got lost."

"Poor old thing!" said Norah, absently. "Never mind; sit down and read dear old Brownie's letter. It takes one straight back to Billabong."

"Well, that's no bad thing—though I'd like to see a little more of Ireland," said Wally, subsiding upon grass. "Poor old Brownie! can't you see her, Nor, struggling over this in the kitchen at home. She'd be so much happier over tackling a day's baking."

"She would, indeed," Norah assented, her eyes a little misty. She touched the scrawled pages of the old nurse-housekeeper's letter, her hand resting on it as though it were a living thing. Brownie had been all the mother she had known, and the bond between them was very close. The ill-written sheets brought vividly to her the kind old face, beaming with love as she had always known it.

"Dear Miss Norah," began Brownie, with due formality. Then the formality slumped.

"My dearie, the place is lost without you all everyone arsks me as soon as the male comes wots in the letters and are you coming back soon the hot whether is over thang goodness and we have had good rain and the place is lookin splendid all the horses are in great condishun and Murty says to tell you Bosun is fit to jump out of his skin Murty won't let anyone but himself ride him or Garyowin or Monnuk or the chesnet colt and it keeps him pretty busy keepin them all exercised. Black Billy is no better than he was he is a limb and no mistake it will be a mersy when Mr. Jim comes back to keep that boy in order and your Pa too he will not take no notice of anyone else. We are always wonderin and hopin about the war will it soon be over and that old Kyser hung and how are Mr. Jim and Mr. Wally we all know they will fight as well as any Englishman or any two Germans. But the best of all will be when the old war is over and you all come home to Billabong tell Mr. Wally I have not forgot to make pikelits like he likes they will be waiting for him we got their photergrafs in uniform and dont they look beautiful only so grown up I keep thinking of them just little boys ridin the ponies like they always was in short pants and socks and plenty of darnin they give me to do which it was always a pleasure I'm sure do they look after you well in that old London i hope they feed you proply in that big hotel im told their sheets is always damp do be careful dearie. We try to look after everything the way the master and Mr. Jim would like it juring their absence Murty is sendin word about the stock so i will leave that part of it aloan the garden is lookin grand the ortum roses all out just blazin along the walls and fences there are other flowers but its no good i cant spell them not being no hand with the pen but you will know them all without me tellin the dogs are well but they miss you like all the rest of us also the Wallerby and so my dearie no more at present only come back soon we all send our love and hoppin you are well

"Brownie."

Wally put down the letter, after folding it slowly. Norah, who had read it again over his shoulder, put out her hand for it and tucked it into the pocket of her coat. Neither spoke for awhile. Ireland had faded away: they saw only a long low house with a garden blazing with roses—a kitchen, spotless and shining, where an old woman laboured mightily with the pen. She was a fat old woman, plain and unromantic and very practical; but the thought of her brought home-sickness sharply to the boy and girl sitting on the green slope of Irish turf.

"She's an old brick," said Wally, presently. "By Jove, Nor, won't it be jolly to go back when all this show is over! It makes one feel sort of jumpy to think of driving up to Billabong again!"

"'M," assented Norah, lucidly. Speech was a little difficult just then. Presently she laughed.

"Australian mail-days are lovely, but they always hurt a bit, too. Never mind, we'll all go home together some day, and Billabong will go quite mad, and it will be worth having been away. What do we do this morning, Mr. Second-Lieutenant Meadows?"

"Well, I don't know," Wally answered. "I think you'd better choose your own amusement, Miss Linton-of-Billabong, and I'll fall in with it meekly. Jim and your father have shut themselves up with piles of business letters and stock reports and things like that, and can't come out before lunch."

"Bother the old business!" said Norah, inelegantly, wrinkling her nose, as was her way in deep thought. "Wally, why shouldn't we try Lough Anoor?"

"That's rather an idea—especially as Patsy's engaged to-day, and can't act as boatman. We could paddle round and try Lough Anoor by ourselves. It won't do Lough Nacurra any harm to have a rest."

"No; we've fished it pretty steadily lately," Norah agreed. "It would be rather fun to try a new place. I'd like to take Timsy, if you don't mind, Wally. He's such a jolly little chap, and it would be a tremendous treat for him."

"Good idea!" agreed Wally. "Great man, Timsy; he'll take charge of us and run the whole show, and be entirely happy. Will you find him, Nor, while I get the rods and basket?"

Timsy was never difficult to find, when the seekers were the Australians. He was digging his bare brown toes into the gravel by the front door when Norah and Wally emerged from the garden.

"Are you busy to-day, Timsy?" asked Norah, gravely. One of the things that Timsy liked about these people from the other side of the world was that they always treated him as an equal in age and sense, and did not "talk down" to him. He had bitter memories of an English visitor who had addressed him as "Little boy," and of an elderly lady who had patted him on the head, and called him "dear." His blood still boiled when he thought of it.

"I am not," he replied. "I'm after catching all the chickens me mother wants,—and 'twas themselves give me a fine hunt. Chickens do be always knowing when they're wanted to be kilt."

"Then you can't blame them for running," said Norah. "No more jobs, Timsy?"

"There is not, miss. Me mother's after telling me to get out and play."

"Mr. Wally and I are going to fish Lough Anoor," Norah said. "We haven't been there yet, and we don't know much about it. Would you care to come, too, Timsy?"

Swift delight leaped to the small boy's eyes.

"Is it me? Sure, wouldn't I be in your way, miss?"

"Why, you'll be very useful," said Norah. "You'd to come?"

"Like!" said Timsy. Words failed him, and he could only beam at them speechlessly. As they disappeared into the house they heard suppressed yelps of joy, and presently, from the front windows, beheld Timsy energetically turning handsprings on the path, in the effort to relieve his overcharged feelings.

They took the track across the bog leading to Lough Nacurra, skirted it, following a sheep-path along the shore, and mounted a rise. Below them lay the little lough they sought, a jewel in a setting of gently-rolling hills. In one corner a number of queer, gnarled objects showed above the surface of the water.

"What are those, Timsy?" Wally asked.

"They's ould limbs of trees, sir; the lough does be low, and them ould things sticks out. Me daddy says there was a mighty big forest here, one time: there's bog-wood everywhere in this part. There's a small little landing-stage near them, where the boat is."

They plunged down hill. Arrived at the boat, Wally whistled long and low.

"It must be a boat, I suppose," he said, doubtfully. "Timsy said it was, and he ought to know. But—Did you ever see anything quite like it, Nor?"

"I did not," Norah said.

The boat was flat-bottomed, clumsily and heavily built. The paint which had originally declared her a white vessel had long ago peeled off or faded to a yellowish grey. She squatted on the water like a very flat duck, and water lay in her, and evidently had lain long. There were no oars, and nothing that could be used to bale. Altogether, no craft could have looked less tempting.

"Well, Jim reckoned the boat on Lough Aniller bad, and the Nacurra one only fit for a museum," Wally said. "I'd like him to see this one: it would do his old heart good. Timsy, how does one row a boat in this country when there are no oars?"

Timsy, thus appealed to, gave as his opinion that the paddles would be up at Michael McCarthy's house, beyant; further, that if Patsy knew how the said Michael McCarthy had the boat left, he'd have him destroyed. "Let ye sit down, sir, and Miss Norah, too," concluded the small boy, shouldering the burden of the responsibility. "I'll slip up and bring the paddles and a baling-tin down in no time at all."

"You won't," said Wally, firmly. "I'm in this job, Timsy. Come along and we'll interview Mr. McCarthy."

That gentleman, however, was from home, his place being taken by a lame son, who produced two oars which were not even distantly related to each other, remarking that his father was wore out with keeping the boat in order for the gentry, and none of them coming anigh her. When Wally demanded a baling-tin, he cast about him a wild glance which finally rested on an excellent tin dipper which presumably belonged to his mother.

"Herself is away with the hins—let you take it," he said, thankfully. "Hiven send she do not come back on me before you'd be gone!"

With this pious hope echoing in their ears, the marauding party withdrew, Timsy racing ahead with the dipper, lest "herself" should make an untimely appearance and demand her cherished vessel. When Norah and Wally arrived at the boat he was baling furiously, and clung to his job until he was too breathless to argue the question further with Wally.

A flat-bottomed boat, built on elementary principles, is not the easiest thing to empty. They tilted her sideways, getting very wet in the process, and wielded the dipper until it scraped dismally against the boards; but a large residue of water still lingered, defying anything but a pump or a bath-sponge, equipment which they lacked. When they restored her to an even keel the water slapped dismally across the sodden bottom boards.

"I'm afraid we'll never get her dry," Wally said, ruefully. "Tell you what, Norah—I'll put in a few bits of wood, and you can put your feet on them; that will keep them out of the water, at any rate."

Wood is scarce in Donegal. There was not a bit to be found except the tough lumps of bog-wood sticking out of the water, and of these Wally managed to secure enough for his purpose.

"They aren't lovely," he said, looking at the uneven logs. "Still, they ought to keep your feet dry, and that's something." He worked the unwieldy boat round until her stern pointed to the shore, so that Norah could get in without being compelled to walk along the wet floor. Timsy hopped in, bare-legged and cheery, and they shoved off, moving gingerly among the half-submerged wood, which threatened momentarily to rip a hole in the rotten flooring.

"I'd hate to say a word against Ireland," Wally remarked. "But you'd wonder why they'd build the landing-stage in the very middle of a submerged forest."

"The stones did be a thrifle more convanient there." Timsy offered as a solution.

"Well—maybe. Still it would be no great lift to take them a little further," said Wally. "Does the boat never get snagged, Timsy?"

"She do, sir. Many's the time me daddy's mended her, and he at home. There's no one to do it now, till I get a bit bigger—Patsy he's destroyed with work, he says, and he can't be lugging tools all this way, says he. And that Michael McCarthy, he's no use at all in the world." Timsy knitted his brows, a worried little figure. "It'll be a good thing when the ould war is over and all them Germans kilt. Then me daddy'll come back and fix everything."

"Would you rather he hadn't gone, Timsy?"

The small boy's lip trembled.

" 'Twas awful when he went. Me mother cried, and so did old Nanny and Bridget. But me mother and me daddy they says there's no dacint man can stop out of it. I wisht I was big enough to go too. Will they take drummer-boys in your regiment, Mr. Wally? I'm pretty big when I howld meself straight."

"I'm afraid you've got to be a bit bigger yet, old man," Wally told him. "But you've got to be here, to keep an eye on the place; it must be a great comfort to your daddy to know you're here, to look after your mother. There must be a certain number of fellows at home to mind Ireland in case the Germans should send troops here, you know; so we leave those at home who are too young or too old to march fast, and carry heavy loads, and do rough digging. You're doing your bit as long as you're helping at home."

"Is that so, truly?" said Timsy, much cheered. "And could I go when I'm bigger?"

"Of course you could, if the war is still there," Wally answered, cheerfully. "Only we hope it won't be. You'll be able to fight much better in the next war if you have your daddy home to train you first. It isn't every fellow who can have a sergeant all on himself to train him, you know."

"I'd be in great luck, wouldn't I?" said the small boy, hopefully. "But sure, we'll all be in the heighth of luck once we get daddy home."

Wally had poled the old boat out of the submerged trees, with many a bump and scrape that made him look apprehensively at the boards. The gaunt and stunted tree-ghosts ceased, and the water deepened, so he took to the oars. They pulled up against a freshening breeze to the head of the lough, where Wally shipped the paddles thankfully.

"That's a great pair of oars," said he. "One weighs a ton and the other only a hundredweight, so pulling becomes a matter of scientific adjustment. Well, we'll drift down, Nor, and see what Lough Anoor holds."

That the little lough held trout was made clear within the first five minutes, when a fish rose at Norah, who struck too hard and missed it, to her intense disgust. Luck favoured her, however, for it was a hungry trout and came at her gamely on the next cast, this time departing with an annoying mouthful of steel and feathers instead of the plump fly he had hoped to engulf. He came to the surface after an exciting few minutes, and, being very thoroughly hooked, survived three ineffectual attempts by Wally to get the landing-net under him. The fourth landed him in the bottom of the boat, both operators slightly breathless, while Timsy, scarlet with excitement, jigged on his seat and uttered sage counsel which no one heard.

"Awfully sorry, Nor,—I nearly lost that fellow for you," Wally exclaimed. "Scooping up a jumping fish with that old net is much harder than playing him, I think: I have the utmost respect for Patsy every time he uses it. Never saw him make a mistake yet. I say, young Norah, what's the good of my putting down a floor of bog-wood for you? Your feet are soaking!"

Norah glanced down, still flushed with the pride of capture.

"I'm sorry, truly," she said, laughing. "You see, I can't possibly play a fish sitting down; I've just got to stand up. And I tried to stand on those old lumps of wood, but they simply turned over and deposited me in the water. Never mind, Wally, it isn't the first time I've had wet feet."

"Don't go and collect a cold, or your father and Jim will have my blood," said Wally, doubtfully. "You'll have to land and run about if you get chilly."

"If I said, 'Land my grandmother!' it would be rude, so I won't," said Norah, who was casting again vigorously. "Quick, Wally, there's a rise near you!"—and Mr. Meadows forgot prudence in the excitement of trout. At the end of the drift the basket held four fish, while a fifth had made his escape at the very edge of the boat, and was doubtless in some snug hole, reflecting on the Providence which helps little trout by entrusting the landing-net to inexperienced hands.

The wind had risen, and to pull the heavy, water-logged old boat up the lough was no easy task. There was no rudder, and she steered very badly, her awkwardness intensified by the unequal oars. The waves slapped against her side, and occasionally flung in a little cloud of spray, and she leaked fast. Norah baled energetically, with poor results.

"She's a noble vessel," said Wally, pulling with a will. "Feel her wallow in the trough of these silly little waves. I guess we'll call her 'The Walloping Window-Blind,' Nor, after the boat in the song. Can you swim, Timsy?"

"I cannot, sir," said Timsy, grinning. "Sure that one won't sink on us."

"Blest if I know," Wally answered, doubtfully. "I wouldn't be surprised at any old thing she'd do. Anyhow, Miss Norah and I can rescue you if she goes down; and the water isn't very cold. Timsy, did you ever hear the sergeant's opinion of this boat?"

Timsy's grin widened.

"I did, sir," he said, with probably prudent reticence. "Sure, there's no one does be liking her in these parts. She's not an aisy puller at all."

"True for you," said Wally, panting. "Thank goodness, here's the end of the lough. Hurry up, Nor, she'll drift back quickly before this wind, and they ought to be rising." His flies whistled out over the dancing water.

"If you'd let me have the net itself I could be landing the fish for you," said Timsy, eagerly. "I've landed 'em for me daddy many a time—he taught me."

"Good man—what the sergeant taught you is good enough for us," said Wally. "Stand by, then—I've got a beauty on. He's pulling like fury." He played the fish dexterously, his keen, brown face eager. "Come on, you monster—I'd bet he weighs a pound, Norah! Ready, Timsy?—he's about done—ah, good kid!" as the small boy slipped the net under the struggling fish with all the deftness of Mr. Burke himself. "Oh, a beauty! And to think we used to imagine that a hand-line was sport!"

"You live and learn," said Norah, sagely. "That's the biggest yet, Wally, and didn't he fight! Oh, I've got one!—be ready, Timsy."

Timsy crouched, alert, his hard little hand gripping the net. The fish was a strong one and fought hard for his life; again and again he ran the line out, even when almost at the side of the boat. Norah reeled him in at last, almost done, but still fighting.

"Oh, be careful, and he lepping!" Timsy uttered. "If you take the strain off when he's hooked slightly he'll get off on you. Isn't he the great fighter entirely! Quick, miss, I'll get him!"

He dived at him with the net. The trout leaped to one side, a wave hiding his flashing golden-brown body; and Timsy, following a thought too far, overbalanced, and shot head first into the water. Wally, casting in the bow, did not see. Norah had a moment's vision of the slight childish body as the brown water closed over him. He had not uttered a sound.

"Wally, quick—the oars!" she gasped, dropping her rod. The boat was drifting fast before the wind. She watched, knowing that Timsy would be far beyond their reach when he came to the surface. Then the little head appeared for an instant and she sprang into the water.

A year earlier, Wally would have followed without a thought. But training and experience had steadied him; he knew that in the boat he would be far more use than in the rough water, with the wind taking the 'Walloping Window-Blind,' their one refuge, swiftly away from them. He flung himself at the oars and steadied her, watching, his heart in his mouth. Norah swam like a fish, he knew; but the water was rough, and Timsy would be a dead weight, even supposing that she had been able to grip him.

Then, to his utter relief, the two heads broke the water together. He heard Norah's voice: "Hold my shoulder, Timsy—you're all right. Don't be scared."

"I'll be beside you in a second, Nor," Wally shouted. "Just keep paddling." He pulled the clumsy boat frantically up the lough, and let her drop down to Norah, shipping the oars as he reached her. Leaning over, he gripped Timsy firmly.

"Hold on to the kid, and I'll pull you both to the boat," he said. "Can you catch it?—I've got him." He waited until Norah's hand gripped the side. "That's right—let him go. Come on, Timsy." He hauled the silent small boy into the boat and turned back to Norah. "Hang on to me, old girl—thank goodness we can't pull this old tub over."

There was a struggle, and Norah came over the side, scrambling in with difficulty.

"Is Timsy all right?"

"I am, miss," said a small voice, between chattering teeth.

Wally flung off his coat, and wrapped it round the child.

"Poor old chap—that will keep the wind off you a bit," he said. "Norah, get hold of the oars and pull in—you'll be nearly as quick as I would be, and it will keep you warmer. My Aunt! that kid hung on to the landing-net all the time! Well, you are a good sort, Timsy!"

"I dunno why would I let it go," shivered Timsy. "Bad enough for me to be such an omadhaun, to be falling in—and herself going after me! Me mother'll be fit to tear the face off me!"

"She'll be too glad to see you alive," said Wally, reassuringly. "We'll——"

Timsy interrupted him with a cry. He caught Norah's neglected rod.

"Howly Mother, but the fish is in it yet!" he shouted. "Oh, will ye come, please, sir!"

They landed the trout between them, Timsy recovering some measure of his self-respect by being allowed to use the net.

"He had it nearly swallowed—if he hadn't, he'd have been gone this long time," he chattered, watching Wally disengage the hook. "Isn't it the grand luck we're in! and he the beautifullest trout! Oh, why would I want to be falling in, and the fish rising!" He looked wistfully at Norah. "Tis all wet ye are, and the day spoilt on ye," he said, sadly. "You won't never take me out again, Miss Norah."

"Won't we just!" said Norah, smiling at him through a tangle of wet hair. "We don't get out of friends because of a trifle like that, Timsy." She brought the "Walloping Window-Blind" floundering against the shore. "There! it would warm an iceberg to pull that old tub. Come along, Timsy, and I'll race you home."

Wally put a detaining hand on her arm as he turned from securing the boat.

"Sure you're all right, Nor?"

"Right as—as anything," said Norah, laughing at the anxious face. "I believe you're growing careful, Wally—what's come to you?"

"It's all very well," said Wally, unhappily. "Do you think it's jolly for a fellow to see you pitching into a beastly lough? And I'm going home dry, and you and the kid wet. If there was any sense in it I'd jump in and get wet, too!"

"Only there isn't," said Norah—"and it was lucky for the two wet ones that you were dry in the boat. An old and hardened warrior like you ought to have more common sense."

"I suppose I ought," said Wally, relapsing into a smile. "Only . . . Oh, well. Now we've got to run, or we'll never catch young Timsy."

"Norah had read it over his shoulder."

"Then the little head appeared for an instant and she sprang into the water."

CHAPTER VIII
JOHN O'NEILL
"A fiery soul, which, working out its way,

Fretted the pigmy body to decay."

Dryden.

"And we're hanging out the sign

From the Leeuwin to the Line:

'This bit of the world belongs to US!' "

THE words came floating down the hillside at the top of a cheery young baritone. Also down the hillside came sounds of haste—heavy footsteps, crashing undergrowth, and rustling of bracken.

The hill sloped steeply, ending with an abrupt plunge into a boreen below: a little winding lane, walled in by high banks, clad with heather and furze, and all abloom with wild flowers. The main road ran westward, dusty and hot in the June sunlight; but the boreen was all in shade, twisting its way in and out between the hills. The dew was yet on its grass, though in the blossoming furze above, fringing the banks, the bees droned heavily, winging their busy way among the hot sweetness.

The noise overhead came nearer, and there came into the song staccato notes never intended by the composer, as the singer half-slid, half-plunged, down the hillside, taking inequalities in the ground with long strides. Nevertheless, the voice persevered, happy, if disjointed, until it was just above the boreen. Then the song and the hurrying footsteps ceased together, and there was a pause.

"Wire!" said Wally's disgusted tones. "And barbed, at that! Didn't we have enough in France!"

The wire was half-hidden in the tangle of grass and furze; a tense strand twanged as his boot caught it in clambering over. His thin face showed for a moment, peeping over into the boreen. There was nothing to do but slither, and slither he did, landing in the little lane with a mighty thud, and bringing with him a shower of furze blossoms, and clattering stones and clods. They fell close to a man sitting on a fragment of rock and leaning back against the bank. He had not stirred at the commotion overhead, and now he sat motionless, looking up at the tall lad with a faint smile.

"I beg your pardon!" said Wally, abashed. "I say. I hope nothing hit you?"

The man on the boulder shook his head. It was a big head, with a wide brow and lines of pain round the eyes; but he was a small man, and the hand lying on the knee of his rough tweed suit was startlingly thin. Even as he leaned back against the bank it was easy to see that his shoulders were misshapen and humped. Wally glanced once, and withdrew his eyes hurriedly, with a boy's instinctive dread of appearing to notice anything amiss.

"Beastly careless of me!" he said, apologetically. "I never thought of anyone being down below."

"Well, you gave enough warning that you were coming," said the man. "Anyone remaining below did so entirely at his own risk. Do you always come down a hill in that fashion, may I ask?"

Wally grinned.

"Not always," he admitted. "But it was a jolly hill; and it had taken me such a time to climb up it that I had a fancy to see how quickly I could get down. And I was feeling awfully fit. It's so jolly to be feeling well—makes you act like a kid."

"It must be jolly," said the other, laconically.

Wally flushed hotly, in dread of having hurt him. It was painfully clear that to feel well was not a common experience for the man on the boulder. He had a sudden wild desire to undo the impression of exuberant health and spirits. The tired eyes were even harder to face than the twisted shoulders.

"Been an awful crock, really," he said, sitting down on another fragment of rock. "Gassed—over there." He nodded vaguely in the direction—more or less—of Europe. "Makes you feel like nothing on earth."

"It's pretty bad, isn't it?" asked the other, with swift interest.

"Rather. We didn't get anything like a full dose, of course, or we wouldn't be here. But even a little is rather beastly. And the worst of it is, that it hangs on to you long after you're better—it seems to lurk down somewhere inside you, and gets hold of you just as you're beginning to think you're really all right. It actually makes a fellow think he's got nerves!"

"You don't look like it," said the man, laughing for the first time. The brown, boyish face did not suggest such attributes.

"Well, it truly does make one pretty queer," said Wally, laughing too. "However, I believe we've nearly got rid of it—this country of yours is enough to make us forget it."

"You're Australian, aren't you?" the man asked.

Wally nodded. "How did you know?"

"Oh, this is a little place," said the other. "Strangers are our only excitement, and since the war started we haven't had nearly so many. All the people who used to come here to fish are away fighting." He sighed. "Most of them will not come back any more. You were quite a godsend to us. Your boatman told one of my men about you; and the baker's boy tells the cook; and the butcher tells every one; and the postmistress is simply full of news about you. As for the shops, they are fairly buzzing!"

"Why, there are only two," said Wally, laughing.

"That's why they buzz," said the man. "I don't go into shops, myself; but I have been altogether unable to repress the delighted confidences of my chauffeur. He tells me that you're all very keen fishermen——"

"And don't know a thing about it!" said Wally. "Did he tell you that, too?"

"He said you were getting on," said the other, guardedly, his eyes twinkling. The chauffeur's confidences had probably been ample. "But your stories of Australia have them all fascinated, and if they weren't—most of them—grandfathers, they would probably emigrate in a body. Thank goodness, though, we've not many slackers here: almost all our young men are fighting. My chauffeur, poor lad, lost a leg at Ypres. His wooden leg is fairly satisfactory, but of course he can't go back, much as he wants to. We're nearly all old men or—cripples"—his voice was suddenly bitter: "and it's rather pleasant to see young faces again. You bring the stir of the world with you."

"We've had so much stir that we were uncommonly glad to get away from it," Wally answered. "And this is a jolly place; if there were more big timber it would be nearly as good as our bush-country." He paused, cheerfully certain of having paid Ireland the highest possible compliment: then he rose. "I must be getting back."

The man on the boulder rose also, slowly. When he stood up, his crooked shoulders became more evident. He took one or two steps slowly and painfully. Then he staggered, stretching an uncertain hand towards the bank.

"Can I help you?" It was impossible to pretend any longer not to notice: he was swaying, and Wally was beside him with a swift stride. The other caught at the strong young arm.

"Thank you," he said, presently. There were drops of perspiration on his brow, but his voice was steady. "I'm something of a crock myself, and this happens to be one of my bad days. I came up here because I couldn't stand the car any more—it's waiting for me on the road. If you would not mind helping me——?"

They went along the boreen slowly, between the blossoming banks. The man rested heavily on Wally's arm.

"Sure I'm not tiring you?" he asked, once. "You're not fit yourself, yet."

"Oh, I'm all right," Wally answered. "Please lean as much as you like. Would you like a rest?"

"No—we're nearly there. And I'm better." His face was white, but he smiled up at the tall boy. Then a turn in the lane brought the high road in view, and, drawn up by the side, a big touring-car. The chauffeur, drowsing in his seat in the sun, became suddenly awake. He limped quickly towards his master.

"Sure I knew you had no right to be going up there alone," he said, reproachfully. "Will you give me the other arm, sir?"

"I'm all right, Con. This gentleman has helped me splendidly." But he put a hand on the chauffeur's sleeve, more, Wally fancied, to pacify him than because he needed extra help.

In the car, he leaned back with a sigh of relief. It was luxuriously padded, and there were special cushions that the chauffeur adjusted with a practised hand.

"Awfully sorry to have been such a nuisance," he said. "Thanks ever so much; you saved me a rather nasty five minutes." He looked wistfully at Wally. "I suppose you wouldn't come home with me?"

Wally hesitated. He wanted badly to get back to his party and to the trout that were so tantalizing and so engrossing. But there was something hard to resist in the tired eyes.

"You would be doing me a real kindness," said the other. "I can send word to your friends——" He broke off. "Oh, it's hardly fair to ask you—you didn't come here to muddle about with a sick man. Never mind—I'll get you to come over some day when I'm more fit."

"I'd like to," said Wally, cheerfully; "but I'm coming now, as well, if I may." He hopped into the car, and sat down. "If you could let them know, I should be glad—they may be waiting for me."

"Where are they?—at the hotel?"

"No, they're fishing Lough Nacurra. I said I would turn up about twelve and hail them; it's Australian mail-day, and I've been posting the family's letters."

"If doesn't seem fair to keep you," said the car's owner. "But these days I dread my own company. So if you'll come to lunch with me I'll send you back to them in good time to get a few trout before the evening. Home, Con." The car started gently, and he leaned back and closed his eyes.

Wally felt slightly bewildered. Here was he, in company with a man whose name he did not know, and who was apparently going to sleep—both of them being whisked through the peaceful Irish landscape at an astonishing rate of speed in a motor which surpassed anything he had ever imagined in luxury of fittings. It was a very large car: four people could easily have found room in the seat he shared with his silent host, and there were, in addition, three little arm-chairs which folded flat when not in use. It was splendidly upholstered, and there were electric lamps in cunning places, and many of what Wally termed "contraptions"; pockets and flaps for holding papers, a clock and speedometer, and a silver vase in which nodded two perfect roses. Wally infinitely preferred horses to motors: but this was indeed a motor to be respected, and he gazed about him with frank interest, which did not abate when he found that his host was looking at him.

"I was admiring your car," he said. "It's a beauty; I don't think I ever saw such a big one."

"Well, I use it as a bedroom very often," said the other. "I like knocking about in it; and I hate hotels; so Con and I live in the car when we go touring, and he cooks for me, camp-fashion. This seat makes a very good bed; and I have various travelling fixtures that screw on here and there when they are needed, or live under the seat. I planned it myself, and I don't think there's a foot of waste space in it. Con sleeps in the front seat. We have an electric cooker, and he turns out uncommonly good meals. Of course, if we encounter really bad weather we have to put in for shelter, but I'm glad to say that doesn't often happen to us."

"How jolly!" Wally exclaimed. "I suppose you've been all over Ireland in that way?"

"Ireland—Scotland—England: and most of Europe and America," said his host. "I'm an idle man, you see, and travelling, if I can do it in my own fashion, makes amends for a good many things I can't have." The weariness came back into his face. "I might as well introduce myself," he said; "I forgot that I had kidnapped you without the civility of telling you my name, which is O'Neill—John O'Neill. I live at Rathcullen House, where we shall be in another minute or two."

Memory came back to Wally of a road perched above the lough, and of a little runabout car driven by a man in motor-goggles: and of the boatman's confidences.

"Then you're Sir John O'Neill?" he asked.

"Yes—the first part of it doesn't matter. The line goes back a good way, but I'm the last of it. But the old house is rather jolly; I hope you will all come and see it as often as you can spare the time."

The car swung off the road as he spoke, and through a great gateway where beautiful gates of wrought iron stood open between massive stone pillars. A little gabled lodge, with windows of diamond lattice-work, was just within: a pleasant-faced woman in pursuit of a fleeing mischievous child stopped, smiled, and dropped a curtsey, while the three-year-old atom she had been chasing bobbed down in ridiculous imitation, her elfish face breaking into smiles in its tangle of dark curls. John O'Neill smiled in return; and the car sped on smoothly, up a wide avenue lined with enormous beech-trees, arching and meeting overhead so that they seemed to be driving into a tunnel of perfect green. Between their mighty trunks Wally caught glimpses of a wide park, where little black Kerry cattle grazed.

For over a mile the avenue ran its winding way through the park. Then the trees ceased, and they came out into a clear space of terraced lawn, blazing with flower-beds, and sloping down to a lake fringed with ornamental plants, and dotted with many-coloured water-lilies, among which paddled lazily some curious waterfowl which Wally had never seen. Beyond the lawn stood a long grey house; a house of old grey stone, of many gables, clad in ivy and Virginia creeper. Even to the Australian boy's eyes it was mellow with the dignity of centuries. It was not imposing or majestic, like the old houses he had seen in England; but about it hovered an atmosphere of high breeding and of quiet peace: a house of memories, tranquil in its beauty and in its dreams.

The car came to rest gently beside a stone step, and in an instant a white-haired old butler was at the door, offering his arm to his master. John O'Neill got out slowly, and limped up the steps to the great doorway, where an Irish wolf-hound stood, looking at him with liquid eyes of welcome.

"I say—what a jolly dog!" Wally uttered.

"Yes, he's rather a nice old chap," said his host. "Shake hands, Lomair"; and the big dog put a paw gravely into Wally's hand. He followed his master into the house.

The great square hall was panelled with old oak, almost black in the subdued light within. A staircase, with wide, shallow steps, wound its way in a long curve to a gallery overhead: and at the far end, an enormous fireplace was filled with evergreens. Eastern rugs lay on the polished oaken floor; in one corner a stand of flowering plants made a sheet of colour. On the walls were splendid heads—deer of many kinds, markhor, ibex, koodoo, and two heads with enormous spreading antlers, stretching, from tip to tip, fully eleven feet. They drew an exclamation from Wally.

"They belonged to the old Irish elk," O'Neill explained. "He must have been a pretty big fellow; a pity civilization proved too much for him. He has been extinct thousands of years."

"Fancy seeing a herd of those fellows!" Wally exclaimed, gazing in admiration at the noble head. "But however would he get those antlers through timber?"

"I don't think he frequented forests much," O'Neill said. "The plains suited him better. But he must have been able to lay his horns right back—all deer can do that when necessary. I dare say he could dodge through trees at a good rate."

"Well, he looks as if he could hardly have got through the doorway of a Town Hall," Wally commented. "You have a splendid lot of heads. Did you shoot them yourself?"

"A few—I can't do much stalking," O'Neill said. "I got those two tigers, but that was from the back of an elephant. My father shot most of the others; he was a mighty hunter. The trout were mine"—he indicated some huge stuffed specimens, in glass cases, on the wall.

"They're splendid," Wally said, regarding his host with much admiration. "And you actually shot the tigers! Was it very exciting?"

"No—the trout took far more killing. The elephants and the beaters did most of the work so far as the tigers were concerned; it was only a sort of arm-chair performance on my part. I simply sat in a fairly comfortable howdah and fired when I was told to do so."

"It sounds simple, but—well, I'd like to have the chance. And you must have shot straight," Wally said. He glanced from the grim masks to the slight figure with ungainly shoulders, marvelling in his heart at the contrast between hunter and hunted. At the moment John O'Neill did not look capable of killing a mouse.

He dropped in to a big arm-chair, motioning Wally to another. The colour was returning to his face, and his eyes began to lose their pain-filled expression. In the big chair's depths he looked smaller than ever; but his eyes were very bright, and soon Wally forgot his morning's fishing and altogether lost sight of his host's infirmities in the fascination of his talk. Half-crippled as he was, he had been everywhere, and done many things that stronger men long vainly to do. He had travelled widely, and not as the average tourist, who skims over many experiences without gathering the cream of any. John O'Neill had gone off the beaten track in search of the unusual, and he had found it in a dozen different countries. He had hunted and fished; had shot big game in India and made his way up unknown rivers in South America, until sickness had forced him to abandon enterprise and return to civilization to save his life. Wandering in the bypaths of the world, he had brought home a harvest of queer experiences; he told them simply, with a twinkle in his eye and a quick joy in the humorous that often left his hearer shaking with laughter.

Wally listened in growing wonderment and a great sense of pity. If this man, so cruelly handicapped, had already done so much, what might he not have done, given a straight and sound body! Yet how he had accomplished even the tenth part of what he had done was a mystery. Wally looked at the frail, slight figure with respectful amazement.

John O'Neill broke off presently.

"I rattle along at a terrible rate when I'm lucky enough to find a listener," he said. "And lately I've been horribly sick of my own society. You see, they wouldn't have me in any capacity at the Front; I offered to do anything, and I did think they might have let me drive an ambulance; but an ambulance driver over there really has to be a hefty chap, able to put his shoulder literally to the wheel when a road goes to pieces in front of him, owing to a shell lobbing on it; and of course they said I wouldn't do, so soon as they looked at me. So I went to London and did Red Cross work and recruiting—and overdid it, like a silly ass. Broke down, and had to crawl home and be ill."

"Hard luck!" said Wally, sympathetically.

"Stupidity, you mean," remarked his host. "A man ought to know when he has had enough, whether it's work or beer. But it's not easy to stand aside when all the lucky people—like you—are playing the real game. At best, mine was only an imitation."

"I don't agree with you," Wally said, warmly. "We can't all fight—the rest of the country has to carry on."

"Oh, well, there are enough slackers and shirkers to do that," O'Neill said. "And anyhow, I couldn't even carry on at what I did attempt to do. Never mind—tell me your own adventures."

Wally's story of war did not take long in the telling; but he spun it out as much as possible, switching from war to Australia in response to the eager questions of the man in the big leather chair. John O'Neill was a curious blending: at one moment almost savagely cynical and despondent, as his own physical handicap weighed upon him: at the next, laughing like a boy, and full of a boy's keen interest in what he had not seen. Australian talk held him closely attentive: it was almost the only corner of the world that he had not visited, but he meant to go there, he said, after the war. Travelling by sea was unpleasant enough at any time without the added chance of an impromptu ducking if a submarine or a mine came across you.

"Do they all buck—your horses?" he asked. "I can ride a bit, but a buckjumper would be beyond me."

Wally reassured him as to the manners of Australian steeds.

"There's a general impression in England that we all live in red shirts, in the bush, and ride fiery, untamed steeds," said he, laughing. "It goes with the universal belief that all Australia is tropical. I've tried to tell fellows in England that there are parts of Australia where we have a pretty decent imitation of Swiss winter sports—skiing, skating, and all the rest of it; but they look on me with polite disbelief. They can't—or won't—understand that Australia stretches over enough of the map to have a dozen different kinds of climate. Not that it matters, anyhow; I don't think we expect people to be wildly interested in us."

"We'll know more about you by the time the war is over," his host suggested.

"Well—I suppose so. Lots of our fellows will come to London; we're all awfully keen to see it, and it's a great chance for us. I only hope we shall take a lot of your men back with us; they're falling over each other in England—or will be, once the war is over: and we want them. We needed them badly enough before the war: afterwards it will be worse than ever."

"Don't you preach emigration in Ireland," said O'Neill, laughing.

"Why not? They emigrate, whether you preach or not; only they go to America and Canada, because they're near and there's nothing between them and Ireland.

They would probably do much better if they would come to Australia, only they don't know a thing about it. I told one old woman a few things about Australia and wages there, and all she could say was, 'God help us!' When I'd finished, she said. 'And Australy'd be somewhere in Americy, wouldn't it, dear?'"

"Did you say, 'God help us'?" laughed O'Neill.

"I might have," grinned Wally. "They know Canada—but then, look what Canada is!" He gave a mock shiver—Wally had been reared in hot Queensland. "As one Canadian chap said to me, after visiting our irrigation settlements—'I don't know why people come to us instead of to you: just look at the climate you've got—and we have three seasons in the year—July, August, and winter!' But I suppose they seem nearer home, and they can't realize that when you once get on a ship you might as well be there for a month as a week."

The white-haired butler announced luncheon, and they found the table laid in the bow-window of a long and lofty room, whence could be seen the park, ending in a glimpse of bog and heather, with a flash of blue that meant a little lough caught among the hills. Afterwards, they strolled out on the terrace and through the scented garden to the stables, where two fine hunters and some useful ponies made friends with Wally instantly.

"The Government took most of my horses when war broke out; but I managed to keep these two," said O'Neill, his hand on an arching neck while a soft muzzle sought in his pocket for a carrot. "I'd sooner have paid what they were worth than let them go; they're too good for war treatment, unless it were absolutely necessary. And thank goodness this is not a war of horses. Would you care to try one of these fellows, some day?"

"Wouldn't I!" said Wally, beaming. "And—could Jim?"

"Of course—and what about Jim's sister? Does she ride?"

"She does," said Wally, suppressing a smile at that incomplete statement.

"Rides anything that ever looked through a bridle, I suppose," said his host, watching him. "She looks a workmanlike person. That brown pony is pretty good; she might like him. I can show you all a bit of Irish jumping—ditches and banks instead of your fly fences."

"We'll probably fall off," said Wally, with conviction.

"Then you'll find the falling softer than in Australia," O'Neill said, consolingly. "But I don't fancy you will give us much fun that way."

The motor waited at the hall door.

"Con will drop you near your people," O'Neill said. "I'd like to come with you—but if I overdo things to-day I'll pay to-morrow; and I'm anxious to see the last of this attack. Will you tell Mr. Linton I hope to call on him in a few days?"

"We'll be awfully glad to see you," Wally said. "And thanks ever so for giving me such a good time."

O'Neill laughed. "Is it me now, to be giving you a good time?" he said. "I thought 'twas the other way round it was. You have helped me through a stiff day, and I'm very grateful." He shook hands warmly, and the motor whirred away.

"He fell close to a man sitting on a fragment of rock and leaning back against the bank."

CHAPTER IX
PINS AND PORK
"Sure, this is blessed Erin, an' this the same glen;

The gold is on the whin-bush, the wather sings again:

The Fairy Thorn's in flower—an' what ails my heart then?"

Moira O'Neil.

"WELL—of all the deserters!"

"Is it me?" asked Wally, modestly. He made an enormous stride from a half-submerged stone into the boat, and nearly lost his balance, collapsing in the stern.

"You!" said Jim, steadying the boat, which endeavoured, under the assault, to bury her nose in a muddy bank of rushes. "You, that was going to catch several hundred trout, and instead cleared out——"

"In a plutocratic motor," said Norah.

"With a bloated aristocrat," added Jim.

"And never said good-bye!" finished Mr. Linton, with an artistic catch in his voice.

"I did," said Wally: "I did it all. And I didn't want to."

Sounds of disbelief rose from his hearers.

"You needn't snort," said the victim, inelegantly.

"I don't think it betters your case to describe our just indignation as snorting," said Mr. Linton.

"If you were to grovel it would become you better," said Norah.

"Not in this boat," hastily remarked her father. "It isn't planned for gymnastics."

"He's too well-fed to grovel, anyhow," said Jim brutally. "What did you have in the ducal castle, Wal? ortolans and plovers' eggs, and things?"

"Chops," said Wally.

"Shades of Australia!" ejaculated Mr. Linton. "Is that what one eats in company with dukes?"

"I don't know," Wally answered, patiently. "He isn't a duke, anyhow. Where did you people get your soaring ideas?"

"From a lame chauffeur who seemed to think you were getting a great deal more than you deserved——" Jim began.

"That's what I'm getting now!" said Wally.

"Well, he said you had gone off in the mothor to the big house. We inferred from his tone that it was not merely big, but enormous. The master had tuk you, he said; we further gathered that you might come back when the master had finished with you. It sounded rather like Jack and the Giant, and if we had known who had kidnapped you we might have organized a search party. As we didn't, we caught trout—lots of 'em."

"Did you, indeed?" said Wally, with open envy. "Lucky beggars—I wish I had!"

"And you rioting in baronial halls!" said Norah. "Some people don't know when they are well off."

"If we let Wally have a word in edgeways for a few minutes we might find out a little more about the baronial halls," said Mr. Linton. "Tell us what happened to you, Wally. Was it a duke?"

"It was not—only a poor hump backed chap with some sort of a handle to his name. He's Sir John O'Neill, and he has a lovely place; but you never saw a man with less 'frill,' " Wally remarked. "Simple as anyone could be. And I don't think I've ever been so sorry for anyone."

"Is he badly crippled?" Jim asked.

"No—only he seems awfully delicate, and subject to beastly fits of illness. He's got any amount of pluck—rides and shoots and fishes, and has motored half over the world. But of course he's terribly handicapped; the wonder is that he has done half as much."

"That must be the man Patsy was talking about—only he called him the young masther," Norah said. "Is he quite young?"

"Oh, I'd put him down at about forty," said Wally, to whom that age was close on senile decay: "I think the old hands here would call a man the young master until he died of old age. He's queer: at times he's like a kid; and then I suppose the pain gets hold of him, because, in a minute he seems to grow quite old, and he drops laughing and gets bitter."

"Poor fellow!" said Mr. Linton. "How did you find him, Wally?"

"Why, I nearly fell on top of him getting down a bank into a lane," Wally answered. "He was sitting on a stone, hating himself, but he didn't seem to mind my sudden appearance at all, though I'm sure clods hit him. Then we yarned, and I helped him back to his car, and he got me to go back to lunch with him—I didn't want to, but——" He was silent.

"I expect he was glad of someone to talk to," Mr. Linton said.

"That's it—he's just as lonely as he can be. All his people are fighting, and he's knocked himself out over Red Cross work, and has had to come back to Ireland and get fit. He's coming to call on you, sir—and he wants us all to go over to Rathcullen—his place—as much as we can."

"H'm," said Jim and Norah, together.

"I wish baronial halls appealed more to my family," said Mr. Linton, laughing.

"I didn't mean to be horrid; but trout and loughs and bogs appeal so much more," said Norah. "Of course we'll go, if he wants us."

"Well, it's a jolly place, and he's horribly lonely," Wally answered. "And I don't know about his halls being baronial, but certainly his stables are: they're simply topping. He hasn't many horses left—the Government took most of them for the war; but there are two ripping hunters, and some extra good ponies. And he wants to lend 'em to us."

"Eh!" said Jim, sitting up. "Wally, my child, how did you manage it?"

"Didn't have to," said Wally, grinning. "He simply threw them at me. Asked me if you could ride, Norah, so I suggested that if he had a quiet donkey it might do."

"We have one that is not quiet," said Norah, regarding him with a fixed eye. "Tell me the truth, Wally—is there something I can ride?"

"Wait till you see it—that's all. And he's going to teach us to jump banks and ditches and things."

"Oh-h!" said Norah, blissfully, "I said this place only wanted horses to make it perfect!"

"Well, now you're going to have the horses, little as you both deserve 'em," said Wally; "and now, perhaps, you'll all apologize humbly for calling me unpleasant names!"

"Certainly not," Jim said, firmly. "If you didn't deserve them at the moment (and I'm not sure that you didn't), you're sure to deserve them before long. Never mind, look at this!"

He opened his fishing-basket carefully and showed a mass of damp grass, among which could be seen glimpses of many trout. Jim dived in with his finger and thumb, and drew out a speckled beauty, which he dangled before Wally's envious gaze.

"A pound and a half, by my patent spring-balance!" he declared, triumphantly. "I played him for what seemed like three hours, and I never was so scared of anything in my life. He got tired at last, however, and Norah officiated with the landing-net."

"Yes, and missed him twice," said Norah, shame-faced. "It was the greatest wonder he didn't get off. But a big trout on the end of a little line does wobble so much when it's coming towards the net. It's much worse than a screwing ball at tennis."

"I know—and you feel perfectly certain the line is going to break, if the rod doesn't," Wally said. "I feel like that over a quarter-pounder: I don't know how you ever managed to make a collected effort for that big fellow."

"It wasn't collected at all—I just swiped wildly, and got him by the sheerest good luck," Norah answered. "I mean to practise with a cricket ball on a string, hung from the big tree outside my window: it would be awful to miss another beauty like that."

They were drifting down the little lough very slowly. There were purple shadows under the hills, lying across the strip of bog that stretched westward, where the curlew and golden plover were calling. A little breeze sprang up, just rippling the surface of the water. Wally got out his rod hastily; but though the conditions seemed ideal, the trout had apparently gone to sleep, and when an hour's casting had not yielded so much as a rise, it was decided that there might be better things than fishing, and the party returned to the shore. A small boy, lurking about the landing stage, was entrusted with the rods and baskets, and disappeared slowly among the trees fringing the path that led to the hotel.

"What are we going to do?" Jim asked.

"I'm going to Gortbeg," Norah said. "I want some pins."

"Pins?" Jim echoed. "Why ever must you walk two miles for pins? I'm sure you don't use one in a year."

"No, and so I haven't got any," Norah said. "And I must have some, because I want to shorten my bog-lepping skirt, and I can't turn up the edge without pins to keep it in place."

"But you sew that sort of thing, don't you?" Jim asked, wrestling with masculine obtuseness.

"Of course—after you've pinned it in place. Jimmy, you had better let me attack that skirt in my own way!" said Norah, justly incensed. "If you'd tried climbing a mountain in a too-long skirt you wouldn't argue about making it shorter."

"I guess I would cut a foot off it without arguing at all," said Jim, laughing. "Skirts are fool-things out of a house. Well, lead on, my child: I suppose we're all going pin-hunting."

The road to Gortbeg lay between high banks, with occasional gaps through which could be seen pleasant moors and fields, and sometimes an old mansion, almost hidden by enormous beech-trees. Most of the great houses of the country were silent and closely-shuttered; the men of the family away fighting, the women doing Red Cross work in London, or nursing as near the firing-line as they could manage to establish themselves. In a few were faint signs of occupation: a white-haired old lady on a lawn, an old man, surrounded by a number of dogs, of many breeds, wandering through the woods; but even in these houses there was an air of brooding quiet and expectancy, of silent daily watching for news. The gardens were gay with summer flowers, and nothing could spoil the beauty of the trees; but there were weeds in the mould, and the paths were unkempt and moss-grown. The district was never a rich one, and now the war had taken all its men and money.

Down the road, to meet them, came a boy on a donkey: a cheery small boy, sitting very far back with his knees well in. The donkey was guiltless of bridle or saddle, obeying, with meekness, if not with alacrity, suggestions conveyed to it by the pressure of the bare knees and occasional blows with an ash cudgel.

"The asses of Ireland are a patient race," remarked Wally.

"They had need to be," Jim answered.

"It's up to the ass to be patient in most places," remarked Mr. Linton. "Life isn't exactly a picnic to him anywhere. On the whole, the Irish donkeys seem well enough cared for; I have seen their brothers in other countries far worse treated. That's a nice donkey you have, sonny"—to the small rider, who passed them, grinning cheerfully.

"He is, sorr"; and the grin widened.

"They're such jolly kids in these parts," Wally said. "They always greet you as if you were the one person they had wanted to see for years; and they're so interested in you. It doesn't seem like curiosity, either, but real, genuine interest."

"So it is, as far as it goes," Jim said.

"Well it may not go far, but it's comforting while it lasts—and it generally lasts as long as one is there oneself. It's just as well it doesn't go deeper, or visitors would leave an awful trail of unrequited affection behind them. As it is, one feels they recover after one has gone, after doing all they can to make one's stay pleasant. Yes,

I think Ireland's a nice, friendly country," Wally finished. "And there's Gortbeg, looking as if it had forgotten to wake up for about five hundred years."

There was not much of Gortbeg. A busy little river flowed past it hurriedly, and the village had sprung up along one bank: one winding street, with a few cottages and a whitewashed inn which called itself the Fisherman's Arms. Some boats were moored in the stream near the inn, where a crazy landing-stage jutted out. Scarcely anyone was to be seen except a few children, playing on the green, which they shared with numerous geese, a few donkeys, and some long-haired goats; while over the half-door of one of the cabins a knot of shawled women gossiped.

"There's your shop, Norah," Mr. Linton said, indicating a dingy building which bore in its window a curious assortment of cheap sweets, slates, apples, red flannel, and bacon.

"It looks a bit queer," Norah commented, regarding the emporium rather doubtfully. "However, it's sure to have pins."

The shop was prudently secured, by a bolted half-door, against the ravages of predatory geese or goats. Within, it was very dark, and prolonged hammering on the counter failed to bring any response. Finally Jim found his way into a back room and cooee'd lustily, returning in some haste.

"Phew-w! There's a gentleman in corduroys, asleep on a bed, and two dead pigs hanging by their heels," he said. "None of them took any notice of me; but some one out at the back answered. Here he comes."

The proprietor of the shop entered hurriedly: a plump little man, very breathless and apologetic, and more than a little damp.

"I left a bit of a young gossoon to mind the shop," he said—"and I washin' meself. It's gone he is, playin' with the other boys—sure I'll teach him to play when I get a holt of him. Pins, miss? Is it hairpins, now, you'd be wanting?"

"No, just ordinary pins," Norah told him.

"H'm," said the shopman, doubtfully. "I dunno would I have them, at all. If it was hairpins, now, there's not a place in Donegal where you'd get a finer selection. Pins . . ." He pondered deeply, and rummaged in a box that seemed sacred to extremely sticky bull's eyes. "Well, well, we'd better look for them. It might be they'd be in some odd corner."

The wall behind him was divided into innumerable little compartments, and he looked faithfully through them all, striking match after match to illumine his progress. There were assorted goods in the compartments: nails and screws, tin saucepan-lids, marbles, boots, soap, oranges, reels of cotton, biscuits, socks, and ass's shoes; he searched them all, turning over the contents of each until the match burned down to his fingers, when he would throw it hastily on the floor, strike another, and move on to the next collection. The box of matches was nearly exhausted when at length he gave up his quest.

"They're not in it at all," he said, despondently. "I did have some, one time, but I expect they're sold on me. When the traveller comes I could be getting some in from Belfast, if there was no hurry."

Norah indicated that there was hurry, and asked if there were another shop.

"There's Mary Doody's," said the man of business, sadly; "at the least, you might call it a shop, though it's only herself knows what she sells. That's the only one." He came to the doorway, and pointed down the street. "The last house, it is. If 'twas anything in the wurruld now, except pins, I'd have it."

A little way from the shop, he caught them up, breathless, but aflame with business enterprise.

"Is it from Moroney's ye are? Would ye tell Mrs. Moroney that I've the grandest bit of pork ever she seen—killed yesterday, an' they me own pigs that I rared on the place. Peter Grogan—sure, she'll know me."

"Thank you," Jim said, hurriedly. "Good night."

"Good night," responded Mr. Grogan. "Tell her to-morrow's early closing day, an' I could bring one over in the little ass-cart as aisy as not." The last words were uttered in a high shriek as the distance widened between himself and the Linton party.

"Pork is a good thing," said Mr. Linton, sententiously. "Isn't it, Jim?"

"If you'd seen the room I saw!" said his son, with feeling. "Such a bedroom: and the gentleman in bed, and I should say very drunk. No, I don't think I'll deliver that message."

"I wouldn't," said Mr. Linton.

Mary Doody's place of business stood back a little from the road. There was no window for the display of goods, and the door was shut. The uninitiated might, indeed, have been pardoned for failing to regard it as a shop, or for passing by, unnoticed, the brief legend over the door which stated that Mrs. Doody's residence was a Generil Store, and added that she was further empowered to sell stout and porter. The inhabitants of Gortbeg, however, were clearly to be numbered among the initiated, for sounds of conviviality came, muffled, from within, and once a voice broke into a snatch of a song. Norah hesitated.

"I suppose I needn't knock."

"They might not hear you, if you did," Jim said. He opened the door.

Within, a long, low room was dim with a mixture of turf and tobacco smoke, and heavy with the fumes of porter. A swinging lamp shed a depressed ray over the scene. As her eyes grew accustomed to the smoky twilight, Norah made out a number of men and a few women sitting on benches near the fire, each with a mug that evidently held comforting liquor. Every one seemed to be talking at once; but a dead silence fell as the door opened on the unfamiliar figures. Norah resisted an inclination to turn and seek fresh air. An immensely fat woman, with a grimy shawl pinned across her bosom, waddled forward.

"Good evening, dear," she said, dividing the greeting impartially between Jim and Norah.

"Good evening," Norah responded. "This is a shop, isn't it?"

"It is, dear," Mrs. Doody said, bridling a little at any doubt being cast on her emporium. "Were you wantin'——?"

"Pins," Norah said hastily. "Do you keep them?"

"I dunno would I," said Mary Doody, unconsciously echoing Mr. Grogan. "Pins. Would they be small pins, now?"

"Yes—just common pins."

"Pins," said Mary Doody, reflecting deeply. She turned and sought in unsavoury boxes which held a stock as varied, if not so numerous, as that of Mr. Grogan. The porter-drinkers became immensely interested. Some of the women came nearer and stared at the strangers, and one or two, catching Norah's eye, smiled a greeting.

Mary Doody heaved her mighty form up from the box over which she had been crouching.

"I had some, wanst," she said. "But 'tis gone they are, or may be them gerrls has them taken. Wouldn't anything else do for you, dear?"

"No, thank you," Norah said, hastily. She turned to go, pursued by Mrs. Doody, who suddenly became interested in the case.

"Did you try Peter Grogan?" she asked. "He have a little shop up yonder."

Norah admitted having tried and failed.

"My, my!" said Mary Doody. " 'Tis puttin' a bad direction on a counthry when you can't buy a paper of pins in it, isn't it, dear?"

Norah laughed. "I'm sorry you haven't got them," she said.

"No. There's no call for them here, dear. We do be using buttons," said Mary Doody, blandly.

Under cover of this broadside Norah made a confused exit, to find Jim and Wally helpless with laughter without.

"Never did I see anyone taught her place so beautifully!" said Jim, ecstatically. "That will teach you to be tidy, young Norah!"

"Buttons!" said Norah, laughing. "I'd like to see Mary Doody shorten a skirt with the aid of buttons. Anyhow, I've got to do it without the aid of pins, that's evident. Come home, you unsympathetic frivollers!"

It was two days later, that, coming in late and ravenously hungry after a long tramp across the bog, the Lintons made a hurried toilet and a still more hurried descent to the dining-room. Dinner had been kept waiting for them, and they applied themselves to it with an energy born of a long day in the open air and a sandwich lunch. It was when the first edge of appetite had been taken off, and they were toying with a mammoth apple-pie, that Mrs. Moroney bore down upon them.

"I'm afraid we were very late, Mrs. Moroney," said Mr. Linton.

"Ah, 'tis no matter," said the lady of the house, waving away the suggestion. "In the heighth of the season there's many a one roaring for dinner, and it ten o'clock at night. Did you enjoy your dinner, now?"

"We did, indeed," said Mr. Linton; "it was most excellent pork——"

He stopped, catching Jim's eye, into which had come a sudden light of comprehension.

"Pork!" said Jim faintly. "Yes, it was pork. Mrs. Moroney, . . . I wonder . . . did you . . . ?"

"Don't tell me there was anything wrong with it," said Mrs. Moroney, aflame in the defence of the pork. "I never see better pigs than them ones of Peter Grogan's; and he after killing them only last Tuesday!"

CHAPTER X
THE ROCK OF DOON
"Hills o' my heart!

Let the herdsman who walks in your high haunted places

Give him strength and courage, and weave his dreams alway:

Let your cairn-heaped hero-dead reveal their grand exultant faces.

And the Gentle Folk be good to him betwixt the dark and day."

Ethna Carbery.

SIR John O'Neill paid his formal call on the Australians, tactfully choosing a day so hopelessly wet as to forbid any thought of fishing or "bog-lepping." Bog excursions had a peculiar fascination for Norah and the boys, who loved rambling among the deep brown pools, leaping from tuft to tuft of sound grass, and making experiments—frequently disastrous—in mossy surfaces that looked sound, but were very likely to prove quagmires which effectually removed any lurking doubt in Norah's mind that an Irish bog could be boggy. They sought the bogs in almost all weathers. But the day that brought Sir John to the old house on Lough Aniller was one of such pitiless rain that prudence, in the shape of Mr. Linton, forbade any excursion to patients so newly recovered as Jim and Wally.

Even in the most homelike of boarding-houses a wet day is apt to be depressing to open-air people. It was with relief, mingled with amazement, that they saw the motor coming up the dripping avenue in the afternoon; and a moment later Bridget, obviously impressed, ushered Sir John into the drawing-room. The Lintons were established as favourites in the household on their own merits; but it was placing them on quite a different standard of respect to find that they were visited by the "ould stock."

Every one enjoyed the visit. Sir John was better, the lines of pain that Wally had seen nearly gone from his face. There was an almost boyish eagerness about him; he was keen to know them all, to hear their frank talk, to make friends with them. David Linton and his son liked him from the moment they met his eyes; brown eyes, with something of the mute appeal that lies in the eyes of a dog. As for Norah, in all her life she had not known what it meant to be so sorry for anyone as she felt for this brave, crippled man, with his high-bred face and gallant bearing. Afterwards, when John O'Neill looked back at heir meeting, one of his memories of Norah was that she had never seemed to see his misshapen shoulders.

That first visit had stretched over the whole afternoon, no one quite knew how. Outside, the rain streamed down the window-panes and lashed the lough into waves; but within the old house a fire of turf and bog-wood blazed, casting ruddy lights on the furniture, and sending its pleasant, acrid smell into the room. They gathered round it in a half-circle and "yarned"—exchanging stories of Ireland, and Australia, and London and war. There could be no talk in those grim days without war-stories and war-rumours; but after a time they drifted away to far-off times, and Sir John, beginning half-timidly with an old Irish legend, found that he had a suddenly enthralled circle of listeners, who demanded more, and yet more—tales of high and far-off times and of the mighty heroes of Ireland: Finn MacCool and the Fianna, Cuchulain, Angus Og, and the half-real, half-legendary past that holds Ireland in a mist of romance. He knew it all, and loved it, telling the stories with the quiet pride of a descendant of a race whose roots were deep in the soil of the land that had borne them: and the children of the country that had no history hung upon his words.

"What must you think of me?" he said at last, when, in a pause, the clock in the hall boomed out six strokes. "I come to call, and I remain to an unseemly hour spinning yarns. The fact is, you—well, you just aren't strangers at all, and I certainly knew you before. Were you in Ireland in a previous incarnation, Miss Norah?"

Norah laughed.

"I would love to think so," she said. "One would like to have had some part in the Ireland you can talk about. Will you come again and tell us more, Sir John?"

His eyes were grateful.

"If I don't bore you. I fastened upon this poor boy"—indicating Wally with a friendly nod—"the other day when I was desperately sick of my own company, and now I seem to have done the same to you all; and you're very good to a lonely man. But I want all of you at Rathcullen."

"We're coming," said Wally, solemnly.

"Will you? I timed my call to-day, because I didn't think even half-amphibious Australians would be out in such weather—and see what luck I've had!" He looked no older than the boys, his eager face glowing in the firelight. "But please don't come to Rathcullen formally, Mr. Linton; if I bring the car over can I carry you all off to-morrow for lunch? There are horses simply spoiling to be ridden, Miss Norah."

"Oh-h!" said Norah. "But I've no riding-things with me."

"That doesn't matter: I have two young cousins who occasionally pay me a visit, and their riding-kit is at Rathcullen, since they can't use it in London. I'm sure you can manage with it; details of fit don't signify much in Donegal." He rose, and stood on the hearthrug looking eagerly at them. When he was sitting, his finely-modelled head and clever face made it easy to forget his dwarfed body: standing, among the lithe, tall Australians, it was suddenly pitifully evident. He felt it, for he flushed, and for a moment his eyes dropped; then he faced them again, bravely. Mr. Linton spoke, hurriedly.

"We would be delighted to go to you. But are we not rather a numerous party? I think we ought to send a detachment!"

"No, indeed—I wouldn't know which to choose!" returned the Irishman, whimsically. "You see, you are just a godsend to me, if you will spare me a little of your time; I have been so long shut up alone. And it's not good to be alone when one is spoiling to be in the thick of things; I grow horribly bad-tempered. When I know that these young giants are out of the hunt, too, I become more reconciled to circumstances. You see my complete selfishness!" He smiled at them delightfully. "So, may I come for you all to-morrow?"

"Thanks—but there is really no reason why we should trouble you to bring the motor. We can easily walk over."

"There's every reason; I'll get you earlier!" said O'Neill, laughing.

The motor slid down the avenue in the driving rain, and the Australians looked at each other.

"Did you ever make friends so quickly with anyone, dad?" Jim asked.

"I don't think I did," David Linton answered. "There's something about him one can't quite express: so much of the child left in the man. Poor fellow—poor fellow!"

"I think he's the bravest man I ever saw," said Norah.

The day at Rathcullen House was the first of many. Sir John was so frankly eager to have them there, and his welcome was so spontaneous and heart-felt, that the Australians suddenly felt themselves "belong," and the beautiful old house became to them an Irish version of their own Billabong. Ireland, always many-sided, showed them a new and fascinating face. They had loved the lanes and bogs and moors where they had been free to wander. But now they found themselves free of a wide demesne where wealth and art had done all that was possible to aid Nature, with a perfect understanding of where it was best to leave Nature alone. The park, with its splendid old trees, and the well-kept fields around it, gave opportunities for trying Sir John's horses; and Norah and the boys were soon under the spell of jumping the big banks that the hunters took so cleverly,—although, at first, to see them jump on to a bank, change feet with lightning rapidity, and leap down the far side, seemed to Antipodean eyes more like a circus performance than ordinary riding! Beyond the park stretched miles of deer-forest, unlike an ordinary forest in that it had no trees,—being a great expanse of heathery hills and moor, seamed and studded with rocks, streams babbling here and there, half-hidden in deep channels fringed with long grass and heather and ling. As land, it Was worthless; nothing would grow in the stony barren soil save the moorland plants; but it formed a glorious ground for long rambles. O'Neill was fast recovering his normal strength, and his energy was always like a devouring fire; he could not, however, walk far, and he and David Linton would find rocky seats on the moor while Norah and the boys rambled far over the deer-forest, often stalking patiently for an hour, armed with field-glasses, to catch a glimpse of the shy red-deer.

"A don't know why people want to shoot them," Norah said, after a long crawl through the rough heather, which had resulted in a splendid view of a magnificent stag. "They're so beautiful; and it's just as much fun to stalk them like this!" To which Jim and Wally returned non-committal grunts, and exchanged, privately, glances of amazement at the strangeness of the feminine outlook.

Sometimes there were days on the lough at the far end of the Rathcullen bog: a well-stocked lough where no outside fishing was permitted, and which yielded them trout of a weight far beyond their dreams; and there were motor-drives far afield, exploring the country-side, with Sir John always ready with legends and stories of the "ould ancient" times. Even on wet days the big Rolls-Royce would appear early in the morning, bearing an urgent invitation; and wet days were easy to spend in Rathcullen—in the great hall, the well-stocked library, the conservatories, or the picture-gallery, where faces of long-dead O'Neills, some of them startlingly like their host, stared down at them from the panelled walls. In the billiard-room Wally and Jim fought cheerful battles, while Mr. Linton would write Australian letters in the library, and Norah and Sir John explore other nooks and corners of the great house, or discourse music after their own fashion. His friendship seemed fitted to each: with Mr. Linton he could be the man of affairs, deeply-read and thoughtful; while to the boys and Norah he was the most delightful of chums, as full of fun even as Wally.

"He fits in so," said Jim. "He's never in our way, and—what is a good deal more wonderful—I don't believe we're ever in his!"

Many times Sir John begged them to transfer themselves altogether to Rathcullen. But something of Australian independence held them back; they preferred to retain their rooms at the Lough Aniller house, though it saw less and less of them in the daytime, and Timsy openly bewailed their constant absence—until the sergeant came home on furlough, when Timsy promptly forgot every one else in the world, and walked with his head in clouds of glory.

"Indeed," Mr. Linton said, one day, in answer to a renewed invitation—"I am frequently ashamed to think how completely we seem to have quartered ourselves on you, O'Neill. It's hardly fair to inflict you still further."

"If you could but guess what you have done for me, you might be surprised," Sir John answered.

They were in the motor, running along a smooth high road near the little narrow-gauge railway line. Ahead, Norah and the boys could be seen across a field, riding; they had come across country, taking banks and ditches as they came, and were making towards a point where they were all to meet. John O'Neill looked at the racing trio with a smile.

"I was in a pretty bad way when Wally dropped on me in the boreen that morning," he said, presently.

"He said you were suffering terribly," David Linton said.

"Oh—that was nothing. I'm fairly well used to pain when my stupid attacks come on, though that had certainly been a stiff one. But—well, I think I was beginning to lose heart. My physical disadvantages have always been in my way, naturally; but I have managed to keep them in the background to a certain extent and live a man's life, even in a second-rate fashion. But since the war began I couldn't do it. I was so useless—a cumberer of the ground, when every man was needed. My people have always been fighters, until——until I came, to blot the record."

"You have no right to say that," said David Linton, sharply. "You did more than thousands of men are doing."

"I did what I could. But I wanted to fight, man—to fight! If you knew how I envied every private I saw marching through London! every lucky youngster with a sound heart and a pair of straight shoulders. I had always set my teeth, before, and got through a man's work, somehow or other. But here was something I couldn't do—they wouldn't have me. And even over what work I was able to tackle, I went to pieces. When I came back to Ireland I felt like rubbish, flung out of the way—out of the way of men who were men."

"It's not fair to feel like that," David Linton said. "And it is not true."

"Well—you have all helped me to believe that perhaps I am not altogether on the dust-heap. You came when I was desperate; every day in Rathcullen was making me worse. I couldn't go into the picture-gallery; the fighting-men on the walls seemed to look at me in scorn to see to what a poor thing the old house had come down. And then you all came, and you didn't seem to notice that anything was wrong with me. You made me one of you—even those youngsters, full of all the energy and laughter and youth of that big young country of yours. They have made a chum of me: I haven't laughed for years as I've laughed in the last fortnight. And I'm fitter than I've been for years—I've forgotten to think of myself, and when you all go I also am going back, to work. There must be work, even for me."

"For you! Why, you're a young man, full of energy, even if you can't have active service," said David Linton. "And I am a grey old man, but there's work for me. Don't think that you have no job, because you can't get the job you like; that's an easy attitude to adopt. Every man can find his job if he looks for it with his eyes open."

"Well, you have helped mine to open," O'Neill said. "I was miserable because I had hitched my wagon to a star and had found I couldn't drive it. The old servants—bless their kind hearts!—were purring over me and pitying me, and I was feeling raw; and then you all walked into my life and declined to notice that I was a useless dwarf——"

"Because you aren't," said the other man, sharply. "Don't talk utter nonsense!"

O'Neill laughed.

"Well—I won't forget," he said. "But I am grateful; only I sometimes wonder if I ask for too much of your time. Do you think the youngsters are bored?"

"Bored!" Mr. Linton said in amazement. "Why, they are having the time of their lives! I could not possibly have given them half the pleasure you have Put in their way. You talk of gratitude, but to my mind it should be entirely on our side."

"No," said O'Neill firmly. "Still, I'm glad to think they are enjoying themselves,—not merely being polite and benevolent!" Whereat David Linton broke into laughter.

"I trust they'd be polite in any circumstances," he said. "But even politeness has its limits. You wouldn't call that sort of thing forced, would you? Look."

He pointed across a field. Norah and the boys were galloping to meet them. They flashed up a little hill, dipped down into a hollow, and scurried up another rise, where a stiff bank met them, with a deep drop into the next field. Norah's brown pony got over it with the cleverness of a cat, and she raced ahead of the boys, who set sail after her, vociferating quite unintelligible remarks about people who took unfair short cuts. Their merry voices brought echoes from the hills. Norah maintained her advantage until a low bank brought them out into the road, and all together they trotted towards the waiting motor. Their glowing faces sufficiently answered Sir John's doubts.

"Why, of course you beat them, Norah—easily!" he said, shamelessly ignoring the boys' side of the race. "Didn't I tell you that pony could beat most things in Donegal, if she got the chance?"

"I did cut a corner," Norah admitted, laughing. "But 'tis themselves has the animals of great size—and they flippant leppers!" She dropped into brogue with an ease born of close association with Timsy and his parents. "Sir John, is that the Doon Rock?"

She pointed with her whip to a great rocky eminence half a mile away.

"Yes, that's the Rock," O'Neill answered. "It's rather a landmark, isn't it? We'll wait for you at the foot, if you'll jog on after us."

The riders followed the motor slowly. The road led past the great mass, half hill, half rock, that towered over the little fields. It was about three hundred feet high, with sparse vegetation endeavouring to find a footing on its rugged sides, and grey boulders, weather-worn and clothed with lichen, jutting out, grim and bleak. The motor halted under its shadow, and the groom who occupied the front seat with Con, the lame chauffeur, led the horses away to a cottage close by.

A few hundred yards away a curious sight puzzled the Australians. On a little green, where some grey stones marked a well, was a little plantation of sticks stuck in the ground. Fluttering rags waved from many of them, and ornamented the ragged brambles near the well.

"You haven't seen a holy well, have you?" O'Neill asked. "That is one of the most famous—the Well of Doon."

"But what are the sticks?" Wally asked.

"Come and see."

They walked over to the well. A deeply marked path led to it, and all about it the ground was beaten hard by the feet of many people, save in the patch of ground where the sticks stood upright. There were all kinds of sticks; rough stakes, cut from a hedge, ash-plants, blackthorns—some of no value, others well-finished and costly. Rags, white and coloured, fluttered from them. And there was more than one crutch, standing straight and stiff among the lesser sticks.

"But what is it?" breathed Norah.

"It's a holy well. Hundreds of years ago there was a great sickness in the country, and the people sent to a saint who had originally come from these parts, begging him to come and help them. The saint was in Rome, and he could not come. But he was sorry for the people; and the legend goes that he threw his staff into a well in Rome, and it sank, and emerged from the water of the Well of Doon here: and ever since then the people believe that the water has healing power, and that it will heal anyone who pilgrimages to it barefoot."

"But does it?" asked Wally, incredulously.

"Well—they say the age of miracles is past. But the age of faith-healing is not; and you won't find an Irishman, whatever his religion, sneering at the old holy places of Ireland. I don't pretend to understand these things, but I respect them. And then—there is no doubt whatever as to the genuineness, and the permanence, of many of the cures." He pointed to the little forest of sticks. "Look at those sticks: each one left here by a grateful man or woman who came leaning on the stick, and went away not needing it."

"Great Scott!" said Wally. "And the rags?"

"They are votive offerings. If you look on that flat stone near the well you'll find hundreds of others—tokens, medals, little ornaments, even hairpins: all valueless, but left by people too poor to give even a penny. They believe the saint understands: and I think he would be a hard saint if he did not."

The stone was almost covered with tiny offerings.

"Does no one touch them?" Jim asked.

"They're sacred. If you left money there it would not be touched." He pointed to a handful of wilting daisies. "I expect those were left by children on their way to school. All the poor know that it is the spirit, not the letter, of an offering that counts: and even those daisies are left in perfect faith that the saint will see to the matter if trouble should come to them."

"I never thought such beliefs still existed," said Mr. Linton, greatly interested. "Look at this crutch—it's quite good, and looks newly-planted."

A woman, barefooted and with a shawl over her head, had come across the grass from the cottage. She curtseyed to O'Neill.

"It was left this morning, sir," she said, indicating the crutch. "Sure, the man that owned it was in a bad way: he come from Dublin, an' he crippled in his hip. On a side-car they brought him, and there was two men to lift him on and off it, and he yellow with the dint of the pain he had. I seen him limping on his crutch across to the well. And when he went away he walked over to the car as aisy as you or me, and not a limp on him at all, and him throwing a leg on to the car like a boy."

"You mean to say he went away cured?" exclaimed Mr. Linton.

"Sure, there's his crutch," said the woman, simply. "He'd no more use at all for it."

"Well-l!" The Australians looked blankly at each other.

" 'Tis fourteen years I've been living over beyant," said the woman. "I've seen them come on sticks and on crutches; some of them carried, and some of them put on cars: but they all walked away—all that had faith in the saint. Why wouldn't they?"

It was a brief question that somehow left them without any answer, since simple faith is too big a thing to meddle with. They said good-bye to the woman and went back to the Rock, where the groom was waiting to help his master in the climb—an old groom with a face like a withered rosy apple. The ascent was not difficult: a winding path led to the summit of the Rock, and they were soon at the top.

"Between them, Elizabeth and Cromwell didn't leave us many of our old monuments," said O'Neill, looking away across the country. "But thank goodness they couldn't touch the Doon Rock!"

The summit was almost flat; a long narrow plateau with soft grass growing in its hollows. One end was wider than the other, with a kind of saddle connecting the two: and in the middle of the smaller end was a great flat stone that looked almost like an altar. All about the high, precipitous eminence the country lay like an unrolled map far beneath them: a wide expanse of flat moor and field and fallow, in the midst of which the great Rock showed, almost startling in its rugged steepness. Little villages were dotted here and there, and sometimes could be seen the blue gleam of water. The white smoke of a train made a creeping line against the dark bog.

Con and the groom had placed the luncheon-basket in a grassy hollow where there was shelter from the breeze that swept keenly across the high Rock; and had retreated with the instinctive delicacy of the Irish peasant, who never intrudes upon "the genthry" when eating, and himself prefers to eat alone. After lunch, Norah and Wally collected the débris of the feast and burned it under the lee side of a boulder, in the belief that no decent person leaves such things as picnic-papers for the next comer to see: and then they strolled across the narrow saddle to the stone on the farther side, where the others had already wandered.

"Tell us about it, Sir John, please," Norah begged.

"It was here that the old O'Donnell chiefs were inaugurated," O'Neill said. "They were the rulers of Tyrconnell, which is now north-west Ulster: the old name is still used in a good deal of Irish poetry. All the clan used to gather when a new leader was to be installed, the people clustering down in the plain below, and the chieftain and his principal men up here on the Rock. It must have been worth seeing."

Jim drew a long breath.

"I should just think so," he said, "Tell us more, O'Neill: I want to reconstruct it. This old Rock must have looked just the same as it does to-day. It's something to have seen even that!"

"Just the same," said Sir John, his eyes kindling at the boy's enthusiasm. "The Inauguration Stone may have been in better preservation, but a few dozen centuries can't do much to the Rock. Well—you can picture the people down below, thousands of them. All the country would be a great unfenced plain—no banks and hedges such as you see to-day, and very likely no roads worth calling roads. There would be forests, most probably, and, in them, animals that became extinct long ago, like the wild boar and wolf. The ground below would be a great camp—every one making merry and dressed in their best."

"I should think that even in those days it wouldn't take much to make an Irish crowd merry," Wally said.

"They would have plenty of entertainment: jugglers, fortune-tellers, buffoons in painted masks, and champions, showing feats with weapons and strength—probably 'spoiling for a fight.' Music there would be in abundance: pipes, tube-players, harps, and bands of chorus-singers. There would be any amount of fun in the crowd. But, of course, the Rock would be the centre of everyone's thoughts."

"It's all coming quite distinctly," said Norah, who was sitting on the grass, gazing out over the plain. "If you look hard you can see them all, in saffron kilts and flowing cloaks like you told us, Sir John. Now tell us who is up here on the Rock."

"The new chief is where Wally is, sitting on the great stone," said O'Neill, smiling at her. "Do you want to know what he's wearing?"

"Oh, please!"

"Well, you can picture him a goodly man, to begin with, for no chief could reign unless he were a champion, free from the slightest physical defect. 'He was graceful and beautiful of form, without blemish or reproach,' one old chronicle says. 'Fair yellow hair he had, and it bound with a golden band to keep it from loosening. A red buckler upon him, with stars and animals of gold thereon, and fastenings of silver. A crimson cloak in wide descending folds around him, fastened at his neck with precious stones. A torque of gold round his neck'—that's a broad twisted band: you can see them to-day in the Museum in Dublin. 'A white shirt with a full collar upon him, intertwined with red gold thread. A girdle of gold, inlaid with precious stones, around him. Two wonderful shoes of gold, with golden loops, about the feet. Two spears with golden sockets in his hands, with rivets of red bronze.' There—can you see him, Norah?"

"I'm trying, but he dazzles me!" Norah said. "Go on, please. Who else is there?"

"All his nobles and councillors, dressed almost as splendidly as the chief himself. The old books are full of details of the richness of their apparel: gold and silver and fine clothing must have been an ordinary thing with them—and not only was it so, but the workmanship was exquisite. They had 'shirts ribbed with gold thread, crimson fringed cloaks, embroidered coats of rejoicing, clothing of red silk, and shirts of the dearest silk.' They wore helmets, and carried spears, 'sharp, thin, hard-pointed, with rivets of gold and silk thongs for throwing'; 'long swords, with hilts and guards of gold; and shields of silver, with rim and boss of gold.' One man is described as 'having in his hand a small-headed, white-breasted hound, with a collar of rubbed gold and a chain of old silver': and a horse had a bridle of silver rings and a gold bit. They had shoes of white bronze, and great golden brooches, with 'gold chains about their necks and bands of gold above them again.'"

O'Neill stopped and laughed.

"I could go on for a long time," he said. "But I'm afraid it begins to sound like the description of Solomon's Temple!"

"And to think," said Jim, unheeding him, "that we had a vague idea that Ireland had been inhabited only by savages!"

"Schools don't teach you anything about Ireland," said O'Neill, contemptuously. "A few hours among the exquisite old things in the Dublin Museum would open your eyes: the finest goldsmiths and silversmiths of the present world cannot touch the beauty of the workmanship of the treasures there;—and some of them were dug up out of bogs, after lying there no one knows how many hundred or thousand years. They were craftsmen in those days, and they loved the work. You don't get that spirit in Trades Union times!"

"Oh, don't talk about Trades Unions!" Norah cried. "We're on the Doon Rock, and I can see all those people round the chief, and the crowd on the plain below, looking up. What else, Sir John?"

"There would be white-robed Druids," O'Neill said; "and the King's bards or poets would be about him. The bard was a very important person and a high functionary, with wide powers. In a sense he was the war-correspondent of his day: he never fought, but he was always present at a battle, and very much in it, noting the heroic deeds of the warriors, and afterwards recording them in his songs. Poetry in those days was a most business-like and practical thing, for everything of any importance was written in verse, such as the laws, the genealogies of the clans, and their history. The poet held an exalted position, and was educated for it from his boyhood by a course of careful study: and the chief poet ranked next to the king, and went about with almost as fine a retinue. They were the professors of their day, and kept schools for training lads for their order. A man had to be very careful not to offend one, or he would write a satire against the culprit; and these satires were dreaded extremely, since they were believed to cause disaster and desolation to fall not only on a man but on his whole family. Nowadays, editors are said to keep special wastepaper baskets for dealing with poets, but it wouldn't have done in the ould ancient times—the post of an editor would have been too unhealthy!"

"I suppose it is through them that the old stories have come down," Jim said.

"Of course. They had to write the verse-tales, and they had to tell them, too; they were obliged to learn and teach three hundred and fifty kinds of versification, and an Ollave, or chief poet, could recite at any moment any of three hundred and fifty stories. They did a lot of harm, because they abused their power; and at last, in the sixth century, were nearly banished from Ireland altogether. Columcille saved them from that fate, but they were made much less important. However, the poets that you are looking at with your mind's eye, Norah, were ages before that, and you can imagine them as gorgeous and as haughty as possible, and every one is very polite to them."

"I'm going to get off this stone and make room for the chief," said Wally, solemnly, rising. "There's the ghost of a poet, glaring at me, and he's going to burst into a satire." He subsided on the grass beside Norah. "Go on, please."

"Well, that is the crowd on top of the Rock," Sir John said: "nobles, councillors, poets, and Druids, all in order of rank: the Rock would hold three or four hundred, all told. And the crowd below, gazing up. I'm glad you got off the stone, Wally, because the chief wants it now. He takes off his wonderful shoes of gold, and places one foot on the stone, and swears to preserve all ancient customs inviolable, to deliver up the rulership peaceably, when the time comes, to his successor, to rule the people with justice, and to maintain the laws. Then he puts away his weapons, and the highest of his nobles, an hereditary official, gives him a straight white rod in token of authority—straight, to remind him that his administration should be just, and white, that his actions should be pure and upright. Then he gives him new sandals: and keeping one of the golden shoes, he throws the other over the new chief's head and proclaims him O'Donnell. All the nobles repeat the title—can't you hear the mighty shout, and the crowd below taking it up, so that it rings over Tyrconnell!"

"Oh-h!" breathed Norah. "And it was here, where we are sitting!" She put her hand on the ground that had felt the tramp of the hosts of ancient days. "Was that all, Sir John?"

"That ended the ceremony; except that each subject paid a cow as rod-money, a sort of tribute to the new chief. But of course there was high feasting and festival, probably for days. They had splendid feasts, too. Once, when one of the great nobles entertained the chief and all the men of Tyrconnel, the preparations took a whole year. A special house was built, surpassing all other buildings in beauty of architecture, with splendid pillars and carvings: in the banqueting-hall the wainscotting was of bronze thirty feet high, overlaid with gold. It took a wagon-team to carry each beam, and the strength of seven men to fix each pole; and the royal couch was set with precious stones 'radiant with every hue, making night bright as day.'"

O'Neill broke off, and hesitated.

"Do I tell you too much?" he asked. "I'm afraid my tongue runs away with me—but I did want you to realize something of what Ireland was. There were great men in those days, and the fighting-men had high ideals of what great champions should be. It is what kept us all through our lifetime,' one said—'truth that was in our hearts, and strength in our arms, and fulfilment on our tongues.'"

He was silent, looking away. The proud soul, pent in the misshapen body, found comfort in turning from the present, that held so little for him, back to the mighty past when the O'Neills, too, had been chieftains and champions.

Presently he stood up, with a shrug.

"Time we went down, I'm afraid," he said, cheerfully. "Before we go, Norah, I will proceed to relate for your benefit the six womanly gifts which were demanded of properly-brought-up young women in the high and far-off times in Ireland. They were, the gift of modest behaviour, the gift of singing, the gift of sweet speech, the gift of beauty, the gift of wisdom, and the gift of needlework!"

"Wow!" said poor Norah, in dismay. "Perhaps it's as well I got born in Australia!"

CHAPTER XI
NORTHWARD

"Says he to all belongin' him, 'Now happy may ye be!

But I'm off to find me fortune,' sure he says, says he."

Moira O'Neill.

"IS Mr. Linton in, Timsy?"

"He is, sir. Leastways, he's out, down by the lough, and all of them with him." The small boy looked up at Sir John O'Neill with more awe than he was wont to regard most people. "Will I get him for you, sir?"

"No—I'll go down, myself. Is your father well, Timsy?"

"He does be splendid, sir," said Timsy, his eye brightening. "Only they'll be takin' him back soon, to fight them ould Germans."

"I expect Lord Kitchener can't do without him," said Sir John, confidentially. "Never mind,—we'll have him back in Donegal altogether, before long, please goodness. And whisper, Timsy—when he comes back for good, he'll have a splendid medal on his coat!" He patted the small boy on the head and left him speechless before a prospect so tremendous.

The Linton party was discovered by the well on the lough shore, where Wally was scratching the nose of the patient donkey and talking to him, as Norah said, as man to man. He had his back to the path down from the garden, and did not hear Sir John's approach.

"If you'd come back to Australia with us, acushla machree," he said, "I'd guarantee you the best of grass and you wouldn't have any water to draw at, all." The ass drooped his head lower, and appeared, not at all impressed by this dazzling future. "And Murty would love you, and Norah would ride you after cattle." ("I would not!" from Norah.) "And you could tell the horses about Ireland, and we'd tie green ribbons round your neck on St. Patrick's Day, and let you wave a green flag with a harp on it in your pearl-pale hand. Oh, lovely ass——!"

"Were you speaking to me?" asked Sir John, politely, near his ear; and Wally jumped, and joined in the laugh against himself.

"We're twin-souls, this patient person and myself," he explained. "I've found it out, and I'm trying to make the ass see it. Never mind, old chap; we'll continue this profitable conversation when we are alone; unfeeling listeners only make you bashful." He produced a carrot from his pocket, and the ass ate it, despondently.

"I'm awfully sorry to have interrupted your heart-to-heart talk; but the fact is, Mr. Linton, I'm simply bursting with an idea, and I had to hurry over and put it before you." Sir John spoke eagerly, turning to Norah with a laugh. "Is it a good moment to approach him, Norah? I want him to promise to do something."

"He ate a noble breakfast," said Norah, gravely. "And he's nearly finished his pipe. I should think the moment's favourable. Anyway, it will have to be now, because I simply can't wait to hear what it is!"

"You see, we know your ideas, O'Neill," Mr. Linton said, laughing. "They generally combine a great deal of trouble for yourself with something quite new in the way of entertainment for us. This must be particularly outrageous, as you want me to promise beforehand. I think you had better make a clean breast of it."

"Well, it's this," Sir John answered. "The weather is glorious, and the glass is high; it's useless weather for fishing, and I think you have explored this neighbourhood pretty thoroughly. The motor holds six quite easily. What do you say to a trip north—a little tour, to last about a week?"

Subdued gasps came from Norah, Jim, and Wally. Mr. Linton laughed outright.

"What did I tell you?" he demanded.

"Not at all," responded Sir John. "I think"—unblushingly—"that Con needs a change; and it would be an excellent way to give him one, if you would only be kind enough to help me. You surely wouldn't refuse poor Con such a little thing!"

"I've re-cast a good many of my ideas about Ireland," David Linton said. "But to utilize five people to take one chauffeur for a change is certainly what I was brought up to call an Irish way of doing things! Seriously, however, O'Neill, your proposal is a very tempting one. Shall we put it to the committee?"

"The committee says, 'Carried nem. con.' I should say," said Jim. "It would be simply top-hole. But isn't it putting rather a strain on you and the motor?"

"Certainly not—as far as I am concerned, a run in sea-air is all I need to make me quite fit again," O'Neill answered. "What do you say about it, Norah?"

"I'm speechless; and as for Wally, he's leaning up against the ass for support," said Norah, indicating Mr. Meadows, who grasped the hapless donkey fondly. "It's the most glorious plan, Sir John; and it's just like you, to think of it."

O'Neill's delicate face flushed with pleasure.

"You're all such satisfactory people, because you're never bored," he said. "And then, you like Ireland, which makes everything delightful. Well, I thought we might have a look at Horn Head and Sheep Haven, Mr. Linton, and perhaps get across to The Rosses; or would you rather have no fixed plan, but just wander about, seeking what we may find? There are innumerable little bays and inlets up there, all rather fascinating; we should be between mountain and sea scenery, and the inns here and there are fairly good."

"I think we will leave it entirely to you, so far as planning the route goes," Mr. Linton answered. "You know the country, and we don't; and as for us, any part of Ireland is good."

"I vote for having no fixed plan at all," Jim said. "It's when you have no plans that the best things happen to you!"

"We'll leave it at that, then," said Sir John. "Can we start to-morrow?"

"We have only two weeks more leave," said Jim. "So the sooner we go the better."

"And you can be ready, Norah?"

"Me? Oh, certainly," said Norah, who, Wally declared, was always ready at any time for anything.

"Then, I'll be off," Sir John declared. "I left Con hard at work on the car, giving her a thorough overhaul—we could not believe that you would be so hard-hearted as to refuse him the trip! But I have a good many things to see to, and I'll have a busy day."

"Could I help you?" Jim asked. "I'm handy at odd jobs."

"Would you care to? I'll be awfully glad of your company," said Sir John warmly. They went off together, the boy's great shoulders towering above O'Neill's dwarfed form.

Jim did not return until late that night. Norah, just about to blow out her candle, heard his light step on the stair and called to him softly.

"Not asleep yet, kiddie?" Jim said, sitting down on the bed. "You should be; you'll be tired to-morrow."

"I'm all right," said Norah, disregarding this friendly caution. "Jim, I packed your bag; and there's a list of things just inside it, in case I made any mistakes."

"Well, you are a brick!" said Jim, who was accustomed to stern independence, but, like most people, greatly appreciated a little spoiling now and then. "I was looking forward rather dismally to a midnight packing; O'Neill wants to get off quite early in the morning."

"We guessed that was likely. Did you have a good day, Jim?"

"Quite. I don't think I was any particular help to O'Neill; he found a few jobs for me, but I fancy he had to rack his brains for them. But we pottered about together all day, and had a very jolly time; he's such fun when he's in good form, and he was like a kid to-day. Made me laugh no end." Jim pondered, beginning to unlace his boots. "I think it's only when he is alone that those bitter fits get hold of him; and he just dreads being alone. That's why he took me over, of course."

"I thought so," nodded Norah. "But I do think he's happier than he was, Jim."

"I believe he is. Well, we'll try to keep him laughing for the next week or so, anyhow," said Jim. "Now, you go to sleep, old kiddie."

The fine weather held, making it easy to leave trout which would have nothing to do with them; and next day the motor took them away into bypaths of Ireland, with new beauty and new legend at every turn. They passed Gartan, and saw the birthplace of Saint Columba, a tiny stone cell with a curiously indented stone; and Columba's ruined church of grey stone, roofless, and with almost-effaced carvings on its walls. Near it a tall, narrow stone stood crookedly—all that remained of a cross. The ground before it, hard as iron, was hollowed where the knees of thousands of pilgrims had knelt in prayer, and the stone itself was smooth from kisses that had been pressed upon it through century after century. Sir John knew many legends of the hot-tempered, fighting saint, whose warlike proclivities eventually led to his banishment from the Ireland he loved, to work and suffer home-sickness until Death came at last to release him.

"The emigrants pray to him specially, since he, too, knew what it meant to be lonely for Ireland," Sir John said. "He was a worker: he wrote three hundred books and founded the same number of churches. So he came to be called Columcille—cille meaning church. An O'Donnell he was: one of the old house. He made a famous copy of the Psalms, the disputed ownership of which caused the fight that led to his leaving Ireland: and this copy—it was called The Cathach, or Battler—was an heirloom in the O'Donnell family, who always carried it with them into battle, in a shrine. One hates to think of him, exiled, working, and longing for home. The first monastery he founded was near Derry; he was only a young man then, but long afterwards he wrote that the angels of God sang in every glade of Derry's oaks. I always think one can see him in this queer little church—big and powerful, with the fighting face and toilworn hands."

For a time they kept near the railway that creeps through the heart of Donegal: a quaint, narrow-gauge line where the trains saunter, forgetful of time. Its way runs through deep bogs, which made its construction no light matter, since solid foundation was in some places only found eighty feet below the surface, and great causeways, embankments, and viaducts had to be built to carry it. Sometimes, in contrast, the way had to be hewn through solid rock. On one hand lay wild and rugged mountains, with some fine dominating peaks: Muckish—"the hog's back"—with its long, flattened ridge, changing from every angle of vision; and the great peak of Errigal, bare and glistening, the highest mountain in Donegal.

"It's a great old peak," said Sir John, looking at it affectionately. "You can see Scotland from the top—and all over Donegal, and southward to the Sligo and Galway hills."

"How it glistens!" said Norah, watching the great cone as the motor went slowly along. "What makes it so white?"

"That's white quartz; it gives it its name, 'the silver mountain.' It looks a single peak from here, but as we round it you'll see that there are really two heads close together; there is a narrow ridge, with a track about a foot wide, connecting them. Some day, when you all come back to stay with me at Rathcullen, we must arrange an expedition for you to climb it."

Their wandering way led them from the railway line, after a time; and they struck northward into lonely country of moors and bogs, dotted with tiny cabins from which blue turf-smoke curled lazily. Once they passed an old man riding a grey mare, with his wife perched behind him on a pillion, holding under her shawl a turkey in a sack, from the mouth of which protruded the head of the indignant bird, making loud protests. None of the women they met, whether young or old, wore hats: all had the heavy Irish shawl round head and shoulders,—and whether the face that looked from the folds were that of a withered old woman or a fresh and smiling colleen, somehow the shawl seemed the best setting that could have been devised for it.

Often, for miles and miles, they met no one and passed no habitation: or perhaps the loneliness of the way would be broken by a little thatched cabin, where ragged children ran to the doorway, to gaze, round-eyed, at the strangers. In one little town, however, a fair was in progress, and the cobbled street presented a lively spectacle. Men, women and children; asses, ridden and driven; horses, cattle, sheep, and pigs, and a few stray geese, mingled in loud-voiced confusion, while dogs slipped hither and thither, managing to intensify the urgency of any situation. To get the big Rolls-Royce through such a concourse was no easy task, and even with a people so good-humoured, a tactless driver would have achieved swift unpopularity. Sir John, however, was at the wheel himself, and he slowed down to a crawl, sounding the hooter occasionally, more in the manner of a gentle suggestion than anything else. His Irish accent was a shade more in evidence than usual as he exchanged greetings with the crowd.

" 'Tis a fine season we're having, thank God!"

"It is, your honour. G'wan now, Mary Kate; get the little ass out of the way of the mothor."

"Ah, don't be hurrying her. I have plenty of time."

"Sure ye'd need it, your honour, the place is that throng."

"And that's a good sign; it's a great fair you're having!"

"Well indeed, sir, it is not bad, thank God!"

O'Neill swerved to avoid an old woman in an ass-cart, who was talking volubly to some neighbours, while the ass took its own direction among the crowd. Voices broke into swift upbraidings.

"Take a howld of the ass there, will you, Maria Cooney!"

"Oh, wirra, it's desthroyed she'll be!"

"She will not, but the great mothor!"

"Is it to scratch the beautiful paint ye would, with the cart!" cried a wrathful man hauling the ass aside bodily, while the unhappy Mrs. Cooney stammered out excuses that no one heard, and blinked feebly at the Rolls-Royce—which was pardonable, since she had never seen one before.

"God help us, 'tis the heighth of a house!"

"I'm sorry to disturb you, ma'am," said O'Neill, smiling at her distressed face. The crowd broke into smiles in answer.

" 'Tis not like the Englishman he is—the one that galloped his machine over Ellen Clancy's gander, an' he goin' to Rosapenna!" shrilled a voice.

"Watch him now—and the bonnivs under the wheels of him!"—as a drove of fat pink pigs broke through the crowd, scattered, in the infuriating manner peculiar to pigs, and resisted all efforts to collect them out of harm's way. Their owner, a lean, black-whiskered man, lifted up his voice and bewailed them.

"Yerra, he have them thrampled! No—aisy, sir, just a moment, till I get at him with a stick. That one do be always in the wrong place." He hauled a pig bodily from beneath the car, retaining it by one leg, while it drowned any other remarks with its shrieks, and its companions scattered through the crowd, pursued hotly by the dogs.

"Sorry—I ought not to bring a motor through a fair," said O'Neill, willing to concede the right to the road to the "bonnivs."

"An' why wouldn't you?" said their owner, cheerfully. "Many's the time I'd not so much as the one left to me when I'd brang 'em through, an' I scourin' every boreen after them. Let you go on, sir—it's all right."

The motor wormed its way along. When the crowd grew less congested, O'Neill ventured to increase the speed. Just as he did so, a small child, escaping from its mother, who was driving a wordy bargain over a matter of geese, toddled into the road in pursuit of a fat puppy; and having caught it, sat down suddenly, right in the path of the motor.

A girl shrieked, and O'Neill wrenched the car to a standstill, the bonnet not two yards from the baby. Jim was out in the road in a flash, and picked up the urchin, who showed considerable annoyance at the escape of the puppy, but was otherwise quite unmoved, and accepted a penny with a composure worthy of a duke. The crowd collected anew with unbelievable swiftness, and O'Neill groaned.

" 'Tis Maggie O'Hare's baby. Woman, dear, where are ye? an' he after being nearly kilt on ye?"

"Did ye see his honour pull up? An ass wouldn't have done it, an' he dhrawin' a cart!"

"I seen him sit down in the road, in-under the mothor, an' I knew he was dead, only I'd not time to let a bawl out of me!"

"Is it dead? Sure, look at him, an' the big gentleman carryin' him, no less!"

"Grinning he is, the way you'd say he was the best boy in Ireland. Ah, that's the dotey wee thing!"

"Sure, that one has no fear at all. He'll be the boy for the trenches!"

At this point Maggie O'Hare arrived breathlessly, having just become aware of her son's peril—with some difficulty, owing to six of her friends having excitedly explained the matter together. To an unprejudiced onlooker, it would have seemed that her principal maternal emotion was horror at finding her offspring perched on Jim's shoulder.

"Come down out of that, Micky—have behaviour, now, an' don't be throublin' the gentleman! Put him down, sir—I'd not have you annoyed with him." She received Micky with much apparent wrath, but her arms were tight round the little body. "Isn't it the rascal he is!—an' I but lettin' him out of me hand that minute, the way I'd be feedin' the goose!"

In England, Jim had learned to give tips; and for a moment his hand sought his pocket. Fortunately, he checked the impulse in time. The woman's eyes met his with the good breeding that lends something of dignity to the poorest Irish peasant.

"He's a great boy," he said, in his pleasant voice. "Not a bit of fear in him—have you, Micky?" He lifted his cap, and said "Good-bye," striding back to the motor. They moved on, slowly, leaving the little town seething behind them.

"It isn't altogether without incident to drive through a fair!" said O'Neill, dreamily.

Towards evening they came to their halting-place for the night—a grey village, nestling among brown hills.

"The inn used to be very fair, but one can't guarantee anything in war-time," Sir John remarked. "Of course it isn't big enough to suffer from the complaint that suddenly affected all the important hotels—the hurried departure of French cooks and German waiters. Many hotel-keepers will speak until the end of their lives, with tears in their voices, about the awful day when Henri and Gaston, and Fritz and Karl, the props of their establishment, dropped their aprons and fled to their respective Fatherlands. You can't convince those hotel-keepers that they do not know all about the horrors of war!"

"This little place doesn't suggest imported cooks and waiters," said Mr. Linton.

"No, as I remember it, the landlady was the cook, and her daughter the housemaid; and a nondescript gentleman of the 'odd-boy' type doubled the parts of boots, barkeeper, groom, and waiter, with any other varieties of usefulness that might be demanded of him. And there he is still, by the same token, bringing in a load of turf." Sir John indicated a wiry little man leading a shambling old black horse bearing two creels slung across his back, piled high with sods. He turned into the back gateway of the inn as they drew up at the front door; and, hearing the motor, cast a glance over his shoulder, realized the presence of guests, and administered a sounding slap on the black horse's quarter, disappearing hurriedly. They heard his voice, shrilly summoning the unseen.

"Is himself within?—let ye hurry! There's a pack of gentry at the door, in a mothor-car!" And a voice yet more shrill:

"Wirra! An' me fire black out—an' what in the world, at all, 'll I give 'em for their dinners!"

They made acquaintance with the problem a little later when, hungry and cheerful, they gathered in the long, low dining-room, where last year's heather and ling filled the fireless grate. The "odd-boy," cleansed beyond belief, awaited them.

"What can we have for dinner?" O'Neill inquired.

"Is it dinner? Sure, anything you'd fancy, sir," said the "odd-boy," with a nervous briskness that somehow induced disbelief.

"H'm," said Sir John, remembering the cry of woe that had floated through the air, earlier. "Chops or steaks?"

The "odd-boy" shifted from one foot to the other.

"I'm afeard there's none in the house, sir," he said. " 'Tis the way the butcher——"

"Oh well—cold meat," O'Neill said, cutting short the butcher's iniquities.

"Yes, sir—certainly, sir!" said the "odd boy," and disappeared. There was an interval during which the party admired the view and endeavoured to repress the pangs of hunger. Finally the messenger reappeared.

"I'm sorry, sir," he said, nervously. "Cold meat is off, they do be tellin' me."

"Well, what can we have?" O'Neill said, losing the finer edge of his patience.

The "odd-boy" grew confidential.

" 'Tis this way, sir," he said. "The fair was yesterday: an' them cattle-jobbers have us ate out of the house. So there's just three things ye can have, sir: an' the first eggs; an' the second's bacon; and third is eggs and bacon. An' ye can have your choice-thing of them three!"

CHAPTER XII
ASS-CART VERSUS MOTOR

"The grand road from the mountain goes shining to the sea,

And there is traffic on it, and many a horse and cart:

But the little roads of Cloonagh are dearer far to me,

And the little roads of Cloonagh go rambling through my heart."

Eva Gore-Booth.

THROUGH the tiny window of Norah's room came the soft sunlight which makes an Irish morning so perfect a thing that to stay in bed a moment longer than necessary would be criminal. Norah woke up, and looked at it sleepily for a few minutes, wishing the window were bigger. It had altogether declined to remain open the night before, until she had propped it with the water-jug, which now stood rakishly on the sill, and had already excited considerable interest and speculation in the street below. She dressed quickly, somewhat embittered by the fact that investigation discovered no sign of a bathroom. The search was a nervous one, since the corridor seemed principally to consist of shut doors; and after cautiously opening one which looked promising, but which revealed a tousled head on a pillow, with loud snores saluting her, she was seized with panic, and fled back to her own room.

When she emerged, fully dressed, she still seemed the only person awake. Downstairs, however, she encountered the "odd-boy," who was sweeping the hall with a lofty disregard of corners, wherein the dust of many sweepings had accumulated in depressing heaps. Through a cloud of dust he blinked in amazement at her.

"Were you wantin' anything, miss?"

"No, thanks," Norah answered; "I was going for a walk. Is there anything to see in the village?"

The "odd-boy" thought deeply, and finally replied with gloom that he didn't know why anybody would be looking at it at all. Then, suddenly inspired, he hastened to the door in Norah's wake.

"There's Willy Gallaher's ould pig, miss, an' she after having eleven of the finest little ones yesterday. Ye'd ought to see them. Willy's the proud man. 'Twas himself was due for a bit of good luck, though, with twins not a week old!"

"Thanks," said Norah, laughing. "But I'd rather see the twins." Which astounding preference left the "odd-boy" gaping. Twins were a regrettable everyday occurrence, but eleven "bonnivs" were the gift of Providence, and not to be lightly regarded.

Norah made her way up the narrow street. The air was full of the pleasant smell of newly-lit turf fires, and in the cottages the women were beginning their day's work. Children ran to peep over the half-door at the stranger, and Norah, peeping over in her turn, saw fat babies crawling about the earthen floors and made friends with them until their mothers picked them up and brought them to the half-door for further admiration. Thus her progress up the street was slow, and it was some time before she came to the outskirts of the village and crossed a green where asses, geese, fowls, and long-haired goats wandered sociably.

Beyond the green the high road curved, and, following it, Norah came upon a narrow river that tumbled from the hills, racing under an old bridge of grey stone in a mass of foaming rapids. On the other side was a little ruined castle, upon which she advanced joyfully, with the passion for anything old which gave the Australians the keenest enjoyment of all their experiences of travel.

It was not much of a castle; the walls had long since collapsed into heaps of broken stone, most of which had been carried away to build cabins and were now concealed under the whitewash of years. A small square tower yet stood, but was obviously unsafe, since the crumbling stairway that wound upwards inside it had been shut off by rusty iron bars. It was not easy to make out the outlines of what had been rooms, for the stones had fallen in all directions, and grass and brambles grew wildly over them. But everywhere, softening the cruelty and destruction of time, ivy clambered; a kindly cloak of green that blotted out harsh outlines and turned the whole into something exquisite.

Norah crossed the bridge and climbed upon a half-fallen wall, perching herself on a huge flat stone that lay bathed in sunshine. Above her the jackdaws which nested in the ivy-covered tower chattered and scolded, flying in and out to their homes; below was no sound save the hurried babble of the river, where now and then came the flash of a leaping trout. It was very peaceful. She tried to "reconstruct" it in the way they loved, seeing again the old days when the castle stood proudly, and chieftains and fair ladies, richly clad, moved about the rooms and looked through the narrow window slits at the river, running just as it ran to-day. It was a fascinating employment; so that she did not hear a light step, until a falling stone brought her back to the present with a jump.

"Did I startle you?" Sir John asked, looking up at her. "They told me you had gone out, and I guessed that if you weren't somewhere playing with a baby you would have found the ruin!"

"The babies and the ruin are both lovely," Norah said, smiling. "I'm taking them in turn."

"Did you sleep well?" Sir John asked, climbing up to the wall, and lighting a cigarette.

"Oh, yes, thanks; only the morning was too nice to stay in bed. I had such a funny little room, all nooks and corners."

"I had a feather bed!" said Sir John, with a wry face. "Awful things; I don't know how people ever slept on them. It was very huge and puffy, and I sank down into its depths, and felt as if the waters were closing over my head. Then I dreamed wild dreams of battle. Altogether, I feel as if I had an adventurous night."

"I read once of an old woman who slept on a turkey-feather bed for twenty years, until at last all the feathers stuck together in a solid mass like a mat, and he had a sealskin coat made out of it!" said Norah.

"I'd love to believe it, but it beats any fishing-yarn I ever heard," said Sir John, regarding her fixedly. "Do you believe it yourself?"

"I don't know anything about the ways of featherbeds," Norah said, laughing. "But I always thought she must have been an unpleasant old lady, for it showed clearly that she hadn't shaken up her mattress for twenty years. Oh, Sir John, did you find a bathroom?"

"I did not; there isn't one. I'm sorry, Norah. We ought to have better luck at our stopping-place to-night."

"I suppose one can't expect baths everywhere," Norah said. "The queer part to us is being charged extra for one's tub; no hotel in Australia ever does anything so ungracious. They rather encourage one to take baths there."

"It's a ridiculous charge, especially where a water-supply is no trouble," O'Neill answered. "Did I ever tell you the story of a friend of mine who was staying in a very old-fashioned country-house, where his early cup of tea was brought in by a very old butler? My friend asked for a bath, and was told there was no hot water available—'the pipes have froze on us,' said the butler, sadly. Next day it was the same; but the third morning the butler came in with triumph in his eye.

" 'Sure, the bath will be all right this morning, sir,' he said, confidentially. 'I have the hot wather beyant.'

"He went out, and returned panting under an enormous bath of the flat tin-saucer variety, which he put down with pride, while my friend—who happened to be as big as your father—watched him, much thrilled. Next he laid down a smart bath-mat, and hung over a chair a bath-towel as large as a sheet. Finally, he went out, and brought back a very small can of hot water, which he poured very carefully into the bath; as my friend said, it made a thin film of wet on its great flat surface. The old butler straightened up, beaming.

" 'Now, sir,' he said, proudly—'ye can have your little dive!' "

Norah's shout of laughter was echoed by Wally and Jim, whose heads suddenly appeared over the ivy-covered wall.

"I don't see why you retire to ruins to tell your best stories, O'Neill," Jim said. "Also, we feel that it's breakfast-time, and we've been scouring the country for you both."

"I begin to feel that way myself," Norah said, jumping down.

Mr. Linton was smoking in front of the hotel. In the dining-room, the "odd-boy," again thinly disguised for the moment as a waiter, hovered about their table for orders, a procedure which seemed superfluous, since the possibilities of the house did not exceed the inevitable bacon and eggs. No one, however, was disposed to quarrel with the meal; and very soon after, they were again on the road, leaving the friendly little village by a winding highway that soon brought them within sight and sound of the sea—one of the deep inlets that thrust themselves far into the wild northern coast of Ireland. The road led, now close to the shore, now striking across country to find a short cut over the neck of a peninsula. They skirted little bays where a golden beach gleamed invitingly, and ran out on rocky headlands, on which the sullen sea thundered. Inland, the country grew more and more lonely and desolate.

"How on earth do these people get a living?" Jim ejaculated, looking at the wretched cabins in a tumbledown village. "The soil is nearly all stone—and how horribly bleak it must be in winter! This is July, and still the wind is wild enough."

"I don't think they get much of a living at all," Sir John said. "Fishing helps, of course; and all the able-bodied men hire themselves out for the harvesting to Scotch and English farmers, and bring home what seems a big sum in these parts, together with stories of the wealth across the water:

"The people that's in England is richer nor the Jews—

"There's not the smallest young gossoon but thravels in his shoes!"

"Indeed, they don't do that here," said Mr. Linton, looking at the ragged boy by the wayside.

118

"Not they—shoes only come with years of discretion, and often, not then. But don't they look rosy and well?—nothing of the pinched look of the youngsters in a city slum."

"No—I think the air must be nourishing!" remarked Wally.

"You're quite right; it is. But they grow little crops, in tiny corners between the stones. The soil is bad enough; they are lucky if they are near the sea, for then they can bring up mussels and kelp as manure. There's a woman bringing some now"; and Sir John pointed to a bent figure, bare-legged, a red shawl over head, and on her back a huge basket, beneath which she was labouring up a steep cliff-path. "She has a kish full of shell-fish there—you wouldn't find it a light load, even on the level, but they carry hundreds of them up these cliffs. There are parts of Donegal so bleak that they have to warm the ground before sowing the seed; they burn the dried sea-weed on the prepared soil, and sow the crop while the ashes are still smoking."

"Great Scott!" said Jim, feebly. "Fancy an Australian doing that!"

Sir John laughed grimly.

"I fancy an Australian would flee in horror if he were offered as a gift a tract of land that supports hundreds of these people," he said. "You should see them reaping their tiny, pocket-handkerchief crops; they do it with a little reaping-hook, and, upon my word, some of them are so small that you might harvest them with a pair of scissors! Of course they're not worth much; but then these people are accustomed to live on very little, and they scarcely need more than they have, if the sea is kind and the fishing fair. They look wild enough; but they are intelligent, even if ignorant, and you will always meet with courtesy among them."

"They would make great fighting men," Jim observed, watching a broad-shouldered, dark-faced young fellow who was digging in a tiny field by the road. He had paused to look at the motor, one foot on the spade, and his splendid young body upright.

"Oh, every sound Irishman is that naturally," Sir John said, with a laugh. "And the women could do their bit if occasion arose. Did you hear, by the way, of the women of Limerick, when some of the disaffected idiots of whom there are too many in the country made a pro-German demonstration there lately? They chose a day when most of the loyal men of the city were away; these fellows were from Dublin, and they made a procession and planned quite a little show. But they reckoned without the women."

"What—did they take a hand?" asked Mr. Linton.

"They did, indeed, with sticks and stones and whatever other missiles came handy. It was most effective: they broke up the procession completely, and the gallant rebels had to be rescued by the police. The women had a great day. I asked one why they didn't leave the matter entirely to the police, and she looked at me in scorn and asked why would they accommodate themselves with the ignorance of policemen? And indeed, I didn't know. After all, some things are managed much better without the law."

The road had for some time been leading away from the sea, and now began to climb up a steep cutting, between rock-walls fringed with ferns and mosses. On the hills above them a few goats browsed, their kids cutting capers among the boulders, with complete enjoyment of the game. They mounted steadily for awhile; then, topping the rise, began to glide downwards. The road turned and twisted as they neared the level ground, following the course of a little stream that came rushing from some unseen source. Sir John, who was driving, sounded his horn steadily.

"There are not many people on these roads," he said, over his shoulder. "But it doesn't do to take risks with the country folk."

"No. Still, I never saw a more desolate road, so far as traffic goes," Mr. Linton answered. "We have not seen a soul for miles on it."

"I don't think there is a soul on it," said Sir John, laughing.

The motor swung round a corner, with a prolonged hoot; and there, so close that the bonnet of the car seemed almost to be touching the ass's nose, came an old woman, nodding sleepily in a cart. There was no time to stop, and no room to turn. The ass planted all four feet stubbornly, stopping dead, and they heard a faint cry from the shawled old figure.

"Sit tight," said O'Neill between his teeth.

The brake jammed hard on as he spoke; they had been running down-hill slowly, with the power shut off. The ass backed indignantly; and the great motor swerved to one side, where there was a little more room in the cutting, bumped heavily over dry channels worn by the winter rains, and rammed her bonnet gently into the rock wall. The occupants of the tonneau found themselves in a heap on the floor. The car throbbed to silence, and the old woman in the ass-cart said, "God help us!" loudly.

"Well, indeed, He did," said O'Neill, under his breath. "Are you all right, all of you?"

"We're mixed, but undamaged," Jim answered. "What about you, O'Neill?"

"I'm all right. How is she, Con?"

Con had swung himself out before the car finally stopped, and was examining the battered bonnet dismally, finally appealing for help to push her away from the wall.

"In a minute," O'Neill said.

He walked over to the old woman, who still sat motionless on the floor of the ass-cart, her withered face pitifully afraid.

"Did you not hear the horn?" O'Neill asked.

"I did, sir—but I didn't rightly know what it was, an' I half asleep." She rocked herself to and fro, wretchedly. "Oh, wirra, the great mothor! Is it desthroyed entirely, sir?"

"It is not—but it's the mercy of Heaven we're not all killed, and you and the little ass, too. When you hear that horn, mother, get to one side of a road quickly: and don't be afraid to call out, if it happens to be a narrow road."

"I . . . I . . ." She looked at him helplessly, her voice breaking.

"Don't worry—you're all right," he said gently. "Is it tired you are?"

"I been sittin' up with my son these two nights," she said, finding words. "Mortal ill he was, an' the woman he married no more use than a yalla-haired doll. An' when they're sick they do be wantin' their mothers again, like as if they'd gone back to be little boys." Just for a moment he caught a gleam of triumph in her dulled eyes.

"And is he better?"

"He is, sir, God be praised, and I'm gettin' home to me man; there's no knowin' what he'll have done to himself, not used to bein' alone and all."

Something passed from O'Neill's palm into the trembling, work-worn old hand.

"That's to bring you luck for your son," he said, forestalling her protests. "Let you get home, mother, and have a meal. Wait a moment."

He unscrewed the cap of his flask, and made her drink out of the silver cup, to her own great horror.

"If I'd a tin, itself!" she protested. "But your honour's cup!"

"Drink it up," said O'Neill, unmoved. He took back the cup and stood aside; and the little ass moved on, the old woman calling down blessings upon him, with tears finding well-accustomed furrows down her cheeks.

"Sitting up two nights, and probably doing the work of the house during the day, in addition to nursing; and most likely on bread and stewed black tea!" said O'Neill, indignantly, striding back to the motor. "You wouldn't wonder if she went to sleep in front of the car of Juggernaut. Poor old soul! I say, you people have been busy!"

They had levered the heavy car back, chocking the wheels with great stones, and the chauffeur was making explorations into her vital parts. Sir John joined him, and they discoursed unintelligibly in technical language.

"Well, it might be worse, but it's not too good," Sir John said, at last, emerging from the investigation and wiping his hands on a ball of cotton-waste. "There's no moving her without men and horses, and no getting her going again until we get some spare parts; and they're no nearer than Belfast or Dublin; possibly we shall have to telegraph to London for them."

"But she's not desthroyed entirely?" Norah said, happily.

"She is not. Hadn't we the luck of the world that it happened where it did, just on level ground and where there was a little room to manœuvre! If it had been three minutes earlier, on the side of the hill, in the narrow cutting, we should simply have gone clean over the poor old soul and her ass. Nothing could have saved them."

"It might easily have been infinitely worse," Mr. Linton said. "But I'm sorry for the car, O'Neill."

"Oh, the car's nothing," Sir John answered, cheerfully. "I'm only sorry for the interruption to our trip. However, things might be more uncomfortable. We're only three or four miles from Carrignarone, where I meant to stop the night: there is quite a passable inn there, small and homely, but it's clean and comfortable enough. We could stay there for a few days, while Con goes to Belfast to get what is necessary—that is, if you like. The coast is interesting, and we might get some sea-fishing. Of course, if you thought that too slow, we could drive to the railway, and get back to Killard." He looked rather wistful. "I had hoped this was going to be such a jolly trip," he said.

"Why, so it is," Jim responded. "I'm awfully sorry for the damage to the motor, but we're going to have plenty of fun all the same. It will be rather good fun to be on a coast again, and we're all keen on sea-fishing. And you know, O'Neill, we wouldn't make any definite plans, so that the unexpected could take charge of us!"

"It has certainly done that," Sir John said, laughing. "Well, I think the next thing is lunch: a good thing I got the hotel to put us up something, though it will probably be only hard-boiled eggs."

It was hard-boiled eggs, and they ate them merrily, sitting on the bank of the little stream, where lichen-covered boulders, smooth and weather-worn, made convenient seats.

"I am perfectly certain," Mr. Linton said, "that if I were in London and ate an enormous meal of soda-bread, eggs like bullets, and very black tea out of a

Thermos, I should have dyspepsia. Not that I ever had it; but the mixture sounds dyspeptic when you couple it with London. But sitting on the bank of a Donegal river it seems quite the proper thing, and I shall be very well after it."

"No one could be anything but well in Donegal," Wally said, decisively. "Whew-w, Jim! think of the trenches, in a fortnight!"

"I'd rather not, if you don't mind," said Jim, lighting his pipe. "I want my little hit-back at Brer Boche, but I'd much rather it was in the open: there's no romance in war when you carry it on in an over-populated ditch."

"Lucky young animals!" said Sir John, openly envious—and the boys flushed a little. As a rule, they were careful not to talk of the Front in the presence of the man whose whole soul longed to be out there with them. "But you'll all come back, won't you? and Mr. Linton, when the war is over, or when these ancient campaigners next get leave, you will bring them back to Rathcullen? I want to know that that is a settled thing."

"That is a matter which I don't need to put to the committee," Mr. Linton replied, looking at the cheery faces. "We'll certainly come, O'Neill, since you are so good. And then, when we pack up finally for Australia and Billabong, what about you? You know it's high time you visited that little country of ours."

"He's coming with us," said Norah, with decision. "Say you are, Sir John—please!"

"Well, indeed, I begin to think I am," O'Neill answered. "I was getting terribly old when you invaded Donegal, but now I believe I shall soon be nearly as young as Mr. Linton! At any rate, I might follow you out." But the boys protested, arguing that there was no point in travelling alone when they might make a family party.

"It would be miles jollier," said Wally. "Then we could 'personally conduct' you to Billabong, and you would have the unforgettable experience of seeing Brownie go mad. I'm quite certain she and Murty will be delirious on the day that Norah comes marching home again!" So they planned happily, in gay defiance of the guns thundering across the Channel. That sullen menace was only a fortnight ahead, and already Norah dreamed of it at night. But in the daytime it was better to pretend that it did not exist.

Con was left with the motor, to administer what "first-aid" was possible: and after lunch the rest of the party set off along the road to Carrignarone, which was reached after an easy walk of an hour and a half. It was a little fishing-village, boasting a better inn than others of its type, since in normal years the sport to be obtained brought a small harvest of visitors. War, however, had meant lean times—wherefore the people of the inn fell thankfully on the windfall afforded them by a stranded party of six, and ran three ways at once in preparing for their comfort. A cart, with a couple of strong horses, was forthcoming, and under the charge of Jim and Wally, set off to the rescue of the motor—which was eventually towed into the village, where it caused what the war-reports term "a certain liveliness." At the steering-wheel sat Con, a picture of humiliation—deepening to disgust when the carter politely offered him a whip!

"Them machines do be all very well to play with, for genthry an' for them that have too much money," said the carter, drawing a distinction that was not lost on his hearers. "But 'tis mighty glad they are of the ould horses when annything goes wrong with the works!" Which was so obviously true at the moment that no one had any spirit to contradict him.

CHAPTER XIII
THE CAVE AMONG THE ROCKS
"The great waves of the Atlantic sweep storming on their way,

Shining green and silver with the hidden herring-shoal;

But the Little Waves of Breffny have drenched my heart in spray

And the Little Waves of Breffny go stumbling through my soul."

Eva Gore-Booth.

WALLY ran out upon a point of rock that ended abruptly in a sheer face, under which the outgoing tide ran swiftly, deep and green. For a moment he stood motionless, his slim body gleaming white against sea and rock; then he curved forward and shot into the water in a clean dive that made scarcely any splash. He reappeared, shaking the water from his eyes, his brown face glowing.

"Coo-ee, Jim! Come on—it's ripping!"

Jim appeared from a cave, shedding the last of his raiment. There was no pause in his dive; his swift rush along the point ended in a leap that carried him far out, and when he emerged, strong over-arm strokes carried him quickly in towards a tiny bay where hard yellow sand made a perfect landing-place. Wally gave chase, unavailingly: when his feet touched the shore Jim was already racing again along the rocks, his dive this time beginning with a complete somersault in the air, before, with a mighty splash, he disappeared once more. Wally came hard upon his heels, springing in, in a sitting position, his hands locked under his knees; and for the next twenty minutes the chums sported in the water like a couple of seals, racing, playing tricks upon each other, and practising the dozen different dives taught them in schoolboy days in Australia. Finally they rubbed themselves down with dry, warm sand, donned their clothes, and subsided, glowing, on a sunny rock, to light their pipes.

"What a perfect place for a swim!" Jim said, looking at the long, narrow inlet with its twin headlands. "That point only needs one thing, Wal—a really good spring-board."

"Yes. Do you remember the big spring-board in the St. Kilda baths—the one you broke when you were trying how high you could spring before diving?"

"Do I not!" said Jim ruefully. "It was the pride of the baths, and replacing it made me a poor man for the rest of the term!" He pitched a shell far out into the sea. "Doesn't that seem ages ago!"

"So it is: anything that happened before the war is ages ago," Wally answered. "And I suppose, when we get back to Billabong, all this"—he swept a comprehensive gesture that included Ireland and Europe—"will seem a kind of prehistoric dream. Anyhow it's a good dream while it lasts."

"Yes, it's all too good to have missed it," Jim said. "Ireland has been jolly, beyond our hopes, thanks to O'Neill—what a brick that poor chap is! Now if we can only finish up by a bit of real fighting, it will all be a huge lark. I'm not a scrap sorry to have been in the trenches; it was all good experience. But I say, Wal, I do want to get going above ground!"

"Rather!" Wally answered. "I want to take a hand in a general worry, and afterwards to be in it when we chase the lovely Hun back to his happy home. And I specially want to be there when we chase 'em out of Brussels: I'd like to see that plucky Belgian King marching down his main street again. Won't they howl!"

"We'll all howl when that day comes," said Jim. "You know, Ireland has been just topping, and it's jolly to be with old dad and Norah again; but I'm beginning to think it's about time we got back to work. We're fit as possible now; and we didn't sign on to play about. This sort of thing"—he touched his rough tweed clothes—"was all very well when we were crocks. But we aren't crocks now. I think, of course, that it was only common sense to get quite fit; they don't want half-cured people over yonder. Still——"

"Still, being cured, it's time we dug out our khaki again," Wally said, nodding. "I quite agree: one would begin to feel a shirker if one stayed much longer. And Australians haven't shown themselves shirkers in this war."

"No. It's funny, you know," Jim reflected. "I did hate the trenches—the filth, and the flies, and the smells, and the vermin; and I used to wonder if I was a tin-soldier, and had no business to have come at all, because lots of chaps say they love it, no matter what the conditions are. Well, I didn't love it; I'd sooner have driven bullocks, any day."

"Same here," said Wally.

"It used to buck me that you felt the same," Jim said, "because of course I knew you weren't any tin-soldier, and the other fellows used to say how keen you were, and that you'd get on well."

"But they said just the same to me about you, you old ass!" said Wally laughing. "Who got a special pat on the back at the last inspection, I'd like to know?"

"Oh, that was only luck," said Jim, much embarrassed. "Bit of eye-wash for the C.O. Anyway, I used to worry for fear I wasn't any good at the game; and it worried me that I was so awfully glad to come away, after they gassed us. But lately, I've been a bit bucked, because I'm getting no end keen to be back. We'll hate it again, I'm certain. But one has got to see the job through. You feel it too, don't you?"

" 'M," nodded Wally. "I suppose it's just the beastliness one hates, but one likes one's job."

"I expect so. I used to get horribly annoyed with young Wilson, in my platoon, but I'd like uncommonly to know how the little beggar is shaping now, and who has the handling of him. He's a queer-tempered, obstinate, cross-grained varmint, but he'll do anything for you if you treat him like a human being. Only you can't drive him. I hope we'll get our old crowds back—though I'm afraid it's rather too much to hope for."

"I'm afraid so," Wally agreed. "My corporal was a dear old thing; only he would persist periodically in forgetting that I was grown-up. I don't blame them—the old N.C.O.'s know ever so much more than we do. That chap had been all over the world, and seen no end of service; he'd have had a commission if he could have kept off beer. It was when he was drunk that he used to think I was his small boy. I had my own troubles with him"—and Wally grinned reminiscently.

"They were such a good lot of fellows," Jim said. "Oh, it will be pretty good to get back; and to see Anstruther and Garrett and Blake, and all the crowd again, and make them fight their battles over for us. It's one of the annoying parts about our dose of gas that I haven't the slightest recollection of our own little scrap. I used to remember the beginning; but now my only memory is of you sitting on a biscuit-tin eating bully, and I'm sure that happened before the fun began. I wonder if the other fellows will have much to talk about?"

"Well, we won't, anyhow," Wally said. "Ireland isn't the place for adventures. Let's hope we may get some good specimens of our own in Flanders—and in Germany—and then we needn't envy any of 'em."

"Rather!" assented Jim. "I say, suppose we move on—the sun isn't as hot as it was, or I'm colder than I was; and anyhow, we may as well explore." He sprang up, followed by his chum, and they strolled across the rocks.

The party had been at Carrignarone for three days, and there was, as yet, no word from Con, who had departed on an outside car, en route to Belfast, to obtain what was necessary to restore the motor to health. Not that anyone minded the delay. The little inn was clean and well-kept; the sea-fishing was good, and the bathing perfect; while the shore, with its alternating strand and rock, was a never-failing fascination. Wally and Jim had made friends with an old fisherman, who had taken them out with him very early that morning; and luck had been so good that they had come in some hours earlier than they were expected, so that the big haul they brought could be taken to the railway and landed in Dublin in time for the next morning's market. At the inn, they found that Sir John, Norah, and Mr. Linton had gone out, leaving no word of their movements; so the boys, after an enormous lunch, had departed to explore the shore farther than their previous walks had led them, until the long narrow inlet had tempted them to bathe.

They strolled round the beach from the point where they had dived, now and then picking up a curious shell or some sea-treasure that might be included in the parcels that went periodically to Billabong, where Brownie would have cherished the veriest rubbish if only her nurslings had gathered it for her. The tide was almost out, and at the farther headland the rocks lay uncovered for a long way, full of alluring rock-pools, gleaming with sea-anemones. It was impossible to round the point, however, for it was higher than the other headland, and the water roared at its base, even at low tide; so they strolled back across the rocks, looking for the nearest place where it would be possible to climb up and cross the point.

The crags above them grew more accessible presently, and they scrambled up, slipping and clambering until they found themselves on a jutting rock with a wide flat surface, which, bathed in sunshine, invited them to stop and rest. Loose fragments of rock lay about the flat top, and Wally perched on one, but rose hastily.

"That thing wriggled under me," he said, "It's just on the balance: I believe I could push it over."

" 'That Master Wally have the mischieviousness of ten boys,' as Brownie used to say," Jim remarked, lazily. "Sit down, and don't play tricks with the landscape."

"It would be considerably like hard work, so I don't think I will," said Wally, sitting down on another fragment. "This old table of a rock wants tidying up, I think—did you ever see so many loose chunks scattered about?"

"I expect a bit of the cliff fell on it from above, and flew into bits," said Jim. "Anyhow, it's warm and jolly. What's that?"

Something tinkled on the rock, and Wally uttered a sharp exclamation of annoyance.

"Botheration! That's my knife."

"Hard luck!" said Jim, looking at a cleft in the surface, down which the knife had vanished. "Never mind; I've got two with me, and you can have one."

"Thanks, but I don't want to lose that fellow," Wally said, vexedly. "It's that extra-special knife Norah gave me when I was going out—the big one she called 'the lethal weapon.' It's full of all sorts of dodges. I'd sooner lose a lot of odd things than that knife."

He lay flat, and put his eye to the cleft in the rock, peering downwards.

"Afraid it's gone for good, old man," Jim said. "It's hard luck—but Norah will understand. She'll probably jump at the chance of giving you another."

"I want this one," said Wally, his voice slightly muffled. He peered harder. "I say, Jim, I can see daylight down here."

"I don't see how you can," Jim said, leaning over in his turn. "This old rock seems pretty solid. Let's look." He applied his eye to the cleft, in his turn.

"Well, there is light," he said presently, sitting up. "I wonder if there's some opening below, Wal?"

"Don't know, but I'm going to see," Wally answered. He swung himself over the edge of the flat rock and climbed down, followed by his chum. They hunted about the great pile, seeking for some opening that might explain the glimmer of daylight that had greeted them above.

On one side of the mass was the long stretch of rock from which they had first climbed up; but on the other they found smooth hard sand, only lately under water. There were openings here and there among the boulders, but they led to nothing, and had no communication with the upper air; they explored them in turn, but found no solution of the problem. Then, as Wally was backing out on hands and knees from one of these false scents, he heard a low whistle from Jim, and hurried round a boulder, to find him regarding what looked like a slit, about three feet high, between two masses of rock.

"There's some sort of a cave in there," Jim said. "I've been in a little way, and it looks rather interesting, so I came back for you. There's light far above one's head; I believe we'll find your knife there."

They crawled into the narrow passage. Almost immediately it turned, so sharply that a casual searcher might easily have been misled into thinking it ended: and then it widened and they found themselves in a long, narrow cave. They could see no roof; but far above, a faint bar of light glimmered, and made it possible to see where they were going. Underfoot was hard sand. The walls were dripping with wet and encrusted with seaweeds and limpets.

"This is a real sea-cave," Wally said cheerfully.

An echo took his voice and went muttering round the rocks, the mutter rising at length almost to a cry. It was an eerie sound, in the wet dusk of the cave, with the dark smell of a submerged place in their nostrils; and the boys jumped.

"I guess this isn't a place to raise one's voice in," Wally said, dropping his to a whisper. "That's a nice, tame echo; I'd like to take it back to Billabong!"

"Would you!" uttered Jim, with feeling. "The blacks would say it was the Bunyip come back; and anyhow, you'd get into trouble for bringing out a prohibited immigrant." He made a quick pounce on an object that glittered faintly on the sand. "There's your knife, old man!"

"Bless you!" said Wally, thankfully receiving his property. "I say, what luck! and haven't you the eye of a hawk?"

"Why, I kicked it," said Jim. "A good thing it's so big: I always thought Norah gave it to you with the idea that you might club a few Germans with it, if you got the chance—and scalp 'em afterwards. Get out!—" as Wally tipped his cap off. "Remember that you're in a subterranean locality, and behave as such. Hark at that echo!"

He had raised his voice, unwittingly, and the echo had sent it shrieking round the cave. It was quite a relief when the sound died away to a low murmur.

"I'm not at all sure that it isn't the Bunyip, an' he livin' here at his aise, as Con would say," Wally muttered. "Come on; we'll see how far this place goes."

The light grew dimmer as they moved on, away from the crack overhead. Fortunately, Jim was never to be found without a tiny electric torch in his pocket, and its little beam of light was sufficiently to guide them. But for the torch their explorations would certainly have come to an end immediately, for it was not half a minute before they found themselves against a wall that apparently ended the cave.

"Well, it isn't much of a cavern, after all," Jim remarked. "Not bad as a dressing-room for Norah, if she wants to bathe from this beach—there's clear sand right down to the water from the entrance in one place. She will have to come at low tide, though."

He flashed his torch into the corners as they turned to retrace their steps. One was plainly nothing but solid wall: but in the other something caught his eye; a darker patch of shadow that was not quite like the rock.

"Why, I believe there's an opening in that corner," he said. "It must be another cave, communicating with this one. Come and see."

The opening was only wide enough to admit one at a time, and so screened by a jutting boulder that it was almost invisible. Within was a cave very like the first one, though much larger; differing from it, too, in that the sand ended, and the floor was of fairly smooth rock, which, in the middle, held a great pool of water. This time there was no doubt that they were at the end of their subterranean journey; Jim flashed the light right round the wall, but there was no break in the solid rock, glistening with wet.

"Well, that's the finish," Wally said. "It isn't a wildly exciting place, except for that demoniacal echo. We'll bring Norah and the others here and make it talk. I'd like to hear what its little efforts would be like if one gave a football yell!"

"Something would break," said Jim, suppressing a laugh. He strolled across to the pool, and turned the light on its black surface.

"That is a deep and mysterious and probably, haunted water-hole and you'd better be careful," said Wally in a sepulchral whisper. "Most likely the Bunyip lives there, and in a moment we shall see his grisly head emerge from the unfathomed depths, and then all will be over with two promising young officers of His Majesty's Army." He paused for breath.

"Idiot!" said Jim, pleasantly. "I wonder if it's deep. Lend me your stick, Wal."

He leaned over the pool and thrust the stick into its depths. It went in for its full length. Then came a sound which made the boys look at each other in bewilderment.

"It sounds as if the Bunyip had been chucking his old tins in," Wally said.

"It's tin, I'll swear," Jim answered. "And solid at that; I can't move it."

He took off his coat, rolled his shirt-sleeve to the shoulder, and recommenced investigations. It was easy enough to feel the stick scraping on tin; beyond that, he could make out nothing, save that there was plenty of tin to scrape. Jim desisted at length, and stood pondering.

"I think this is pretty queer," he said, presently. "Wonder if we've stumbled on a smuggler's cave, Wal. Look here, I'm going to paddle."

"Well, you don't know the depth of that beastly place," Wally said. "For all we know it may be miles deep."

"Well, can't I swim?" Jim queried in amazement.

"Yes, a little. Anyhow, I'm coming, too."

Jim laughed softly.

"I thought that was it," he said. "Look here—you stay at the edge with the light, and I'll hold one end of the stick, and you can hang on to the other. That will make it all right. There's no sense in out both paddling in."

Wally assented, more or less reluctantly; and Jim took off his boots and stockings and rolled his trouser-legs high. Then, he stepped carefully into the black pool.

"By Jove, it's cold!" he said.

"What's the bottom like?"

"Fairly smooth." He moved on, becoming less cautious. Then he uttered an exclamation.

"What's up?" came from Wally.

"I've stubbed my silly toe against something—my own fault." Jim answered. "Why, it's another tin!"

He stooped, feeling in the water. Presently he let go of the stick, and plunged both hands in: and in a moment turned, carrying something that was evidently heavy. He put it on the rock at the edge of the pool, and stepped out of the water. Wally flashed the light on the treasure-trove, and then whistled softly.

"Petrol!"

Jim nodded.

"The pool is full of it, I believe: I felt lots of other tins." He turned the big square can over and over, finding no mark upon it. "H'm. Now I'm going to put it back."

"Why are you in such a hurry?"

"Because I don't know whom we have to deal with," Jim said. He waded in again and replaced the heavy tin, returning quickly, and picking up his boots and stockings.

"Slip out and reconnoitre, carefully," he said. "Take care that you aren't seen. Find out if anyone is in sight."

Wally returned in a few minutes.

"Not a soul," he reported. "And there's not a footmark visible on the sand, except our own."

"That's good, anyhow," Jim said. "We'll get out of this."

He led the way out, not speaking until they were clear of the rocks near the cave. Then he sat down, and for the first time the two boys looked at each other. Their faces were grave.

"It's submarines, of course?" Wally asked. "Germans?"

131

"Couldn't be anything else. And what a depôt! Look at this inlet—shut in by the headlands, with a perfect sandy bottom: a submarine could come in here and lie in complete safety, and no one would ever dream of looking for her. The cave is not five minutes from the water's edge, even at low tide—of course, no one could get in to it at all unless the tide were right out: when it is in there's a foot of water over the entrance."

"Yes—and at low tide the sand is as hard as iron," Wally said, excitedly. "They could fill their collapsible boat with petrol tins in ten minutes with two or three men to fish them out of the water and a few more to carry them down. Oh, Jimmy, we've got to bag them!"

"Rather!" Jim answered. "The question is, how?"

He thought deeply.

"We must be awfully careful," he said, at last.

"It's much too big and important for us to mess up by trying to keep it to ourselves. But there isn't a policeman in the district, and if there were, he might mess it up as badly as ourselves. We've got to get a patrol-boat round to the inlet somehow; you know they're all round the coast, and it wouldn't take long to bring one here. But one doesn't know whom to trust. The Germans may be getting help from on shore, for all we can tell."

"Of course they may," Wally cried. "People say there are plenty of pro-Germans about; and they'd pay well enough to tempt these peasantry. But all the people we've talked to in Carrignarone seem just as keen as we are about the war. I don't believe they're in it."

"Neither do I, but it's hard to tell," Jim answered. "Oh, it's maddening!—the brutes may come in to-night, for all we know! We can telegraph to the nearest coastguard station, of course, or wherever one can catch a patrol-boat—there are some sort of instructions about submarines and aeroplanes posted up in every post-office. But she might not be in time."

"I suppose we can trust the postmistress?"

"If we can't, we're done," Jim said. "If only the motor were all right we needn't trust anyone. Isn't it simply sickening to think we may do the wrong thing altogether? And if we make a mistake, and the submarine gets away with a fresh supply of petrol, she may sink half a dozen Lusitanias before she is caught!"

"We've just got to get her," Wally said, between his teeth. "It seems to me there's only one thing to do: we must telegraph for the patrol-boat, and, meanwhile, watch every night at low tide. It's a comfort that they can't get into the cave at any other time, isn't it? I say, Jim, your father said we were kids to bring our revolvers with us—but isn't it a mercy we did!"

"Rather!" Jim said. The revolvers had been new toys; they had not felt able to part from them. "And O'Neill has one, too—you remember, he said we might have some shooting-practice in these lonely parts and teach Norah how to use one." He became silent, suddenly, and Wally, watching his thoughtful face, did not interrupt him. After a while he spoke, half-apologetically.

"I say, Wal, old chap."

"Yes?"

"Look here," Jim said. "It's your show as much as mine, of course, and I won't do anything to which you don't agree. But——" he stopped again.

"Oh, do go on!" said Wally. "Say it!"

"Well, it's just this. We'll get lots of shows later on, if we've any luck: not so important as this, perhaps, but still, there ought to be chances. Anyhow, we're able to go out to the Front and do our bit. And that poor chap isn't."

"O'Neill?" Wally said. "No."

"Well—do you see what I mean?"

"It takes brains," said Wally, laughing. "But I think I do. You want to make this his show?"

Jim nodded.

"It wouldn't hurt us," he said. "He is such a brick, and he's eating his heart out over the whole thing. It's just the toughest sort of luck—and here he is, knocking about with us and giving us a ripping time, and you'd think that every time he looks at us it must remind him of what he wants to have and can't. And now here's a thing he could be right in."

"Rather!" Wally said. "I'm jolly glad you thought of it, old man. And it isn't any beautiful sacrifice on our parts, either, for he has tons more brains than we have, and he's a first-class shot. Let's get him to run it altogether, and we'll be his subalterns."

Jim sighed with relief.

"It seemed a bit hard to ask you to give up the credit," he said.

"And what about you?" grinned Wally

"Oh, credit be hanged!" said Jim, laughing. "Anyhow, we'll get all the fun!"

"Wally flashed the light on the treasure-trove, and then whistled softly."

CHAPTER XIV
A FAMILY MATTER
"To count the life of battle good,

   And clear the land that gave you birth,

   And dearer yet the brotherhood

   That binds the brave of all the earth."

Henry Newbolt.

    JOHN O'NEILL was dressing for dinner: an operation which consisted in putting on a clean soft collar and brushing his hair, since the travellers' possibilities of toilet were limited to one small kit-bag apiece. To him there came a discreet knock on the door; and Wally and Jim, suitably apologetic, appeared.

"You look like conspirators," said Sir John, surveying the pair. "What's the matter?"

"We've struck a job that's a size too large for us," Jim answered. "So we've come meekly to you."

O'Neill's short laugh was rather bitter.

"Too large for you!" he said. "If that's the case, it would be rather an out-size for me, I should say." His look travelled over the two tall lads, wiry and powerful. "Unless—it isn't money, I suppose, Jim?"

"No, indeed; it's brains!" Jim answered. "And we haven't got any. Anyhow, we don't know how to handle this situation."

"Well, I'm at your disposal," Sir John said. "Fire away—there's plenty of time before dinner."

"We've found a little submarine supply-depôt," Jim said. "What does one do?"

O'Neill dropped his brush, and stared at him.

"You say it much as you might say, 'We've found a mushroom: how do we cook it?' " he uttered. "It isn't a joke, Jim?"

"Indeed it's not," the boy said, quickly. "It's because it's so horribly serious that we've come to you."

"But—where?"

"In a little inlet about a couple of miles up the coast," Jim said. "Funny little shut-in place: you could sail past it outside and never notice it, the headlands are so close together." He described their discovery briefly.

O'Neill sat down on the side of his bed and knitted his brows.

"Of course, the first thing is to get a patrol-boat down," he said. "As it happens, I know Bob Aylwin, who is in command of one of them: his headquarters are at Port Brandon, and he could get here quite quickly."

"Then we must telegraph, I suppose," Jim said. "But we were wondering if it would be safe; things leak out so quickly in a tiny place like this, and you know that people ashore are said to be helping the submarines in some districts. One doesn't like to misjudge anyone, but——" He paused, knitting his brows.

"One has to suspect every one," O'Neill said, shortly. "And telegrams are horribly public things."

"If only the motor were available!" Wally said, anxiously.

"But it is!"

They stared at him.

"Didn't you know Con was back? He turned up early this morning, with the things he went for: and he and a handy man he picked up have been inside her bonnet ever since. He came in just now to report that she is ready to start."

"Oh, good business!" ejaculated Jim. "Will you send him?"

O'Neill thought swiftly.

"I can trust Con absolutely," he said. "But he's an ignorant lad, and he is lame. Would your father go with him, do you think?"

"He'll do anything," Jim said, quickly.

"Wally, will you bring him here?" O'Neill asked. "Hurry!" He sprang to the table and opened a touring map of Donegal. "Where's your inlet, Jim?"

"Here," Jim replied, promptly, indicating a tiny indentation on the rugged coast-line.

O'Neill drew a line round it with a red pencil.

"It will be quite clear on Aylwin's charts, of course," he said. "This will be sufficient guide to begin with. Now can you draw a rough plan of the cave and the path down to the water? I'll explain to your father."

Mr. Linton came hurrying in, and at Sir John's request Wally told him the story, illustrating it with Jim's drawing.

"I know the inlet," David Linton said; "I walked past it the other day when I was out for an early-morning stroll. Queer, land-locked corner: I marked it down as a good bathing-place for you youngsters."

"That's excellent, for you'll be able to direct them by land, if necessary. Now, will you go in the motor to Port Brandon, Mr. Linton? it's only twenty miles, and Con knows the roads. They're not good, but he'll get you there quickly."

"I'll do anything you like," David Linton said. "What will you do here?"

Sir John had taken instinctive command of the situation. For a few moments he did not speak.

"Aylwin must use his own judgment about coming," he said. "He may not want to appear here in daylight, for fear of scaring the enemy away; on the other hand, they may be here already, lying snugly on the bottom of the inlet, and only waiting for night and low water to get the petrol. You say the pool was full of it, Jim?"

"So far as I could tell. I poked with a stick from one side, and waded in from the other. The tins are stacked in it; I don't think they can have taken any out."

"All the more likely that they will soon be in," O'Neill said. "I knew they had been in the north lately; the brutes nearly got one of our transports. But if Aylwin shows up off the mouth of the inlet he may scare them away altogether. If one knew what was best to do! We've got to bag them!" His eyes were dancing. "Great Scott! what a chance it is!"

There came a knock at the door, and Norah's voice.

"Is dad here?"

The conspirators looked at each other guiltily.

"Norah must be told," Jim said. "She's perfectly safe; and we can't carry on this without explaining to her, poor kid. May she come in, O'Neill?"

Sir John was already at the door. Norah, her face troubled, spoke hurriedly.

"I've been looking everywhere for dad or the boys. Are they here, Sir John?"

"Come in, if you don't mind," O'Neill said, holding the door open. He closed it carefully behind her. "We're having a council of war, Norah, and———"

Jim interrupted him, watching his sister's face.

"Is there anything wrong with you, Nor?"

"There's something I thought I'd better tell you," Norah said. "I went along the road just now with some sweets for those babies in the end cottage, beyond the village; and coming back I got over the bank into the field to get some wild flowers. Just as I was going to climb back I heard voices, and I peeped through the hedge and saw two men—men in rough clothes. They had been buying things in the village, for they had parcels, and some bread that wasn't wrapped up. So I bobbed down behind the hedge until they had gone past—they didn't look nice, somehow."

"Yes," said Jim. "Did they see you?"

"No, it's a lonely bit of the road, and there are no houses. I don't suppose they even thought of any one being there. And, Jim, they were talking in German!"

"Are you sure?"

"Perfectly. I couldn't make out what they said, for their voices were very low—and anyhow I never learned enough German at school to understand it when spoken. But I do know the sound of it, and I caught one or two words."

O'Neill drew a long breath.

"If that U-boat isn't lying on the bottom of the inlet I'll eat my hat!" he said. "Probably they put up a collapsible boat last night and sent her round to some other beach—they'll take risks to get fresh food. And to-night she'll paddle back and get her cargo of petrol, and the submarine will take her on board and slide out to do a little more pirate-work. But we may have a few remarks to make first. If I only knew what Aylwin would want to do!"

He sat down, and put his face in his hands. Presently he looked up.

"Jim—is there driftwood on the shore?"

"Lots," said Jim, briefly.

"That's all right. Could we get some up on one of the headlands?"

"Oh—easily. We were bathing off the northern point, and there's quite an easy way up—it isn't nearly as high as the southern headland. Do you mean enough for a fire?"

"Yes. Mr. Linton, will you tell Captain Aylwin that he need not come right in to shore. We will build a signal-fire on the northern headland, and watch the cave at low tide—that will be about two o'clock in the morning. If the Germans come ashore, we'll light the fire—we can carry up a few bottles of petrol from the motor supply to soak the drift-wood. Aylwin can have a boat ready and come in if he sees the blaze; unless he sees it he will know they won't land for another twenty-four hours, for they'll never try it in the daytime. Is that clear?"

"Quite. I have only to describe the place to Captain Aylwin, tell him about the signal-fire, and accompany him if he needs me. Otherwise, I suppose I may break the speed-limit in coming back?"

"Of course. There's a wireless station up there—they'll get Aylwin for you. If he should be away they will know where to send a message."

"Very well. And what will you three do?" David Linton's eyes lingered hungrily on his son.

138

"We can only get the beacon ready, and then watch. Two of us can hide near the cave, and the third must be up on the point to light the fire if he hears a shot. If they come—well, we must let them land and get to the cave; and then we must try to prevent their getting back."

"You will be heavily outnumbered."

"Yes—but the advantage of surprise will be on our side, and we can take cover. I do not dare to get help; it may not be safe to trust anyone."

"Very well," David Lint on said, quietly. "Will you order the motor, O'Neill? I can be off in three minutes."

He shook hands with the boys, wishing them luck very gravely knowing that in all probability it was the last time he should speak to them. Jim went downstairs with him, without a word.

Con and the motor were at the door.

"You'll be there by eight o'clock, with luck," O'Neill said. "Remember, you're racing, Con. And——" He dropped his voice. "I'll keep him safe for you if I can, sir."

"Thanks," said David Linton. He shook hands with his boy again. The motor whirred off in a cloud of dust.

They went up the staircase in silence, to where Norah and Wally waited for them.

"Wally has told me all about it," said Norah, pale, but steady-eyed. "Oh, Sir John, I could help! Do let me."

"You can help by keeping out of harm's way," he told her, gently.

"And you all fighting!"

"Norah, dear, we can't have you in it," O'Neill said. "I know it's hard: far harder than anything we have to do. But you have too much sense not to know that this isn't woman's work."

Norah choked back a sob.

"I know you couldn't have me where there's shooting," she said. "But I can do something, if you'll let me: and in Australia women always did help men when there was need, and they didn't talk about things being 'women's work.' Women had to fight the blacks, too."

"Norah, we can't let you fight," Jim said. "Be sensible, old kiddie."

"I don't want to fight," said poor Norah. "At least, I do, but I know that's out of the question. But why on earth shouldn't I light the beacon?"

"Because there would be risk," O'Neill said roughly. "Norah, I hate hurting you. Don't make it harder for us."

"I don't want to, indeed I don't," Norah faltered. "But . . ." There was a lump in her throat, and she turned away, fighting for her voice. Jim's arm round her shoulders steadied her.

"You know you'll be outnumbered," she said. "You can't tell any of these people, and there are only the three of you until daddy brings help. And one of you is going to light the beacon! If you let me do it, it leaves you all free to fight; and there's no risk to me. No one will be on the point. I'd only have to light a match and get out of the way."

"No," said Wally, his young voice strained. "You aren't going to do it."

"I know what it will be," Norah said. "The one of you who lights the beacon will come tearing down the rocks to help the others, and the Germans will just shoot him easily. I needn't do that; I can hide up on the point. There isn't any risk—not a bit."

"Oh, Norah, Norah, I wish you'd gone to bed!" uttered Jim. "Don't you see we can't let you?"

"No, I don't," said his sister. "You haven't any right to stop me. You know it will be only a chance if you three can stop the submarine going out if help doesn't come in time. And if there are only two of you, it's so much less chance. Dad's gone away looking dreadful, only he wouldn't say a word, because he knows he hasn't any right to hinder you." Norah was sobbing openly now. "And you have no right to lose any chances. We can't let that beastly thing go out, to sink other ships full of women and kiddies like the Lusitania babies. Goodness knows I'm f-fool enough," said poor Norah. "But at least I can put a match to a fire!"

"She's quite right," Jim said, quietly. "All serene, Nor. Buck up, old kiddie!"

"Jim—you can't———!" Wally burst out.

"I can't agree to it," John O'Neill said, wretchedly.

"She's quite right," Jim repeated. "The job is bigger than we are. It's only a question, as she says, if all three of us can check those people at the cave: and if we can get the beacon lit in any other way, we simply have no right to reduce our number by one-third. There really should be no danger: she has only to put a match to it, and get away before the firelight shows her up." He spoke firmly, but his young face was drawn and haggard. "I am quite sure dad would say the same."

"I know he would," Norah said.

"And I thought this was rather a lark!" said Wally, with a groan. He turned and walked to the window.

"If you are certain your father would be satisfied, I have no more to say," O'Neill said. "It certainly makes an enormous difference: three can stop a rush where two would be hopelessly outclassed. And the man coming down from the headland wouldn't have a chance: the people on the submarine would get him in a minute."

"Remember," said Wally sharply, turning from the window, "as soon as your match is lit, duck, and crawl away. That old wood will flare wildly directly it's lit, if it's soaked in petrol. Don't wait a second."

"I won't," said Norah, and nodded at him cheerfully. "Don't worry; I'll be all right."

"All right! I think it's awful to let you do it!" Wally uttered.

"Wally, I've got to. Don't you see I have?" Norah put her hand on his arm.

"Yes, I suppose I do," he said. "All our lives put together don't matter twopence if we can put an end to even one submarine. I know we must let you. But I wish to goodness we'd left you in Australia!"

"Wally!" Norah flushed scarlet.

"I say . . . I didn't mean to be a beast," the boy said, contritely. "Only—I just can't stand it!" He went out, his swift strides echoing down the corridor.

"Don't mind him, little chap: he's only worried about you," Jim said, gently. "He'll be all right when he comes back."

"At any rate, we mustn't have you bothered," Sir John said, patting Norah's shoulder. "You'll need to be quite calm and cool for your job, and for getting away quietly after it. And I really don't believe you'll be in any danger; the Germans can't possibly rake that point with gunfire from the submarine. They might hit a standing figure, but not one lying flat. And I hope the men on shore will be too busy to take interest in beacons." There was a grim note in his voice, but his face was extraordinarily happy.

"The more I think of it," Jim said, "the more likely it seems that we're here just in time. You see, they can't get into the cave except at low tide; and of course they want darkness. But there's very little darkness just now; it's twilight until nearly ten o'clock, and then dawn comes not long after three, or even earlier. The tide is out just before dawn: the very best time for them to work. In a few days it would not suit them nearly so well."

"Quite so," O'Neill said. "Everything seems to point to to-night or to-morrow. I would hope with all my heart for to-night if I were sure of Aylwin getting here in time; for every day means more risk of their suspecting us, especially if they are in league with any of the people on shore. The Irish peasants are very quick to suspect a stranger."

"Oh, I hope it's to-night!" Norah cried. "But, Sir John, supposing we can—I mean, you and the boys can——"

"Not a bit of it—it's certainly 'we,'" said O'Neill, laughing.

"Well, supposing we can cut off the men who come ashore. What will the submarine do? We can't touch her."

"There's where Aylwin comes in, of course," O'Neill said. "If we can cut off the shore party and keep them from rejoining the submarine, I don't think she can get away. She would not have much fuel, for one thing; and for another, she does not carry enough men to spare those we may have the luck to bag. She would probably submerge; but she can't remain below more than twenty-four hours; and then the destroyer would get her easily. Of course, there is a lot of supposition about it all. I am calculating by the little I know of submarines, but the Germans may have a later and more powerful pattern that I don't understand, with a larger crew. We can only do our best. It ought to be a good fight, anyhow."

A knock came, and Jim opened the door.

"The misthress is afther sending me up to say the dinner'll be spoilt on ye," said a patient voice. "Them little chickens do be boiled to rags; 'tis that tender they are they'd fall asunder if you did but prod them with your finger!"

"We'll hurry, Mary," said Jim. "Come on, you people."

"Dinner!" said Norah. "Oh, I don't believe I could eat any."

"Yes, you could," said Wally, appearing suddenly. "Little girls who won't eat dinner can't light bonfires!" He tucked her hand into his arm and raced her down the staircase. At the foot, he stopped.

"Norah, I'm sorry," he said. "Is it all right?"

"Of course it's all right," said Norah. "But you were never cross with me before, in all your life, and don't you do it again!"

"I never got you mixed up in a war before!" said Wally soberly. "Don't you do it again, either!"

CHAPTER XV
PLANS OF CAMPAIGN

"They are fighting in the heavens: they're at war beneath the sea—

Ay, their ways are mighty different from the ways o' you an' me!"

Dudley Clark.

DINNER at the Carrignarone Hotel, where the Australians and Sir John were the only guests, was apt to be a lengthy and hilarious affair, with everybody very hungry and very merry, and with jokes flying, much to the disorganization of the waitress, who was wont to spend much of her time in clapping her hand over her mouth and rushing from the room. When the necessities of the meal forbade these hasty retreats, the waitress was apt to explode in short, sharp gasps, greatly endangering whatever dish she happened to be handing.

This evening, however, the younger members of the party were inclined to be unusually silent. Mr. Linton's vacant seat was in itself depressing; and since it was impossible to talk of the subject seething in their minds, conversation of any kind was not easy. But John O'Neill was like a child; and before long they all fell under the spell of his merriment. Never had they seen him in such a happy mood. Every line was smoothed from his worn face, and his eyes danced with an eager joy that was almost uncanny. All his being seemed transformed in the complete contentment that had possession of him. Deliberately he set himself to make the others laugh; and succeeded so well that they astonished themselves by making an extremely good dinner and feeling, at its conclusion, considerably reinforced for the work that lay before them.

O'Neill led the way out to the little landing-stage near the inn, where the fishing-boats were anchored, their brown nets drying on rough fences on the beach. They sat down on some upturned fish-boxes, looking westward across the water, where the sun was preparing to set in a glory of golden cloud.

"Now I'm going to be sensible," Sir John said. "I've been thinking out a plan of campaign, and I want your views."

He brought out from his pocket a plan of the inlet, drawn by Jim—a companion to the one Mr. Linton had carried to Captain Aylwin.

"You have 'Flat Rock' marked here over the cave," he said. "Is that the rock you were sitting on when Wally dropped his knife?"

"Yes, that's the one," Jim answered. "It has a cleft in it through which the knife went down—just wide enough to admit the knife. It's really a kind of lid over the rocks that form the first cave."

"And you said there were loose boulders lying on it?"

"Yes; big fragments of rock. I should think that a big chunk of the cliff must have fallen on it once, probably splitting it and making the crack, and breaking itself as well. A lot of it went down: the biggest piece buried itself partly in the sand."

"That's the boulder that almost hides the entrance, then?"

Jim nodded assent.

"It's about three feet from the entrance and a good deal wider than it," he said. "There are so many similar rocks lying about that it would be quite easy to miss the cave altogether."

"Then I take it that the top of the flat rock is above high-water mark?"

"Oh, yes," Jim answered. "High-water mark is about a foot over the top of the entrance, and the rock is quite four feet higher than that. Otherwise I don't fancy the waves would have left those big pieces of loose rock lying on it."

"That's what I wanted to know. Now listen. Suppose the Germans land, and most of them disappear into the caves, to fish for petrol. What is to hinder two active people, armed with levers, from sending down from the top of the rock enough boulders to block the entrance?"

Jim started, his pipe falling from his hand.

"By—Jove!" he uttered. "What a ripping idea!"

"Why, we could do it as easily as possible," Wally said, excitedly. "The rocks are quite close to the edge: one of them is so loose that we were rocking it this afternoon. We've pretty hefty muscles—we could send half a dozen over in no time with a couple of iron bars. Glory, O'Neill, you have a head!"

"Yes," said Jim, his eyes dancing—"and they could hardly miss the entrance, because the big boulder in front would prevent their rolling out too far. What chumps we were, not to think of it, Wal!"

"Then you'd have the Germans like rats in a trap—and with no shooting at all!" Norah cried, delightedly.

"Something like that: with luck," said O'Neill. "Of course, they would have a guard posted outside, and another at the boat. But the main crowd would be inside, I should think."

"It's really rather a staggering notion, it's so simple," Jim said. "And I don't see how it can go wrong."

"It certainly simplifies our plan of action," O'Neill remarked. "And it doesn't beat us, even if it fails; you would have to jump down among the boulders, in that case, and do the best you could with your revolvers as the people inside came out—which they would do in a hurry. My own little game must be the boat and the guard at it. It's rather important that it should not be allowed to get back; a submarine without a collapsible is rather like a horse with a lame leg." He turned his face towards the sunset, its expression of child-like happiness stronger than ever. "Wow! isn't it going to be a jewel of a fight!"

Jim laughed.

"Aren't you the Berserk!" he said. "But I don't much like being separated. You'll be careful, O'Neill, won't you, and keep well behind cover? There are plenty of boulders near where they must land."

"Rather!" Sir John answered. "For once in my life I have a job that matters, and I'm certainly not going to risk carrying it out by getting shot unnecessarily. They won't leave a strong guard at the boat: a submarine crew is too limited to use many men, and then, so far as we know, they feel perfectly safe, and have no reason to take extra precautions. Speed will be their main idea; they must make the most of the short time between low-water and daylight." He swung round towards Norah, smiling at her. "How are you feeling, mate?"

"I'm feeling very cheerful," said Norah, whose face bore out her words. "There isn't nearly so much danger for the boys on top of the rock, is there, Sir John?"

"Certainly not; if they can block the entrance from above they may not even have to use their revolvers—which will be a sad blow to them," O'Neill answered. "I'm always against promiscuous shooting, especially when there are ladies present—even to satisfy fire-eaters like Wally and Jim!"

"Are you sure you'll be all right, Sir John?"

"I'll be as right as possible," he assured her, laughing at her anxious face. "All I have to do is to sit comfortably behind my little rock and pot at fat Germans; and when you hear me potting, you can light the beacon and crawl away with discreet haste. I hope you realize that we couldn't carry out this plan at all if we hadn't you as fire-lighter: we couldn't do without a fourth hand."

"I'm so glad," Norah said, happily. "When do we start, Sir John?"

"We'll slip out about half-past nine," he answered. "You and I will stroll along in one direction, and the boys in another, and we can meet near the northern headland where we must have the beacon. Each of us must carry a bottle of petrol—I'll see to getting them ready; and as we go we can pick up stray bits of wood. There is driftwood everywhere on the beach, and we can collect plenty beyond the inlet: I don't want to go there, nor do I want to show up on the north headland while there is much light. We don't know where the Germans you saw this evening may be hiding—though I would think, judging from the direction in which they were going, that their boat must be hidden in a tiny bay that lies south of the inlet. Still, it doesn't do to risk things."

"I suppose," said Wally, "those fellows with the boat will stay wherever they are hiding until nearly low-water; then they'll pull round to the inlet, and the submarine will bob up, and they'll take the other men on board and go ashore after the petrol."

"That's the most likely thing," O'Neill said. "We must be in position long before that. A good thing it's a warm night: still, we shall have to lie still for a good while, and you'd better dress warmly, all of you." He looked at his watch. "Nine o'clock, and time we began to get ready. There are crowbars in the old shed Con used as a garage, boys; I noticed them this morning. I'm going after bottles for the petrol."

He stood up, looking at the three young faces. They were all eager; but it was as though a living light glowed in his own dark eyes. He held his gallant head high, the twisted body forgotten.

"I'd like to say 'Thank you,' only I don't know how," he said. "If you hadn't come, this wouldn't have happened; and now, whatever comes, I'll always have it to remember that just once in my life I had a chance of a man's job." His light stride carried him quickly across the beach.

CHAPTER XVI
THE FIGHT IN THE DAWN
"The fighting man shall from the sun

    Take warmth, and life from the glowing earth;

Speed with the light-foot winds to run.

    And with the trees to newer birth;

And find, when fighting shall be done,

    Great rest, and fulness after dearth."

Julian Grenfell.

IN the little inlet, shadowed by the high rocks, everything was very quiet. The tide was running out rapidly: foot by foot the smooth boulders came out of the sea, to stand like sentinels until once more the heaving green water should swing back and climb gently until it rippled over their heads. Inch by inch the opening grew, forming the entrance to the cave under the rocks, and the water slid out as though rejoicing to escape from its dark prison within and to seek the laughing freedom of the sea that tumbled beyond the headlands. Overhead a half-moon sailed, now and then blotted out by drifting clouds; and in the East was the faintest glimmer of the coming dawn. But the water of the little bay lay black and formless, and though the sands showed, visible and pale, the shadows that lay about the great boulders were like pools of ink.

On the flat rock over the cave Jim and Wally crouched, now and then moving cautiously to keep their tired limbs from stiffening. It was very cold, in the silent hour before dawn. Two hours earlier they had climbed down from above, making use of the scant moonlight or clinging like limpets to the cliff when the clouds blotted out the moon's faint radiance: glad to arrive at their destination with nothing worse than bruises and torn clothes.

Once on the rock, they had set about their preparations: crawling all over it, making sure of knowing every inch in the dark, and becoming acquainted with each boulder that lay upon its surface. They tested them with their crowbars in the darkness, and found it possible to move all but two or three. The great fragment that balanced near the edge they levered nearer still, so that only a little effort would be needed to send it crashing down; and then they moved others near it, working with caution that was almost painful, lest even a scratch of rock on rock should carry a warning across the dark water. Below them, the waves had at first rippled and splashed against the crags; but gradually they receded, and leaning over, lying flat on the stone, they could make out the position of the great boulder that marked the entrance to the cave, and so make sure that their balanced rock was in the right place. Then there was nothing to do but wait.

How the minutes dragged! Far up on the northern headland, Norah crouched among sparse furze and heather, unheeding the prickly branches that forbade comfort. The edge of the low cliff prevented her seeing the inlet; she could only watch the dim outline of the coast, stretching northward, and the stormy sky with its hurrying clouds. Before her loomed dimly the heap of petrol-soaked wood and furze which they had roughly piled in the darkness behind a boulder that hid it from watching eyes, should any be on the alert. She had expected to be afraid when at last they had all shaken hands with her and wished her luck before creeping away to their posts; but now she found that she had no sense of fear. Jim had stayed behind for a moment and kissed her, calling her "old kiddie" in the way she loved. In the agony of wondering if she would ever hear his voice again there was no room for fear for herself.

John O'Neill had had longer to wait before climbing down to the beach. He had lain on the edge of the high ground, motionless, taking advantage of every moonlit moment to learn by heart the scene below as the tide crawled backward. Jim's plan was fresh in his memory: now he stared at each boulder, studying opportunities for cover and making out the path that the Germans must take to the cave. He knew where it was, though he could not see it: it relieved him, too, that he was unable to discern Jim and Wally, or to hear the faintest sound of their presence, although he knew they must be on the rock. Finally, he made his cautious way to the beach, and followed the tide out yard by yard, creeping from one shadow to another: a shadow himself, white-faced and frail, among the rugged boulders.

It was very cold, on the wet sand; he shivered, and his teeth chattered. He fell to rubbing himself steadily, chafing his wrists and ankles; but it seemed as though the long watch would never end. Once, when the clouds suddenly blew apart and the moon shone more brightly, he fancied he saw a dim shape outside the headlands: a shape that might have been a ship. But before he had time to be certain the dark masses overhead drifted together once more, leaving him in doubt as to whether it had not been his imagination.

The shadow of dawn came in the east, and O'Neill felt his heart sink. They were not coming, after all: soon it would be daylight and the tide would turn and come creeping back to hide the cave for another twelve hours. For a moment the keenness of disappointment made him shiver, suddenly colder than he had ever been; and then his heart thumped and the blood seemed to rush through his veins. Something, long, and grey, and very faint was showing on the water. It was not a dream: he heard a faint plash that he knew was an oar, muffled yet distinct in the deep stillness: and then a low mutter of a voice, coming across the sea to him. He drew a long, satisfied breath, and felt a hatchet that hung at his belt, as he had felt it a hundred times, to make sure that it hung where he could draw it easily. Then his hand closed on the revolver in his coat-pocket and clung to it almost lovingly. For the first time in his life it did not matter in the least that he was a hunchback.

The low sound of oars came nearer, and gradually, out of the darkness, a boat loomed upon the water and grounded softly on the strand. They were not half a dozen yards from where O'Neill crouched in a patch of black shadow, watching between two rocks. The men in her stepped out, quietly, but showing no sense of danger. They were more in number than he had expected; there would be a stiff fight if Jim and Wally failed to trap them. He crouched lower, scarcely daring to breathe. Then one who was evidently in command gave a low curt order and they filed off along the winding path between the strewn boulders, leaving two of their number in the boat.

The rocks hid the main body for a moment. The guards worked the boat round until her bow pointed outwards in readiness for the run back to the submarine; then they came out, stamping on the sand to keep warm. One of them, a thick-set fellow in oilskins, strode inland a few yards, pausing so close to O'Neill that the Irishman could have touched him, and for a sick instant he thought he was discovered; but the sailor strolled back to his companion with a muttered curse at the cold, and they stood by the boat, talking in low tones. O'Neill searched the rocks with his eyes, straining to see the entrance to the cave. Surely it was time for them to have reached it. Would the sound he longed for never come?

Then came a long reverberating crash, and another, and yet another and a long, terrible cry, and above it a shrill whistle. The men on the beach swung round, breaking into a torrent of bewildered furious speech. On the northern headland came a flicker of light that spread upwards and soared in a sheet of flame; and simultaneously Sir John fired at the man nearest him and saw him pitch into the water on his face. The second man rushed at him as he rose from behind the rock, and he fired again, and missed; and the German Was upon him, towering over the slight, misshapen form, and firing as he came. O'Neill felt a sharp agony in his side. The two revolvers rang out together, and the German staggered and fell bodily upon him, crushing him to the sand, while his revolver flew from his hand, splashing into a pool in a rock.

The Irishman twisted himself from under the inert weight, and struggled to his feet. A German was rushing towards the boat, threading his way among the rocks, his face desperate in its bewilderment and rage. The sight gave strength to John O'Neill anew; he ran to the boat, staggering as he ran, and pulling at his hatchet. There were dark stains on it as he grasped it. The German saw his intention and shouted furiously, and shots began to whistle past O'Neill. There was no time to look: he flung himself into the boat, hacking wildly at the bottom, smiling as it split under his blows and he felt the cold inrush of the water round his feet. The German was upon him: just once he glanced aside from his work and saw the cruel face and the levelled revolver very close, somewhere it seemed that Jim and Wally were shouting. He smiled again, turning for a final blow at the boat. Then sea and rock and sky seemed to burst round him, with a deafening roar, in a blaze of white light that turned the grey dawn into a path of glory.

He woke from a dreamless sleep. They were all about him: kind faces that loved him, that bent over him speaking gently. Some one had propped his head, and had spread coats over him: he was glad of it, for he was very cold. The wavering faces steadied as his vision grew clearer, and he saw them all: David Linton and the boys, and Norah kneeling by him, her eyes full of tears. That troubled him, and he groped for her hand, and held it.

"You mustn't cry," he whispered.

Some one raised his head a little, putting a flask to his lips. He drank eagerly. Then he saw another face he knew.

"Hallo, Aylwin!" he said. "Did you get her?"

The sailor nodded. "Don't talk, old man."

O'Neill laughed outright. The brandy had brought life back to him.

"I'm perfectly well," he said. "Tell me, Jim—quick!"

"We got them quite easily," Jim said, his voice shaking. "The first rock blocked the entrance, and they're there yet. We sent down all the rocks, and one fell on one of the two guards they left; the other managed to wing Wally before he ran."

O'Neill started.

"Is he hurt?"

"Only my arm," said Wally. "It's quite all right—don't you worry. It wasn't much to pay for the haul we got—thanks to you." The boyish face twitched, and he put out his hand and took O'Neill's in its grip.

"Go on, please," Sir John begged.

"The other chap ran," Jim said: "of course his idea was to get the boat back to the submarine. The brute got a start of us while we were making sure the others were blocked in securely."

"Have you put a guard there?" O'Neill interrupted, anxiously. "They might break out."

"Half a dozen of my men," Aylwin said, quickly. "It's all right, old chap."

"We saw him begin to fire at you, and we did our best," said Jim, with a groan. "We didn't dare fire, for fear of hitting you, until we were close. Then we got him—but——" His strained voice ceased.

"You needn't worry—his mate had fixed me first," said O'Neill, serenely. "It was great luck I had, to be able to get to the boat at all: your man didn't matter." He laughed happily. "This makes up for having lived. Tell me your part of it, Bob."

"We got down in very good time," Aylwin said. "The ship couldn't come in, of course; but I've a handy motor-boat with a gun rigged in her, and we sneaked in and lay just under the south headland. It was quite simple; we were into the inlet before the first flare died down, and there was the submarine, with nothing doing. It was as easy as shelling peas."

"Then it was your gun . . . ?" O'Neill said.

"Yes. We're on guard, of course; but she won't come up again. When it's light we'll deal with the gentlemen in the cave." The sailor's curt voice became even more abrupt. "Never saw a show better planned—the whole thing went like clockwork. I always knew you had the makings of a general in you, Jack!"

O'Neill gave a quick, happy sigh.

"The boys and Norah did it all," he said. "But it was splendid fun, to be able to take a hand. I said it would be a jewel of a fight!"

A slow wave of weakness stole over him, and he closed his eyes.

"Is the tide coming in?" he said, presently. "I thought I felt it—creeping."

Jim took off his coat and put it on his feet.

"We'll get you up to the motor presently," he said, his young voice unsteady. O'Neill laughed.

"Not before the finish," he said. "It won't be long."

Norah's head went down suddenly on his hand.

"You can't die!" she said,—"we can't spare you, dear Sir John. We're going to make you better!"

"Dying is only a very little matter, dear little mate," O'Neill said. "It's living that hurts. And just think of what I have—a man's finish! That is a great thing, when one has lived a hunchback."

He did not speak for a long time, lying with closed eyes. The dawn was breaking: light grew on the surface of the inlet, where long streaks of oil floated on the ripples. They watched the quiet figure. Under the coats that covered him, all traces of deformity were lost. Something of new beauty had crept into the high-bred features; and when he opened his eyes again they were like the smiling eyes of a child. They met Jim's, and the lips smiled too, while his weak hand rested on Norah's head.

"And I worrying," he said, "because I was out of the war."

"You had your own job," said Aylwin. "And you pulled it off, old man."

"It was great luck," O'Neill said. "God had pity. Enormous luck . . . to finish at a man's job." He did not speak again. The sun, climbing upwards, shone tenderly upon the happy face.

"The German saw his intention and shouted furiously, and shots began to whistle past O'Neill."

Jim and Wally]   [Page 253
The End.

CPSIA information can be obtained
at www.ICGtesting.com
Printed in the USA
LVHW031107250821
696066LV00009B/1425